THE JUNGLE

A John Milton Novel

Mark Dawson

To Mrs D, FD and SD.

PROLOGUE

NADIA BLINKED. It took a moment to realise that her eyes were open. It was completely dark. She was lying down on something hard. She felt her hands folded across her chest, but she couldn't see them. She blinked her eyes again. She unclasped her fingers and brought her right hand right up to her face. All she could see was the suggestion of a shape passing through the thicker black.

She squeezed her eyes shut and listened. She heard her breathing, quick and shallow, and then, beyond that, the low rumble of an engine.

The muscles in her back were sore. Her legs twitched with cramp. She reached up. Her hands could only have been a few inches above her chest when her knuckles grazed something hard. She turned her hands over and probed with her fingers. She felt something solid and rough, an abrasiveness that snagged against her fingernails.

She felt the first icy stabs of fear in her stomach.

Her memory was foggy, clouded with uncertainty, and she tried to make sense of what had happened to her. It came back to her in fragments. She remembered the trip across the desert; she remembered the boat, so loaded with passengers that she had been certain that it would capsize and tip them all into the ocean; she remembered the way that her brother had clasped her hand and told her everything would be all right; she remembered the way that she had felt at the first sight of land, of Europe, at the promise of a new life that it represented. She had knelt down and kissed the concrete of the dock.

And five minutes later she had been picked up and tossed into the back of the van.

She remembered: the men with guns who took her from Samir; the long drive north in the back of the van with two other women, Amena and Rasha; the tented city that teemed with refugees, men and women like her; the tent, and the big man with the shaven head who had looked at her and nodded; her arms being held behind her back, the prick of the needle in her neck, the plunge into darkness.

Nadia opened her eyes again and pressed up once more, tracing the fingers of both hands to the left and right. She felt another panel, perpendicular to the one that was above her. She found the join between them. Her finger caught in the otherwise flat panel and she realised that she had found a knot in the wood.

She realised where she was.

She was in a wooden box.

"Help!"

Her voice was both loud and deadened, all at once.

She became frantic. "Help! Please, help me!"

She banged her fists on the sides of the box and slapped her palms against the lid until her skin burned. Her heart raced and she started to sweat. She kept banging and screaming until she was gasping for breath.

No-one came.

She heard the rumble of the engine again and then the sensation of renewed motion. She banged the lid and kicked out with her legs, her feet thumping against the end of the box, but it was all in vain. No-one came.

She lay back, panting, her eyes stinging with hot tears.

She had been taken. She had been stolen from her brother, their hopes of a better life ruined. She didn't know where she was. She didn't know what was going to happen to her.

She stopped struggling.

There was no point. No-one was coming to help her.

Nadia was alone.

And she was scared.

Part One

Calais and Dover

Chapter One

JOHN MILTON'S SATURDAY MEETING was held in the sports hall of a school in Chelsea. It was one of his favourites: it was early, at eight o'clock, which meant that he had gotten the meeting out of the way before most people were up and about, and had given himself the best possible start to the day that he could; and, just as important, it was a lively, friendly meeting that was full of positive energy. Milton occasionally felt closer to taking a drink at the weekend, and he had found that the meeting was an effective bolster to help him get through to Monday.

He helped himself to a cup of coffee and a biscuit and took a seat in the middle of the room. He recognised many of the other regulars and exchanged smiles and nods of greeting with a few of them.

Milton closed his eyes and relaxed, feeling the usual serenity that he had only ever found in the meetings.

"Good morning, ladies and gentlemen."

Milton opened his eyes. The secretary of the meeting was Tommy McCall, a burly Glaswegian with a shaven head and tattoos on both forearms. He was an imposing character, but Milton had quickly warmed to him as soon as he heard him speak for the first time. He had a thick accent, occasionally impenetrably so, but his almost constitutional dourness was leavened with a quicksilver sense of humour that belied his aggressive appearance. He was ruthlessly funny, lambasting the other attendees and, more often than not, himself.

"A word or two about my appearance," McCall said, holding up his right arm. It was encased in plaster from the wrist all the way up to just below his shoulder. "Despite what you bastards might think, I haven't fallen off the wagon. I was playing football with my son. I tripped, put

5

my arm down to break my fall and…" He left the arm up, nodding to it with a rueful smile. "I know what you're thinking. You're thinking I'm bullshitting you, but I swear to God I'm not. And believe me, the irony that I'd do twenty years of hard *Scottish* drinking and emerge with not even a scratch on me and then I'd trip over a seven-year-old and do my arm in two places like this, well, I can assure you, that's not lost on me at all."

Tommy put his arm down, resting it on the table with a deliberate clunk that drew more good-natured laughter. He started the meeting properly, welcoming newcomers and then beginning the prayers, a familiar routine that Milton had come to find particularly reassuring. He had been to meetings all over the world, and, barring a few minor differences, the structure and content was almost always the same. There was a reassurance in that routine.

Milton closed his eyes and intoned the prayers with the others.

#

THE SPEAKER at the meeting was a young mother who laid out, during the course of her share, an unfortunate life that had seen her fight to bring up her two children after her husband had died of lung cancer. Six months after he had died, she had been diagnosed with breast cancer. She reported, to warm applause, that the cancer was in remission, but that an old predisposition toward alcoholic thinking had been awakened by her struggles.

Milton listened intently throughout, thinking that her experiences cast his own in stark relief. His drinking had been to drown out the clamour of his guilt. But the source of his guilt were the decisions that he had made and the career that he had chosen for himself. Comparing his life to hers seemed selfish and inappropriate, and he started to feel uncomfortable until Tommy reminded everyone that they should focus on the similarities and not the differences. She had relied on drink to solve a problem. Milton had done the same. They had both lost control of their drinking, and both had ended up in the rooms as a last resort. That was what they shared, and, in that knowledge, Milton found his usual measure of peace.

The meeting came to an end and the men and women started to disperse. Some went for breakfast at a greasy spoon on the King's Road. Milton had his running gear in his bag. He had planned to change into it and then go for a long run along the towpath of the Thames, following it into central London and then looping back in a route that he could stretch out to fifteen miles if he was in the mood. It was a beautiful day, clear and crisp, and the prospect of the exercise was very appealing.

He would get changed in the bathroom. He returned his empty cup to the table, thanked the old woman who had taken on the responsibility for the refreshments, and, as he turned, Tommy was behind him.

"Hello, John."

"All right?"

"Not so bad," he said, holding up his arm, "all things considered."

Milton nodded at the cast. "Is that really what happened?" he said with a grin. "You tripped?"

"I'm serious. I caught my foot and went over. Bloody agony. Cried like a baby. Had to turn down the morphine, too. Last thing I want to do is to end up on that again."

Milton could relate to that. He had been on gabapentin and oxycodone for years, a cocktail to take the edge off the pain caused by the long list of injuries that he had suffered during his career with the Group. He had stopped taking those when he decided that he wasn't going to put anything in his body that might artificially alter the way that he felt. He was going to live an entirely unmedicated life from now on. The occasional ache was a welcome reminder of the things that he had done, and a gentle—and sometimes not so gentle—reminder of his need to atone. And, he had discovered, simple things like long runs, meetings and meditation had the same effect as the drugs.

"How are you managing at work?"

"That's the thing," Tommy said. "I'm supposed to be driving to France tomorrow. I've just signed a contract to bring a shipment of furniture over."

Milton remembered. Tommy ran his own import/export business.

"Do you have another driver?"

"Not for tomorrow."

Milton wondered whether he should help. Service was one of the central tenets of being in the rooms, and he knew that he could help Tommy.

He decided that he would offer. "I could do it."

"Thanks, but that won't work—you need an HGV licence."

"I've got one."

"Really?"

"Passed it when I was in the army. Used to drive trucks around Salisbury Plain."

"What about your work?"

Milton had been working in the taximen's shelter in Russell Square until the previous month. "They let me go," he explained. "There wasn't the demand for it to be open nights anymore. Uber is killing black cabs."

"So you're not working?"

"I'm keeping an eye open. Something will come up. Until then, I've got a lot of free time on my hands. Happy to help. It wouldn't be a problem."

"I'll pay you," Tommy said. "I don't expect you to do this for nothing."

"Whatever you like," Milton said. "Just tell me when and where, and I'll be there."

Chapter Two

TOMMY HAD A WAREHOUSE in Hounslow, beneath the Heathrow flight path. He told Milton that they would need to make an early start the next day, so he had risen at four, gone for a thirty-minute run, and then caught the first tube from Bethnal Green.

He arrived at the industrial park at six thirty, just as the sun was rising.

Tommy was preparing the tractor unit. It was an old Scania R480 Topline that looked as if it had already clocked up a good number of miles. Tommy had the bonnet up and was checking the engine oil.

"Morning," Milton said.

Tommy turned. "Morning." He closed the bonnet and wiped his hands on a dirty cloth that he had tucked into his belt. "We're booked on the eleven o'clock ferry from Dover. You ready to go?"

"Whenever you are."

Milton went around to the cab, opened the door and climbed up. The interior was showing its age. The upholstery of the seats was battered, the leather cracked and the padding secured in place with cross-hatches of gaffer tape. The floor was scuffed, one of the mats was missing, and a groove had been worn into the carpeting beneath the clutch from where Tommy, or whoever else had owned the vehicle, had rested his foot. A stack of old newspapers and freight documents sat on the passenger seat.

Tommy opened the passenger door and, using his left hand, awkwardly clambered up.

"She's not much to look at," Tommy admitted as he swept the piles of papers from the passenger seat and onto the floor, "but she's reliable. Never once broken down on me yet. Keys are in the ignition."

Milton reached down and turned the key. The engine grumbled to life. Tommy settled into the seat and then struggled to fasten his seat belt. Milton waited until he was done, clipped his own into place, and put the truck into gear. He pulled out of the yard and started the journey.

#

THE TRIP TO DOVER had been straightforward. They had boarded the ferry and it had departed for Calais on time. Milton and Tommy had enjoyed a late breakfast in the Routemasters café, and now the ferry had arrived in port and they were ready to set off again.

Milton jockeyed the truck out of the maw of the ferry and set off to the south toward Boulogne-sur-Mer. Amiens was two hours on the A26. The law allowed him to drive for only ten hours a day; they had planned for him to have clocked up four hours by the time they reached the warehouse. He would rest while the goods were loaded, and then they would make the return trip. It meant that he would drive for around six hours in total. They were returning on the overnight crossing, so the clock would be reset provided they made it back to the ship before the end of the tenth hour.

Tommy had left spare time to take into account the possibility of delays, but getting out of the port took longer than it should have. Two hours passed before they were even out of the terminal, and Milton was looking at a best case of eight hours behind the wheel to make it back to port. Tommy started to get anxious.

The long queue of trucks was crawling; Milton suspected a crash, but, as they left the facility and joined the main road, he could see that it wasn't that at all.

A crowd of people was clustered around the northbound road. The police and port security were there in force, and the spill over meant that people were on the southbound road, too. Traffic was moving at a few miles an hour.

"Who are they?" Milton asked. "Migrants?"

"Yes," Tommy said. "Trying to get over the Channel. They think it's the land of milk and honey. Suppose it is, compared to what they've got where they've come from. They're desperate to get over. You wouldn't believe some of the things I've seen driving through here."

Milton nudged the nose of the cab out into the road until a gap opened up for them and they could join the slow-moving queue.

"Calais has changed," Tommy said. "I used to love stopping here. We used to call it Beach back in the day. We'd all park our trucks on the front, go and get something to eat and drink, stretch the legs a bit, and sleep in the cab until the ferries started sailing in the morning. We'd never have any trouble. Now, though, you wouldn't dare stop. Some operators don't let their drivers stop anywhere within four hours of here. You know, soon as you get up, you're going to have passengers in the back that you don't want. My old lady worries about me whenever she knows I'm coming through here. I'm a big bloke, John, right? You might think I can look after myself, and you'd be right, but I still worry about it. I've seen them go after drivers with knives when they tell them to get out of the back. But it's serious business. If I get caught with one of them in the back, it's a fine. A big one. My margins are already thin. I can't afford to get stuck with something like that."

The truck in front of them stopped suddenly. Milton braked and brought them to a halt.

"There are thousands of them here," Tommy went on. "The French put them into a camp."

"The Jungle," Milton said. "I've seen the news."

"They come from there, wait by the side of the road, and try to get into a lorry. Some of them go through the tunnel. They get into the freight. I read about one poor bastard, last week, he tried to cling onto the bottom of a trailer. Fell off, got squashed under the wheels."

"And you don't approve?"

"I know they're desperate. But this…" He gestured at the crowds on the other side of the road. "It's chaos."

Tommy was normally an affable man. Milton could tell that this was something that bothered him.

"I don't know," Milton said. "It's difficult. If I was in their situation, if I had a family I couldn't look after, maybe I'd do the same thing."

Tommy nodded. "I get it. I know why they do it. Maybe I'd do the same thing, too. But this—what happens here—it's not right. It's not right for them or for us. You'll see. Wait until we come back through again tonight."

Chapter Three

MILTON MAINTAINED a steady pace, a constant sixty-five that ate up the distance between Calais and Amiens. He had been driving for the better part of four hours, and he was starting to feel tired by the time they finally arrived at the warehouse. He rested while the truck was loaded with the furniture that they had come to collect. Then, after a quick meal and a cup of strong black coffee, he got back into the truck and started back to the port. Google reported that the traffic at Le Touquet was poor, so they had diverted onto the longer—but likely faster—A1 through Arras and Béthune. It was still another two hours behind the wheel, though, and, by the time Calais hove back into view, he was exhausted.

They were five miles from the coast when they saw a solitary figure walking along the side of the road.

"Here we go," Tommy said.

"What is it?" Milton asked him.

"You ready? There's your first migrant."

They saw another man walking through a ploughed field and then another walking down a slip road to the Autoroute.

"Some of the drivers drive close enough to get them to jump back over the barriers. I've gone past some of them who've chucked eggs at the windscreen. I've seen a truck with a smashed window where they chucked a brick."

The truck climbed a hill and, at the top, they were rewarded with a view of the camp where the French had allowed the migrants to gather. Milton slowed. It really was a jungle. There were hundreds of tents and temporary buildings crammed into a space that was too small for them. He saw campfires and hundreds of men and women, some of them with children, milling around.

Milton saw dozens of red brake lights in the gloom ahead and, as they continued on, the traffic started to snarl up. Milton touched the brakes, bringing their speed down to a brisk walking pace.

"Try not to stop," Tommy said.

Milton saw maybe two dozen men on the side of the road. The truck was passing through a cutting, and the ground sloped steeply on both sides. The men had scaled the bank, all the way to the top, and, as Milton watched, they started to clamber down. They were hurrying and looked as if they might slip and tumble down at any time. If they fell, there was a risk that they would roll into the road in front of the truck.

Milton dabbed the brakes.

"No," Tommy said. "Keep driving. Don't stop."

Milton bled a little extra speed off, turned the wheel a little to bring the truck a little farther into the middle of the road, and went by the first two men just as they reached the verge.

The men started to jog after them, but Milton accelerated again and they pulled away. He glanced back in the mirror and watched as they maintained their pursuit.

The traffic had slowed to a crawl ahead of them, a long snake of lorries that were waiting to negotiate a roundabout. The men had all made it over the fence now, and they were all running in their direction.

"They're determined," Milton said.

"Check your door," Tommy advised.

Milton did as he suggested; it was locked. The men reached them. Milton looked back in the mirror as one of them disappeared into the blind spot at the back. The others hurried ahead, four on one side of the cab and seven on the other. One man came alongside and indicated that Milton should roll the window down. Milton looked at him. He was young, no older than his mid-twenties, with jet black skin and bright eyes. He was wearing jeans and boots and a quilted jacket.

"What's he doing?" Tommy asked him.

Milton looked down. "Wants me to open the window."

The others reached the front, all of them indicating that Milton and Tommy should open their doors. Others had joined the group. Milton looked down as one of them stared up at him, putting his two fingers together to make the sign of a gun. He pointed his fingers at Milton and made as if to shoot him. Tommy swivelled as they both heard the slap of a hand against the glass. One of the group had climbed up the side of the cab, knocking against the window.

"Piss off," Tommy shouted.

The man shouted something in return and then spat at the glass. A thick gobbet of phlegm rolled down the window. Milton accelerated gently, the two men in front of the cab slapping their palms against the radiator grille as they stepped aside.

The roundabout cleared and Milton was able to increase their speed to thirty.

They approached the tall fence that marked the start of the port's premises. Milton changed gears and slowed down as Tommy reached across to the dash to collect their papers.

"Want me to check the back?" Milton asked.

Tommy shook his head. "No need. We weren't stopped long enough for them to get inside. And I don't want to stay around here any longer than I have to."

#

THE FERRY left on schedule. Milton and Tommy locked up the truck and went upstairs to the Routemasters drivers' canteen. The food was simple and comforting: steaks, pork chops, béarnaise sauce, chips, mushy peas and gravy. Tommy said he was going to get a bit of sleep. Milton was tired, but his mind was active and he doubted that he would be able to get down. He left Tommy lying across two seats in a quiet lounge and went to explore the ship. He wandered into the duty-free shop and browsed the shelves of cheap perfume, economy French wine and poor quality chocolates, all of them priced to sell. There were other drivers there, and Milton listened to their conversations: French prostitutes, rising fuel prices, tobacco smuggling, bent police and customs officials, migrants. Mostly migrants.

Milton watched as one of the drivers bought a box of chocolates for his wife and, wondering what it would be like to have someone at home that he could buy chocolates for, he went back to the lounge.

Tommy was asleep. Milton went over to the other side of the lounge, where he could watch the sea through the large observation window. The glass was dirty, encrusted with dry salt, and the sea was starting to grow rough. The waves were large, big enough for the ferry to pitch and yaw; spray and spume blasted over the sides and against the glass. Milton felt a little queasy.

He knew now, for sure, that he wouldn't be able to sleep. He went to the café for a polystyrene cup of coffee. He took it to an empty table, put in his headphones, and listened to the Stone Roses as he nursed the drink.

Chapter Four

MILTON DROVE out of the ferry terminal at Eastern Docks and followed Tommy's directions to the overhead roadway. The crossing had been slower than scheduled thanks to the inclement weather, and Milton was tired as he drove the truck down the ferry's ramp and onto the dockside. Tommy had slept for the entire crossing, and, when he awoke, he explained that he had had more than enough practice sleeping regardless of the condition of the sea.

Tommy pointed ahead and Milton followed the signs for EXIT/SORTIE above the two freight lanes until they approached the customs booths. Two officials in high-vis jackets stepped out of the booth and waved for Milton to turn into the inspection bay.

"Here we go," Tommy said.

Milton slowed and brought the lorry to a halt. One of the officials, a man with a frizz of white hair, indicated that Milton and Tommy should get out of the cab. The man's colleague, a young woman, went around to the back of the trailer.

Milton opened the door and climbed down. "Morning," he said.

"Good morning, sir."

"Let's get this over with," Tommy said as he went around to the back.

The man had a clipboard with a sheaf of papers attached to it. He flipped through the papers until he found the one that he wanted and then took out a pen from his inside pocket. "What are you carrying?"

"Furniture," Tommy said. "Just come from Amiens."

The man noted it down. "Destination?"

"Hounslow."

"All right, then. Anything happen in Calais?"

"No."

"You didn't stop?"

"There was traffic outside the port, but we didn't stop. Came straight over. Do you want to have a look in the back?"

"Yes, please, sir. Grateful if you could open it up."

Tommy went around to the back. The mechanical security seal was still in place. It comprised a cable that extended through fixing points on the door, and, when sealed, it generated a unique number that the driver logged. Tommy unfastened the seal, retracted the cable and then opened the two big doors.

The interior of the trailer was lit by the sunlight that glowed through the canvas roof.

Tommy groaned. "Fucking hell."

Milton looked up. A metre-long opening had been cut in the roof. Someone had climbed up with a knife and sliced their way inside.

The official keyed the radio that was fastened to the lapel of his jacket and called for the police.

"Must've happened before we got inside the port," Tommy said. "We were stopped in traffic."

"I don't doubt you, sir."

The interior of the trailer was as Milton remembered it after it had been packed in Dijon. The pallets were arranged along the bed of the trailer, with the cardboard boxes that contained the furniture stacked in neat piles and secured with fabric ties. The first row of boxes was three feet high, but the second—containing larger items—was taller than a man. Milton saw muddy scuff marks on the cardboard where someone had clambered up.

Tommy came up next to Milton. "See what I mean? This is ridiculous."

A Port of Dover police van pulled up to the back of the trailer, and four uniformed officers got out. The customs official explained that he suspected that illegal immigrants were inside the trailer and then stepped aside.

The police stepped up to the back and formed a line.

"Out you come," one of the officers called.

There was no reply.

"We know you're in there."

Milton stood behind the officers and watched. They didn't have long to wait. A pair of hands grasped onto the edge of one of the taller boxes and a man pulled himself up. He was wearing jeans, a lightweight jacket and a beanie. His skin was dark and he wore a wide smile as he slid down onto the pallet, stepped forward and jumped down to the ground. The police attended to him as another two young men clambered up from their hiding place. They were dressed in similar clothes to the first, both shivering a little in the early morning cold.

Milton watched as the three men were cuffed and taken to the police van.

The senior policeman went back to the trailer. "We're going to come in and look," he shouted up. "If there's anyone still inside, it'll be a lot easier to just get out now."

There was a short pause before Milton saw another pair of hands fasten onto the lip of the cardboard box. A fourth man hauled himself up and over, but, instead of jumping down to the ground, he waited inside the trailer.

"Come down, please," the policeman said.

"What will happen to me?"

"You'll be taken to a detention centre, sir. Are you claiming asylum?"

"I'm here to find my sister."

"You can talk about that when you get to the detention centre."

"Please, sir. She has been kidnapped and trafficked here. She is being forced to work as a prostitute."

"Come down. Don't make me come up there."

The man was frantic. "Please, sir. I have to find her. *Please*. If I go to the detention centre, how can I do that?"

The officer turned to the brawniest of his colleagues and

suggested, quietly, that he might have to go up there and bring the man down. The immigrant was young, not even out of his teens, and Milton had no wish to see him manhandled. Before the officer could say anything, he stepped up, braced his palms on the lip of the trailer and boosted himself up.

"Sir," the officer complained, taking a step forward, "please—leave this to us."

The man inside the truck shrank away as Milton stepped onto the pallet. "Help me. I need to find my sister."

Milton spoke evenly and calmly. "You have to come down," he said. "You can't avoid it. Just come down or they'll bring you out. They won't be gentle about it. Come on—make it easy on yourself."

"What about my sister?"

"Claim asylum," Milton suggested.

"And then?"

"You can ask them to help."

"Why would they help me? They don't care."

"You don't have a choice right now."

The big police officer was right up against the lip of the trailer now. "Get down, please," he called up.

The young man looked torn. He glanced at the officer and then back to Milton. "What is your name?"

"John. What about you?"

"Samir."

"Come on then, Samir. We'll get down together."

"Will you help me?"

"Will you come down?"

"If you say you will."

There was something earnest about the young man that Milton found himself drawn to. He meant what he said; his desperation was authentic, and he believed him.

"Okay," Milton said. "I'll help." He turned to the open doorway and addressed the policeman. "He's coming down."

Milton extended his hand and Samir took it, using it to

help him maintain his balance as he negotiated the smaller boxes on the pallet. Milton lowered himself to the ground. "Go easy on him," he said to the officer.

Samir slid down.

The customs official was taking notes.

"I'm going to be fined?" Tommy said to him.

"I'm sorry, sir. Nothing I can do."

"How much?"

"Probably a couple of thousand. That's the going rate."

"What a farce," Tommy said. "Look at what they've done. Who's going to pay for the damage to my roof?"

"You go to the station and make a statement, sir, and maybe the French government will pay."

"And the fine? They'll pay that, too?"

The man shrugged.

"Come on," Milton said, pulling him away.

The officers cuffed Samir and led him to the van.

"Where will they take him?" Milton asked one of the officers.

"Dover immigration centre," the woman replied.

"And then?"

"Depends on his application. Most likely, they'll send him back where he came from. But that's not our problem."

Milton disagreed, although he kept it to himself. Things were different now. They were much simpler. He was interested in helping people who had no other means of helping themselves. Samir had asked him to help, and Milton had said yes.

That made the young man Milton's problem.

Chapter Five

THE BUILDING had been a prison before it was pressed into service as a holding facility for immigrants. It was on the Western Heights on the outskirts of Dover, a monstrous Victorian hulk that presided over the town and the sea beyond it. Milton had driven down from London, leaving at six so that he could arrive in plenty of time for the start of visiting. It was cold when Milton stepped out of the car and looked down from the hill. The town beyond was cloaked in fog, and the sea was invisible, the mournful warning of the foghorn echoing out over the water. Milton drew his jacket tightly around his shoulders, zipped it all the way up to his neck, and set off.

Milton had read through the information on the facility's website before he went to bed last night. The Western Heights had been a fortified area since Roman times, and these buildings occupied the site of fortifications commenced during the reign of Napoleon to counter the threat of a French invasion. The facility was encircled by a high wire mesh fence and Milton made his way to the guardhouse, told the guards that he was here to visit a detainee, waited for the gate to be unlocked and, when it was, he went inside.

He reached the reception area. There was a desk with two clerks processing the details of the visitors. There was a double line of vinyl chairs, each row bolted to the linoleum-covered floor. Milton went to the desk. The clerk asked for proof of identity, and Milton handed over his fake passport.

"Take a seat, please, Mr. Smith. I'll let you know when you can go through."

Milton took an empty seat and looked around. There was only one other visitor, an elderly woman who was still wrapped up in a thick winter coat. That, he supposed, wasn't surprising. If the detainees were young men like the ones who had been removed from the back of Tommy's trailer, then it was likely that they had no relatives here. They would come and seek asylum and, if it was granted, they would apply to bring their families. Others, the economic migrants, had no intention of being detained. They would have tried to sink beneath the surface, evading bureaucracy and taking advantage of the opportunities that would be afforded them. Those men, too, would not normally have family in the country to visit them. They would be left here until their cases were determined. Most would be sent back home.

There was a low coffee table next to the chair, with leaflets spread across it. Milton reached down, took one and read through it as he waited for his details to be processed. The leaflet explained that the centre consisted of five living units—Deal, Sandwich, Romney, Rye and Hastings—and one small separation unit named Hythe. The accommodation was arranged into six-bed dormitories, with a handful of single and double rooms. The leaflet had clearly been written to gloss over the fact that the facility was, in practical terms, a prison. It had a picture of a smiling detainee, and, next to him, a block of text explained that all living accommodation had access to discrete lavatories, power supply and televisions. There were prayer rooms, and all detainees were allowed to keep a mobile phone or borrow one from the centre. Recreational activities were provided in the association areas on each of the units, and detainees were locked up for the least time possible.

A woman took a seat over from him.

"Hello," she said.

"Good morning."

Milton looked at her. She was middle-aged, dressed in a trouser suit, with tousled blonde hair and a gentle face.

"You here to see someone?"

"I am," Milton said. "You?"

"I'm an immigration lawyer."

"Looking for work?"

She frowned a little. "Not chasing ambulances, if that's what you mean."

"Sorry—"

She waved a hand. "It was legal aid before the government made it more difficult to get. It's mostly pro bono now. The men here, the women in the other places they put them, they've got no hope of getting a fair hearing without representation. I don't think that's right."

"That's very noble."

"You're very cynical, Mr…"

"Smith. And no, I'm not. That didn't come out right. Sorry."

She extended a hand across the table between them. "I'm Cynthia Whitchurch."

Milton took her hand. "John. Nice to meet you."

"Who are you here to see?"

"A young man I met yesterday."

"How did you meet him?"

"I was driving the truck he was inside."

"And you're here because…?"

"Because I'd like to help him. If I can."

"And you think I'm noble," she said. "Good for you." She opened her purse, took out a business card and handed it to Milton. "He'll need a lawyer. Tell him to come over and see me. I'm here all morning. If he doesn't want to speak now, that's my office number."

"Thank you," Milton said. "I'll tell him."

A pair of double doors swung open.

"Here we go," Cynthia said. "They're ready for us."

Chapter Six

THE VISITING AREA was a large room with views out over the sea. Some effort had been made to make it look welcoming: there were sofas decorated with colourful throws, a coffee machine offering free drinks, and a plate of biscuits. It was a good attempt, Milton thought, but not enough to deflect attention from the bars on the windows, the guards posted at two doors, and the stifled atmosphere. This was a prison and, despite the attempts to make it something else, it would always be a prison. Cynthia set herself up behind a table with a patterned cloth spread over it to foster an impression, perhaps, of homely friendliness.

The doors were opened and the detainees came inside. There were forty of them, mostly wearing standard-issue prison tracksuits. Some would have been detained as soon as they entered the country, bringing no other belongings with them apart from the clothes that they were wearing. Others would have been detained on the street, with no opportunity to collect their belongings. The majority of them made for Cynthia, waiting patiently to sit at one of the two chairs so that they could discuss their situations. The others helped themselves to the coffee and biscuits and sat around, talking with one another in low voices.

Milton looked, but he didn't see Samir. He was about to get up and ask one of the guards if he could help when he saw him. He was standing in the doorway, peering inside, an expression of wariness on his face. Milton raised his hand to attract his attention and, seeing him, the young man came over.

Milton stood and offered his hand. "Do you remember me?"

"You're the driver," he said, taking his hand.

"That's right," Milton said. "John Smith. And you're

Samir. What's your full name?"

"Samir Al Hamady."

"Sit down. You want a coffee?"

Samir released Milton's hand and sat. "All right."

Milton went over to the coffee machine, slotted a plastic cup beneath the nozzle, and pressed the button for a cappuccino. He turned as the machine started to hiss and churn and looked back at the table. Samir was angled away from him. His hands were clasped on the table and he was looking down at them. He looked younger than he had looked last night. Milton wondered how old he was.

He filled a second cup, put two biscuits on a napkin, and brought everything over. He gave Samir one of the plastic cups, left the biscuits in the middle of the table, and sat down.

"You came."

"I said I would."

"I thought that was just talk. To get me out of the truck."

"No. When I say something, I do it."

"Thank you. But I doubt that there is anything you can do to help me."

"Shall we see about that? What's happened to you so far?"

"They talk to me. They ask am I claiming asylum. I say yes, I am."

"And after that?"

"There are more interviews. I have to meet the person who will look after my case. Then an interview where they decide whether or not I stay. But that is several weeks away. The process can take four months. I have to stay here until they decide, and my sister is still outside. She needs me."

Milton nodded to the busy queues leading to Cynthia. "Have you thought about speaking to a lawyer?"

Samir looked around. "Her?" he said with a sudden derision that took Milton by surprise. "She is here to ease her middle-class conscience. She is here to talk to the poor migrants to make herself feel better, but what do you think she would say if they opened the doors and said we were free to stay in the country?"

"I spoke to her outside. That's not what she thinks. She wants to help."

"She cannot help me, John. And I doubt that you can. The others here"—he gestured around the room at the other detainees—"they say that I have no chance. I will be returned."

Milton looked at him steadily. "Okay, then. What can I do? How can I help?"

"Can you get me out of here?"

"No," Milton said. "Probably not."

"Then there is no point in us talking."

The mood had changed abruptly. Samir looked as if he was about to stand.

"Wait," Milton said.

The young man had been despondent, but something Milton had said had stirred a flash of anger. He was hot-tempered, with more to him than the downcast man Milton had met yesterday.

"What good will it do me?"

"Ten minutes. Just talk to me for ten minutes. What else have you got to do? Sit in your room all day?"

Samir sighed and settled back in the hard plastic chair. He spread his hands on the table.

"Where did you get into the truck? Calais?"

"There was a queue of traffic. You stopped. I followed a man who climbed up."

"You took a big risk."

"I've tried the other ways. They said the trains might work, but others said they were too difficult now. They have guards and dogs. A truck is the best chance of getting over the border. And I nearly did."

"Why are you so desperate?"

He looked away.

"Your sister?" Milton pressed.

Samir stared out of the barred window that looked out onto the sea below, and, for a moment, Milton thought that he was ignoring him. But then he turned back to face him, and Milton saw that his eyes were damp.

"Her name is Nadia," he said. "We… we…" His voice became choked and, as Milton watched, he bowed his head and started to cry. Milton sat there awkwardly. He had never been a particularly empathetic person, and his previous career had cauterised any vestiges of sensitivity that he might once have possessed. He sat quietly, waiting until Samir had composed himself again.

When Samir looked up again, his cheeks were wet. "She is my little sister," he said. "Do you have a sister, John?"

"No," he said.

"Then you will not understand."

"Just tell me."

"We are from Eritrea. It is a dangerous place. My father opposed the regime. That was enough for the government to kill him and my mother. They would have killed us, too, but we were able to get away. We travelled north, through the desert to Libya. We left on a boat. It was dangerous. Many people fell into the water and the boat did not stop to collect them. We watched them try to swim after us until we couldn't see them anymore."

"Where did you land?"

"Italy," he said. "There is an island—Lampedusa. We have a cousin in Turin. He said that we could stay with him until we found work."

Samir paused again, and Milton saw that his hands, resting on the table, were now clenched into tight fists.

"What happened?" he said.

"There were men there," Samir said. "They worked for the smugglers. They said the money we had given them was not enough for the trip. But it *was* enough. They said ten thousand dollars. But we do not have ten thousand. They said that Nadia would have to work for them until the money was all paid. I told them that this was bullshit, that they could not say these things, but they did not listen to me. They took Nadia from me. I tried to stop them, but there were four of them and one of them had a gun. They hit me on the head; they knocked me out. When I woke up, Nadia was gone. I spoke to the others afterwards. They said they put Nadia in a van with three other girls and drove them away."

"Drove them where?"

"I do not know," he replied. "I asked. No one knew anything. No one could help me. I did not know what to do, so I went to Turin to meet my cousin like we had planned. There was nowhere else for me to go."

Samir reached out for his cup, his fingers circling it, but he didn't try to take a drink; he was distracted by the memories that the conversation had recalled.

"What happened next?"

"I waited. Two months, John. I had no idea where Nadia was for two months. She could have been dead. I thought about her every day. I waited and waited for her to contact me, to tell me where she was so that I could go and find her and get her. But nothing came. A week, one month, two months. Nothing. But then I had an email. Two weeks ago. She told me that she was in this country. They took her to Calais and then they sold her and the other girls. She said they were bought by Albanians. They smuggled her over the border with a false passport, and now they make her work in a brothel." He spat the word out. "They said that she would have to work there every day until the money was paid back. They keep her there. She cannot leave. She did not even know where she was for the first month. They say she must stay there; she cannot speak to anyone outside the house."

"So how did she email you?"

"My sister is clever," he said. "She stole the telephone from a man who had been to see her. She used the phone to send me an email, plus a map of where she is. I have saved the map."

"Where is she?"

"A place called Wanstead. Do you know it?"

"It's in London," Milton said.

"That was where I was going to go. I go to the brothel, I find my sister, I get her out."

"Just like that?"

"Why not?"

"I know a little about the Albanians. They are very influential in the underworld here. They're very dangerous. They don't make idle threats, and they won't be pleased to see someone interfering with their business."

"They have her in a house," he said. "Not a prison. I can get her out."

"And then?"

He looked at Milton with an expression of certainty. "And then maybe we make a life for ourselves here. I claimed asylum. If they refuse me, we go back to Turin. The Albanians will never find us."

Milton regarded him critically. He was naïve and he was underestimating the task ahead of him. More important even than that was the impracticality of his plan: he was locked up in the detention centre and there was no guarantee that he would be allowed to leave.

"You asked why I took a risk last night," he said. "Nadia is why. I got this far. She is my sister, John. I love her. I *am* going to find her. I am going to take her away from them."

Milton had already decided what he was going to do. He had seen the desperation in Samir's face as he was dragged away from the truck yesterday morning. It wasn't just the desperation to get into the country, although that was part of it. He had seen panic there, the gut-wrenching fear that he wouldn't be able to do something that was obviously of great importance to him. That was why Milton had come to visit Samir, and hearing the story that the young man related had reinforced his determination that it was the right thing to do.

He would help him.

"I'm going to be brutally honest with you," Milton said. "Is that all right?"

Samir shrugged.

"I don't know much about asylum. Maybe you get it, maybe you don't. But the climate isn't friendly towards asylum seekers at the moment, and I'd say that the odds are against you. If that happens, there's no way you'll be able to try to get your sister."

"Then I come back."

Milton shook his head. "And, assuming that you did get out of here, or you come back again, my guess is that it'll be more difficult than you think to get Nadia away from the Albanians. And if we make another assumption and say that you can do all of that, that you can get out of here and then find her and get *her* out, what's to say that they don't come after you? Are you confident you can hide from them? Two Eritrean refugees won't be that hard to find in London or Turin."

"How is this helpful to me?" he said sourly.

"I'm just laying it out for you. I think you need to be realistic."

Samir stood. "Thank you," he said. "Thank you for coming to see me."

He stood, put the chair beneath the table and made to leave.

Milton stood, too, and stepped out so that he could block Samir's way.

"Get out of my way."

"Relax," Milton said. "I'm trying to help you."

Milton put his hand on Samir's shoulder, but the young man shrugged it aside. "If you want to help," he said, "then get out of the way and leave."

Milton stayed where he was. He stared at the young man, knowing full well the effect that his icy-cold stare would have on him.

"You're not listening, Samir. I'm offering to go and get your sister for you."

That stopped him in his tracks. "What?"

"Sit back down," Milton said gently.

"How can you help me? You're just a truck driver."

Milton stepped out of the way. He went to the other side of the table and pulled Samir's chair out again. "No," he said. "I was just driving to help a friend. That's not what I do. I used to do other things."

"What do you mean? What are you? Police?"

"Military," Milton said, and then added, "To begin with, anyway."

Samir was confused. He lowered himself back down into the chair. "I do not understand."

"I can't tell you everything," Milton said. "But I have some other experience that makes me exactly the kind of person you need."

Part 2

London

Chapter Seven

THE FOLLOWING DAY, when Milton returned home to his small flat after his morning run and opened up his laptop, there was an email waiting for him. It was from Samir. Milton had pressed him to speak to Cynthia and, to his surprise and pleasure, he read that Samir had spent half an hour with her and that she was going to take his application for asylum.

The email continued. Samir said that he was attaching the map that his sister had sent him. Samir explained again that his sister had located herself using the stolen phone.

Milton clicked on the file and a map opened up. The map was of Wanstead, a pleasant suburb to the east of the city, not far from Milton's flat in Bethnal Green. Milton looked more closely. There, in the centre of the map, was the marker that denoted Nadia's location.

Milton opened up his browser and navigated to Google Maps. He dropped the small icon on the A113, to the east of the Green Man roundabout, and waited for the Street View image to appear. He dragged the cursor around the screen and examined the area. There was a large twenty-four-hour emergency veterinary practice that had been established within a large Victorian villa; a petrol station; a busy road, with cars parked half on the pavement and half off it; and, beneath a screen of leafy trees, a small apartment block at number 103. Milton squared the view so that he could look directly at the building and zoomed in. It was three storeys tall, the windows suggesting that there were four flats within. Each flat had a small Juliet balcony, and satellite dishes had been fixed to the walls. Access was via a porch on the ground-floor level, next to a row of garages that had been built adjacent to the main building.

It looked like any other apartment block, the kind of

building that you could find in every London district. It was bland and nondescript, with no suggestion that it was used for anything other than accommodation.

Milton decided that he would pay it a visit.

Chapter Eight

MILTON HAD a beaten-up Volkswagen Polo parked outside his flat. He had bought it for five hundred pounds cash from a dealer on Autotrader.com. It was scruffy and far from comfortable to drive, but it had the benefit of being anonymous and would not stand out during surveillance. He drove east, through Hackney and Homerton, until he was on the A12.

It was two in the afternoon when he came off the roundabout and found the road that he had looked at on his computer. He remembered the vet's. It had a reasonably large car park and he indicated right and turned into it. There were half a dozen cars parked up, and he reversed the Polo into an empty space.

He got out of the car and looked around. The apartment block was opposite him. He walked back to the main road and crossed over. There was a small wall that separated the building's grounds from the pavement and a flagstone path that led to the porch. Milton looked left and right. There were pedestrians on both sides of the road, but he was satisfied that none of them were paying him any attention. He followed the path to the porch. A sign fitted between two lanterns read AGINCOURT. The way inside was through a wooden door with two large glass panels; he put his palm against the frame and gave a gentle push, but the door was locked. There was a keypad set onto the wall to the right of the door.

He leaned forward, putting his face to the glass and cupping his hands around his eyes so that he could see better as he looked inside. There was a row of metal post boxes, a stack of Yellow Pages and clothes catalogues on the floor, and a table that held a dead plant in a small pot. A corridor led away from the porch and, inside, Milton thought he could make out a flight of stairs and the doors to the two ground-floor flats.

"Can I help you?"

Milton turned. An old woman was on the path behind him. She was carrying two heavy plastic bags that were crammed full of shopping and she was looking at him with suspicion.

"Good morning," he said, putting a smile onto his face. "I'm doing customer research. I was really hoping to speak to someone inside the block, but no one is answering."

"Customer research? For who?"

"Sky. I don't suppose you would mind speaking to me?"

She glanced down at her bags. "I've just done my shopping."

"I've only got a few questions. It'll take five minutes."

She paused, considering his offer. Milton gave her another smile. "Those look heavy," he said, nodding down at the bags. "Let me help you take them inside."

"I suppose I could answer a few questions," she said. "Do you have a card?"

"I do, but I'm afraid I left it in the car. Do you need me to go and get it?"

She looked at him shrewdly. "Is there any money involved?"

"There is, actually," Milton said. "Ten pounds."

"Well then," she said. "Why didn't you tell me that? Let's get inside."

Milton stooped down to collect her shopping as she stepped up to the keypad. He watched as she entered the code—5396—and heard the buzz as the lock disengaged.

"This is a nice street," he said as he followed her into the lobby.

"It's all right," she said, opening the post box for number three and checking to see whether anything had been left inside. "Been here twenty years. It's changed."

"How?"

"The neighbours," she said. "You used to know

everyone. Used to be invited in for tea and a biscuit, for a chat—you don't get none of that no more. Don't hardly know who I'm sharing the building with. That's the way of the world these days, though, isn't it? Progress."

"I suppose so," Milton said.

The woman's flat was on the first floor. She climbed the stairs, stopping on the half-landing to catch her breath, and then continued up. They reached the landing. The stairs continued up to the second floor, but she led the way into a dark corridor with two doors facing each other. The doors bore brass numerals: three and four. The woman took a key from a string that she wore around her neck and unlocked the door to number three.

The flat inside was larger than Milton had expected. The door opened onto a long corridor with doors to the left and right and a large lounge at the end. Milton guessed that at least two of the doors were for bedrooms.

"Bring those through here," the woman said, heading into the kitchen. It was a long, thin room with cupboards and a fridge-freezer on the longer walls and an oven at the far end.

"You didn't tell me your name."

The kitchen was spacious, with modern appliances. "It's John Smith," he said.

"I'm Emily. Can I get you a cup of tea?"

"That would be lovely." He put the bags down on the counter. "Do you mind if I quickly use the bathroom?"

"Of course not. Just down the corridor. Next to the sitting room."

Milton left her in the kitchen and made his way down the corridor. The doors to his left and right were ajar, and he pushed them open a little so that he could confirm that they were bedrooms. Both rooms were of decent size. He reached the sitting room, nudged that door open, and noted that it, too, was spacious.

He went into the bathroom, waited a moment, and then flushed the toilet and returned to the kitchen. Emily was pouring hot water into two mugs.

"Sugar is over there," she said, pointing to the counter.

"Not for me," Milton said. He paused for a moment as he considered the best way to bring the conversation around to the topic he was most interested in. "Can I ask what you meant when we were downstairs, Emily? About how it's changed here?"

She leaned back against the counter, her mug clasped in both hands so it could warm them. "It's like I was saying, John, how this place ain't like what it used to be. The flat downstairs, number two—take that for an example. There's a lot of men coming and going there all hours of the day. You see them standing outside sometimes, like you were when I saw you."

"Why are they doing that?"

"Well, I don't like to gossip," she began, although Milton could see from the ease with which she opened up on the subject that gossip was one of her remaining pleasures in life. "But it's obvious, ain't it? That used to belong to a nice old lady. Sweet old dear, she was, until she passed away. Whoever bought it, they've turned it into a brothel. There've been times when I've gone down the stairs to get my post or go out and I've heard them at it, through the door, like bloody animals. Like I said—all hours, day and night."

"Who owns it?"

"Foreigners," she sneered dismissively. "Poles. Eastern Europeans. One of them lot. Can't tell you no more than that. Wouldn't even want to know."

"How many people are in the flat?"

"I don't know," she said. Her salaciousness subsided as she realised something was not as it ought to be. "Wait a minute. I thought you said this was market research?"

"It is," Milton said. "Sort of, anyway."

"What are you? Police?"

Milton replaced the half-finished mug of tea on the counter, took out his wallet and withdrew a ten-pound note.

"Thank you," he said, leaving the note on the counter next to the mug. "You've been very helpful."

"Who are you?" she said as she reached out and took the note. "You said you were from Sky."

"I'll see myself out."

Milton left the kitchen, glanced up and down the corridor one final time, and left the flat. He descended to the ground floor and, instead of walking straight ahead to the door and the road outside, he turned right, into the darkened corridor. There were two doors, each marked with the same brass numerals that he had seen upstairs: here, though, it was one and two.

The door to number two was behind a hinged iron cage. There was a small camera angled down from the wall at the end of the corridor and a peephole in the door. It would be impossible to get inside without the occupants knowing about it.

Milton didn't believe that he was visible to the camera, but he had no desire to dawdle. He turned back and made for the door. The old woman, Emily, was standing on the half-landing, glaring down at him.

He opened the door and stepped down onto the path. A man turned off the pavement and started toward the door. He was dressed in a suit with a grey overcoat and polished black shoes. Milton stepped aside to let him pass. The man saw him and froze.

"Hello," Milton said.

A look of pure panic broke over the man's face. Milton read him at once: someone from the city, headed east for an illicit assignation. The man glanced down at his feet, turned, and went back in the direction from which he had arrived.

Chapter Nine

THE MAN WALKED TO THE NORTHWEST. Milton remembered the geography of the area from his online exploration last night: this road ended at a crossroads with the High Street. To the left was Snaresbrook station; to the right, a little farther, was Wanstead station. Both were on the Central Line, two separate branches that diverged at Leytonstone.

Milton guessed that the man would go left to the nearer station and take a train back into the city.

He followed.

The man passed an almshouse for the elderly and then a series of large Victorian villas that Milton guessed would be worth in excess of a million pounds each. They passed a block of flats from the sixties and an Indian restaurant that had been set up in an old pub.

The man looked back and saw Milton behind him. He walked faster. Milton kept up the pace. He looked ahead. They were approaching a taller block of flats. It was set back from the road, separated from it by a residents' car park.

Milton hurried and closed the distance.

The man turned again.

"What do you want?" the man called back.

Milton followed.

"Leave me alone."

Milton was close now and jogged the final few metres. He reached out with his right hand and grabbed the man around the fleshy part of his left arm, just above the elbow. He found the pressure point and dug into it with his thumb. The man squealed with pain and was helpless as Milton guided him off the pavement and into the car park. There was a red and white security bar that blocked access, but Milton led the man around it until they were up against the side of the building itself. There was a brick enclosure where the building's large industrial waste bins were kept. Milton shoved the man into it. They wouldn't be seen from the road now.

The man looked out of place, up against the foul-smelling bins and dressed in his obviously expensive suit.

"Get away from me!" he said.

"No," Milton said. "I don't think so."

"I'll call the police."

"Go on, then," Milton said. He reached into his pocket and took out his phone. He dialled 999.

"What are you doing?" the man said.

"Calling the police. Better think about what you're going to say. Maybe that I've been following you from the brothel you were about to visit?"

Milton pressed dial and put the call on the speaker.

The operator's voice was audible: "What service do you require?"

The man looked dumbfounded.

Milton muted the microphone. "We both know why you were there," he said.

"What service do you require?"

"You can speak to the police if you want, but I wouldn't recommend it." He offered the phone. "Here. All yours."

"Get away from me."

The man tried to sidestep him, but he was too slow to react as Milton ended the call, reached out with his left hand and caught him around the wrist. Milton turned and pressed into him with his right shoulder, forcing him up against one of the bins and, with him pinned there and helpless, he reached into the man's jacket with his right hand and found his wallet. He took it out and stepped away.

"What are you doing?"

Milton flipped open the wallet and took out the contents. There was a driving licence in the name of Richard Astor, several credit cards in the same name, a security card for Percy, Smith & Williams, and a South West

Trains season ticket.

"Well, then, Richard. I have a name to go with a face now. I've heard of Percy, Smith & Williams. It's a law firm, isn't it? What's their line on their staff using prostitutes?"

The scale of Astor's predicament finally dawned on him. "What do you want?"

Milton dropped the cards, the ticket and the licence on the ground, and Astor knelt down and scrabbled for them amid the rotting trash. Milton splayed the wallet open and took out the remaining items. There was a tightly folded wad of banknotes; Milton opened the wad and thumbed through the six fifties.

"You want money?" Astor said as he looked up, desperation in his voice. "Fine. Take it."

The last thing in the wallet was a folded piece of paper. Milton took it out and unfolded it. It had the word "Agincourt" and a telephone number written on it.

"Agincourt," Milton said. "That was above the door, wasn't it? Who'd answer the phone if I called this number?"

"No," Astor said. "Please don't do that."

Milton took out his phone again. "Who, Mr. Astor? Shall I call and ask them?"

"Please," he begged. "I'll tell you whatever you want. Please. Just don't call them."

"Why not?"

"Because they're dangerous."

Milton put the phone back into his pocket. "Go on, then. Who are they?"

"I don't know. They're Eastern European. I don't know where from."

"How many times have you been there?"

"Four times."

"Names?"

"The guy there is called Drago."

"Surname?"

"I don't know. I don't know anything else about him."

"Describe him."

"Big. Lots of tattoos. Shaven head. He doesn't say much."

"What about the girls?"

He squirmed a little. "There were three last time."

"Keep going."

"I don't know anything about them."

"What about the one that you saw?"

"Her name is Nadia."

Astor was still on his knees. Milton reached down for him, grabbed him by the lapels, and hauled him up. He pushed him back against the bins and held his forearm across his throat. He pressed. "Describe her."

"She's black. Young. Twenty, twenty-one. Pretty."

"When was this?"

"Last week," he choked out.

"And you were going to see her again today?"

"I asked for her. Please—"

"How did you find out about it?"

"Online," he said. "There are forums. Reviews."

"Like TripAdvisor?" Milton said bleakly, quite happy to make Astor squirm a little more.

"Please," he gasped. "I can't breathe."

Milton pulled his arm away and stepped back. He folded the piece of paper and put it into his pocket.

"What are you doing?" Astor said.

Milton eyed him.

"Give that back."

Milton punched him in the gut, a stiff right-hand uppercut that bent him over. He grabbed the lapels of Astor's jacket and hauled him up until they were eye to eye again. "Don't ever go there again."

"I w-w-won't," he gasped out between gasps for breath.

Milton left him there and walked back toward the brothel.

Chapter Ten

MILTON HELD the piece of paper that he had taken from Astor and stared at it, thinking. There didn't seem to be any point in waiting. He had confirmation that Nadia was in the brothel, and he didn't want to leave her there any longer than necessary.

There was little to be gained by planning, either. He had broken into places more heavily secured than the flat, and he could already think of two ways that he could address this one.

The first was the direct approach, but he knew it was unlikely to work. The cage door was a significant obstacle, and, if he was unable to get in, he wasn't interested in leaving a record of his presence on the hard drive that the security camera would be connected to.

The second approach was to use subterfuge and misdirection. That was more appealing. And Milton could do subtle.

He retraced his steps back along New Wanstead until he reached the building. It was four o'clock now and nothing had changed: the same steady flow of traffic, pedestrians walking by on both sides of the road.

He crossed over to the vet's, made his way through the car park to his Polo and got inside. He could see the entrance to the building through the windscreen, together with another twenty metres to the right. The view to the left was obscured by a fence. It was a good enough view for what he needed to do.

He took out his phone and the small Bluetooth speaker he kept in the glove box. He connected the phone and the speaker, found the Faith No More playlist he had put together last night, and, as "Ashes to Ashes" played out, he settled down to wait.

#

MILTON HAD only listened to three tracks before he saw a possible candidate walking toward the block of flats from the east. It was a man dressed much like Astor, in an overcoat and suit. He paused when he was ten metres from the property, took out his phone and referred to something on the screen. A map, perhaps. Directions. He walked on, stopped at the gap in the wall, and looked up and down the road.

Milton could see that he was nervous. He switched off the music and watched as the man turned off the road and made his way down the path to the front door.

Milton took his chance. He stepped out of the car and crossed the car park.

The man hesitated again; Milton waited until he pressed the intercom and leaned forward to speak into it, crossing the road between two cars as the man pushed the door open and walked inside.

Milton walked briskly, crossed the pavement and made his way to the door. He could see the man inside, just making his way through the lobby to the corridor beyond.

Milton entered the code on the keypad, waited for the lock to buzz open and went inside.

He paused at the letterboxes, opened one and pretended to look through the junk mail that had been stuffed inside. He could see the door to number two. The man was waiting there.

Milton knew that he would have to judge this to perfection; timing was everything.

He heard a deadbolt slide back and looked up as the glow of the lights from inside the flat leaked out into the corridor.

Milton heard voices.

"Phillip?"

The name was pronounced with a harsh, guttural accent.

"Yes."

"Come in."

The man stepped back. There was the sound of a second deadlock sliding back and then a creak as the cage was opened. Milton dropped the letters and left the lobby, walking straight on past the staircase and into the corridor. The man he had followed from the street had stepped inside. A second man, well over six feet tall and heavily built, had stepped out into the corridor to let him pass. He was reaching for the cage door when Milton reached him.

"Excuse me," Milton said.

"What do you want?"

Milton assessed him: six two, two hundred and fifty pounds. He was wearing jeans and a cut-off T-shirt that revealed sleeves of tattoos on both arms. He had a nose that looked like it might have been broken a few times in the past; small, mean, dark nuggets for eyes; and, above them, a thick, slab-like brow. A shaven head, with the faded track of a scar that curled from the point of his right ear around to the back of his head.

"This is Agincourt?"

The man glared at him.

"I'm looking for flat three."

"Upstairs," he said.

Milton was smaller than the man: two inches shorter and at least thirty pounds lighter. He doubted that the man would have realised the threat that he presented, and, certainly, he seemed content enough as he reached out for the bars to close the cage.

Milton stepped up, two quick steps, transferring his momentum into the straight jab that he landed square on the man's nose. Milton put his weight behind the punch and followed all the way through, aiming at a point six inches behind the man's head.

The man staggered backwards into the flat, and Milton followed him inside. Phillip was just inside the door, and both Milton and the big man tumbled past him. Milton glanced around quickly and saw the exact same layout as the flat that he had visited upstairs: kitchen to the left, corridor with doors ahead of him on both sides, another two doors at the end.

The big man stumbled back, but quickly recovered his balance. Milton followed up, throwing a left-right-left combination into his ribs and then both sides of his head, but the man had raised his guard and only the left cross into his ribs found its mark. Milton punched again with another right; the man managed to snag Milton's wrist, hauled him closer and butted him in the face.

Milton saw stars and tried to free his wrist. The man had a firm grip, and, before Milton could loosen it, he lashed out with a left hook that caught Milton on the side of his jaw.

Milton opened and closed his mouth, feeling the click of the loosened bones.

Two trailers of blood were running freely from the big man's nostrils; he reached up and swiped the side of his hand across his top lip, looking down at the blood on his finger and then wiping it against his trousers.

"You are dead man."

There was a radiator fixed to the wall of the corridor with a wooden mantel atop it. A mobile phone had been left there, next to a china bowl that contained a handful of change and a set of keys. There was a butterfly knife next to the bowl. The man collected it and, with a nasty flourish, he flicked his wrist and snapped the blade open. The man lowered himself into a well-balanced crouch and, passing the knife from hand to hand, he started forward.

Milton backed away from him.

This hadn't gone quite as well as he had hoped. Maybe he was getting old. Losing his touch.

One of the other doors opened and the face of a young woman peered out.

Milton became aware of movement behind him. He dared not turn, but he knew what had happened as soon as he heard the click of the front door: Philip had made a run for it. He had slammed the door shut. Milton would have to open it before he could leave, and he doubted the man with the knife would allow him the luxury of the time that he would need to do it.

He was committed now.

The man closed in on him.

Milton needed to change the environment. He stepped to the side, into the kitchen. It was the same as the kitchen he had visited earlier: long and narrow, with cupboards on both sides and an oven and hob at the end. He glanced behind him and saw a stack of saucepans, a row of plastic bottles, and microwave meals in cardboard sleeves. There were no windows, and no other way out. He looked for a knife of his own, but he couldn't see anything.

Milton backed farther into the kitchen. It was so narrow that he would have been able to reach out and touch both sides at once. It was claustrophobically small.

The man followed.

"Let's talk about this," Milton said, raising his hands to ward the man off. "No need to do anything rash."

"Too late for that," the man said, the blood still running down his face.

Milton bumped up against the oven.

He was out of room.

The man penned Milton in.

He switched the knife to his right hand and lunged at Milton's gut.

Milton was ready: he blocked down, slapping against the man's wrist and forcing his thrust to the side, the blade scraping a track down the laminate coating on the cupboard door. The man barged forward, leading with his shoulder. There was no room to dodge, and Milton was bounced back against the oven. He gasped for breath and, as the man drew back the knife, he landed a left-hander into the man's broken nose; it wouldn't have been strong enough to damage on its own, but the nose must have been painful and it was enough for the man to fall back.

Milton took his chance. He reached for the bottles on the counter, grabbed the one he wanted, and twisted off the cap. He raised the bottle and squeezed it just as the man raised his knife ready for another thrust. It was bleach; it streamed out in a concentrated jet, splashing against the man's chest until Milton adjusted the aim and played it across his face. He yelled out in pain as the liquid burned his eyes. He dropped the knife to the floor and tried to wipe it away, but it was no good.

Milton reached over to the counter and grabbed a bin liner that had been left there. It contained a little trash; food waste and an empty can fell out onto the floor as Milton upended it. The man stumbled blindly; Milton swept his legs to drop him to the floor and sat atop him, his knees pinning the man's arms to his sides. Milton worked the bag over the man's head, pulling it down and holding it in place with both hands around his neck. The man realised his predicament and tried to release himself. He could not. Milton had leverage; he held the bag in place and started to squeeze, pressing down with both hands and choking the man's air supply. The man bucked beneath him, but Milton was able to stay in place and keep his arms at his sides. He squeezed harder with his hands, harder and harder, the bag pulsing in and out less and less as the man struggled for breath.

Milton held on until he felt the man's body go limp, and then he kept the bag in place for another minute. He let go, rolling away from him and lying on his back to stare up at the ceiling as he regained his breath. The man was still. Milton crouched over him, removed the bag and checked that he was not breathing.

He wasn't. He was dead.

Milton went out into the corridor. Both doors were open now, and two young women looked out at him with their mouths agape. He looked down at himself. Blood from the man's nose had smeared across his right forearm.

"Nadia?"

Neither of them answered.

"Are either of you Nadia?"

The woman to Milton's right shook her head.

"Where is she?"

"Not here. They moved her yesterday."

Milton felt a flash of frustration.

The second woman ducked back into the room.

Milton looked at the woman who had answered his questions. "What's your name?"

"Sarah."

The other woman suddenly appeared in the doorway again. She had put on a coat and was carrying a bag. Before Milton could even think about whether he should stop her, she had bustled by him and hurried to the front door. She twisted the lock, opened it, and disappeared into the hallway beyond.

Sarah watched her go. She showed no signs that she was about to follow.

Milton looked down. There was a lot of potential information lying about in the corridor: the pile of envelopes on the floor, the mobile phone, a spiral-bound notebook. There was a carrier bag on the floor next to the envelopes. Milton collected the bag, scooped up the phone, envelopes and notebook, and dropped them all inside. He turned, saw where the cable from the security camera entered the flat and traced it down to a hard drive that was stored in the cupboard that was pushed up against the right-hand wall of the corridor. Milton pulled out the input cables and the power cord and put the drive into the bag.

Sarah was still watching him.

"You can go too," Milton said. "You don't have to stay here."

She looked confused. "I have nowhere to go."

"But you don't want to stay here?"

"No."

"Get a coat," he said. "And anything you want to take. You can come with me."

Still she paused.

"What is it?"

"What did you do to him?"

"Quickly—make up your mind. I'm going. It's up to you."

"Okay," she said. "I come."

She went into the room and Milton heard the sound of frantic packing. He checked the cupboard where he had found the hard drive, but found nothing else that looked as if it might be useful. He walked along the corridor and pushed open the door of the room from which the second girl had emerged. There was a bed, the sheets disturbed, and clothes strewn across the floor. He heard the sound of cursing from Sarah's room, ignored it, and checked the final two doors. The bathroom was filthy, with stains on the floor and mould growing in the sink and the toilet. The final door, which would normally have led to the sitting room, opened into a converted third bedroom. The curtains were drawn and the room was gloomy, but the light from the corridor fell on a large bed, a rattan sofa and a mirrored dressing table that had been covered with cosmetics and bottles of shampoos and conditioners. Perhaps this had been Nadia's room?

Milton closed the door and saw that the doors of all three bedrooms had been fitted with clasps that would have secured them from the outside. He was fingering the padlock on the sitting room door as Sarah emerged from her bedroom, a coat draped over her arm and a small canvas bag over her shoulder.

"Are you ready?"

"Yes."

"Come on, then."

Milton led the way. As he opened the door to the street, he became aware of someone watching and, as he turned, he saw the old woman from earlier staring down at them from the half-landing with a disapproving expression on her face. Milton wasn't concerned. He doubted that the police would ever become involved—owners of brothels didn't tend to enjoy the attention of the authorities, after all—but, even if they did, all she would be able to do was describe what he looked like. Milton could live with that.

Sarah followed him.

"I have a car on the other side of the road," he said. "Come on."

Chapter Eleven

MILTON DROVE to Bethnal Green Road. The café he had in mind was near the junction with Cambridge Heath Road. It was called E Pellicci, and it was something of a local institution. It was, at its heart, a simple enough greasy spoon, but it was so much more than that. The building itself had been listed by English Heritage, and the lovingly maintained decor was one of the reasons that the place had established such an enduring appeal. Chrome-lined custard-coloured Vitrolite panels covered the façade outside, there were colourful sarsaparilla bottles lined up in the window, and the bearded hipster and his tattooed girlfriend who went inside before them were an indication of how the clientele had evolved in recent years as the area became more and more trendy and authenticity became a prerequisite for commercial success.

Milton opened the door and held it open for the girl to pass inside. The interior was lined with wood panelling, and the same Formica tables had been there for decades. The café had been open since 1900 and had been in the hands of the same family ever since. It had come to prominence in the sixties when the Krays, who lived in nearby Voss Street, held court here. The notoriety of the twins had propelled it into prominence, but it had maintained its popularity thanks to the friendly smiles and banter from Mama Maria and her children, Anna and Nevio Junior.

Anna was behind the counter and she smiled when she saw Milton come inside.

"All right, John?" she said.

"Good, thanks. Can I take the usual table?"

"Course you can, love. What do you want?"

"Two cups of coffee," he said, and, looking down at the desserts inside the glass-fronted cabinet, he pointed at the Portuguese *pasteis de nata* and held up two fingers.

"Sit down," she said. "I'll bring it right over."

Milton led the girl to a table in the corner of the room. The table was beneath a monochrome picture of the original proprietor and his family. He sat down and indicated that she should do the same. She paused for a moment, looking back to the door. Milton could see that she was scared, but that wasn't surprising, under the circumstances. It was possible that she might decide that she was safer on her own. He didn't want her to think that. She would have been wrong.

She put her bag on the floor beneath the table and sat down opposite him.

"It's all right now," he said. "You're safe. And you don't have to worry about me."

"That… m-m-man…" The words came in an awkward stammer. "What did you do to him?"

"He pulled a knife," Milton said.

"What did you do to him?"

"I knocked him out."

"No, you didn't."

"I—"

"If you lie to me, I'm just going to go."

Milton held his tongue.

"You killed him, didn't you?"

"He would have stabbed me."

And, Milton thought, *you don't think he deserved it?* He let that ride.

She looked down at the table and cursed in Arabic.

"I didn't have a choice," Milton said. "He would have killed me."

"Do you know who he is?"

"No," Milton said. "Who?"

"He is one of them. The Albanians who run the brothels. I think he is very senior. They will kill you for what you've done."

"No, they won't," Milton said. "They have no idea who I am."

"They had a camera."

"I took the hard drive. It wouldn't matter. They won't be able to find out who I am. And they won't know where you are, Sarah. Please, try to relax. It's over. You're safe now."

She paused, her fingers tapping against the Formica. "Okay," she said at last. "What do we have to do now?"

"What do you mean?"

"I can't go to the police."

"You don't need to do anything. I told you: you're safe here. No one knows where you are."

"I can't stay here forever. What do I do next?"

"I'll help you."

Anna brought over the drinks and the cake just as the café door opened. The bell tinkled cheerfully and the girl looked up in panic. Milton turned. An elderly man shuffled to the counter with the aid of a stick, took off his flat cap, and ordered a pot of tea.

"Enjoy," Anna said as she went back to the counter to serve the newcomer.

Milton looked back to the girl. He slid the cake across the table. "Have some," he said, with no idea if that was the right thing to do. "It'll make you feel better."

She took the fork, sliced off a portion and put it in her mouth. Milton waited. She finished the first mouthful and quickly took another. She was hungry.

"My name is John," he said. Milton saw that her fingernails had been bitten down to the quicks. He tried to think how he could get her to lower her guard. He was going to need her to trust him. "Where are you from?" he asked.

"Syria."

"Where?"

"Tartus."

"How long have you been here?"

"A month."

"You were there the whole time?"

"Yes."

"The people who ran the house—they brought you into the country?"

"Yes."

Milton indicated that she should elaborate.

"I came over by boat. They said they would help me. They had factory jobs, they said. They took me to France and then brought me to England. When I got here, they said that I owed them money and that the factory jobs had all gone. I was stupid. I knew what would happen, but I ignored it. They said I would have to work to pay them back. They meant I would have to work in the houses."

She reached out for the mug and put it to her lips. Milton waited for her to put the mug back down again.

"In the flat?"

"The brothel. They have lots. All around London."

"Do you know where the others are?"

She shook her head.

"There was a girl in the house," Milton said. "A black girl. Her name is Nadia."

"She is from Eritrea."

"You know her?"

"A little."

"Where is she now?"

"They moved her yesterday night."

"Why?" Milton asked.

"They move all the girls. We work at one place for a while, then we go somewhere else. Variety. So the men do not get bored."

"But you haven't been moved before."

"No," she said. "I haven't been here long enough. But there is talk. The other girl tonight, the one who ran? Her name is Maryana. She's worked for them longer. Months. She said that was her fourth house."

"Would Maryana know where the other houses are?"

"I expect so. You would have to ask her."

"Do you know where she might have gone?"

The girl shook her head.

Milton felt a flicker of frustration. He was getting nowhere fast. "Do you know who they are? The people who ran the house?"

"They are Albanian."

"You said. And their names?"

"The one who was there—" she paused and swallowed "—the one you killed, his name was Drago. He had been with us for a week. The man who normally ran the flat was small and thin, big teeth, like a rat. His name was Ilya. But there had been trouble. A rival gang had threatened to burn down the flat, and Ilya was frightened. Drago was there to make sure the flat was safe. Drago has a brother. A twin brother."

"And his name?"

"Florin. He came now and again to collect the money. Maryana said there were others, like Ilya, but I never met them. I just met Ilya, Drago and Florin."

Milton could see that he was unlikely to get anything much more useful out of her. She was too new to the brothel. She didn't know anything.

"What do I do now?" she said, when she sensed that his questions were at an end.

"I'll take you to the police."

"No," she said, her face losing colour. "I told you. I can't."

"Relax—"

"They said the police would just bring us straight back to them again. It's just like home, in Syria—you can't trust them. The police are corrupt." She rubbed her thumb and forefinger together. "The police can be bought."

Milton understood why she was reluctant. The police in the places that were familiar to her were tools of the regime. They were corrupt, not to be trusted—criminals with a badge. And she had no experience of the police in this country and no reason to think that they would be any different from the authorities at home. It would take time to persuade her otherwise.

"It's not like Syria," he said with as much reassurance as he could muster. "It's different here. They'll look after you."

"And then what? I'm not supposed to be here. The police will hand me over to the immigration people and they'll deport me. And I can't go back to Syria."

Milton paused to think. She had a point, but he wondered whether she was being overly pessimistic. He had read in the newspaper that the government was resettling several thousand Syrians who had fled the conflict. Given that she was already in the country and that she had suffered an ordeal, he suspected that would improve her chances. But he was no expert. She would need a lawyer to help her claim asylum, and he doubted that she had the money for that. He would have to help her.

"Okay," he said. "This is what we'll do. I'll get you fixed up with an immigration lawyer. They'll help you claim asylum, and then you'll be able to stay—get a proper job, away from the Albanians. But you can't stay on the streets. They'll find you."

"So where do I go? I have no money for a hotel."

"You can stay with me."

She looked at him with an expression that looked like disappointment. "And what would you expect in return for that?"

Milton could see what she meant: she thought he was going to ask for sex in return. "No," he said, raising his hands. "Nothing like that. You don't have to do anything."

"Really? I don't believe you. All men are the same. Nothing in life is free."

"I'm not interested in that."

She frowned, and he sensed that he was digging himself into a deeper hole. She thought that his expression of disinterest was a slight.

"That's not what I meant," he stumbled. "I'm not handling this very well. I'm offering to help because it's the right thing to do. I'm making a mess of this, aren't I?"

She smiled and, with that, her face brightened and he saw how pretty she was. "A little."

"No strings. I don't expect anything in return."

He was conscious that he had lost control of the conversation and now he was blundering through it like a fool.

"Where do you live?"

"Bethnal Green. Very close. I've got a little place."

"All right. I will come."

Chapter Twelve

IT WAS ONLY A SHORT DRIVE from Bethnal Green Road to Milton's flat at Arnold Circus. He parked the car in an empty space, the sodium glow of the streetlamp overhead reflecting off the windscreen. He turned to the girl. She had fallen silent again in the car, and now she showed no signs of being ready to move.

"Are you all right?" he asked.

"Why are you doing this?"

"Because I want to help you."

"But you don't know me. I still don't understand."

Milton paused, resting his hands on the wheel as he tried to find the words to explain his motives to her. "I used to have a job where I had to do things that I shouldn't have done. I did it for a long time and I have a lot of things on my conscience. I decided that the only way I could make up for the things that I've done was to help people who needed it."

"Is this your place?"

"Just over there. I have a ground-floor flat. Nothing special, but you'll be safe there."

"And no—"

"And nothing. No obligations and no strings. Just somewhere you can stay until you've worked out what to do next."

She nodded. "Okay."

She opened the door and stepped out.

#

MILTON LED the way across the path to the building. The door to his flat was in a concrete lobby that was often used by the local junkies to shoot up. Milton moved them on whenever he saw them, and he was relieved to see that they were elsewhere tonight. Sarah had followed close behind, and, when he turned to check on her, he saw that she was anxiously looking to the left and right. He was as confident as he could be that they had not been followed, but anxiety on her part was reasonable given what she had experienced.

"Here we are," Milton said. "Home sweet home."

He took his key from his pocket and unlocked the door. He opened it, went inside and then stepped aside so that Sarah could follow.

The flat was small. He had one bedroom, a compact sitting room, a kitchen and a bathroom with a shower. Milton made sure to keep it neat and tidy. He always started his day by making his bed, and the discipline of that routine extended to ensuring that the rest of the flat was kept in good order. It was a hangover from his days in the army, but it had remained important to him.

Sarah stood in the small hallway as Milton came inside and locked the door behind him.

"You can hang your coat up there," he said, pointing to the row of hooks on the wall. There was nothing else on the hooks. Milton had only one coat, and he was wearing it.

She took off her jacket and hung it up.

It didn't take long to show her around. He started with the lounge, then the kitchen and bathroom. He finished in the bedroom.

"You have just one bedroom?" she said.

"Yes. But you can have it. I'll sleep in the lounge."

She didn't argue. She sat down on the edge of the bed, unzipped her knee-high boots and worked them off.

"You know they will try to find you," she said.

"They don't know where we are. You don't need to worry."

"And you don't know them. They are dangerous." She put a hand to her face and scrubbed her eyes. She was tired. "There was one man," she said. "A customer. He beat Maryana. Ilya was there, but the man beat him, too. Drago found him. He said they knew where he worked. Drago and Florin, they visited him. They beat him very badly. They took videos of him, after, and showed them to us. 'We protect you,' they said. 'Don't worry, we look after you.' They are frightening, John. They know things—find things. You say I am safe here, but how can you know that?"

"Because I know that we weren't followed. If you stay inside, there's no way that they could possibly find you here." Milton wanted to add that he was dangerous, too, and that it would take more than an Albanian thug to worry him, but he didn't. He didn't want to make her feel worse for the sake of his own ego.

"Do you want a drink?" he said instead.

"Please. Could I have a coffee?"

He pulled the bedroom door closed and went through into the sitting room. His laptop was on the table and he switched it on. It was an old machine, woefully underspecified by today's standards, and it always took five minutes to boot properly.

Milton went into the kitchen and made two mugs of coffee, then took them and a packet of biscuits to the bedroom. He knocked on the door and, at her quiet response, went inside.

Milton put one of the mugs and the biscuits on the bedside table. "Here," he said.

She reached for the mug and put it to her lips. "Thanks."

"I'm just in the other room," he said. "Shout if you need me."

"What are you doing?"

"Just looking through some stuff. You hungry?"

"A little."

"You like curry?"

"Sure."

"I'll cook. We'll eat in an hour. Okay?"

"Okay," she said.

Milton left the door partially ajar and went to the sitting room. The computer was ready. He took the bag of things that he had taken from the brothel and removed the hard drive that had been attached to the security camera. The USB cable was still plugged into the drive. Milton took the free end and plugged it into his laptop. The icon for the hard drive was visible after a moment. Milton clicked on it. The software that powered the device created new folders for every day that the camera was operational. The hard drive had a capacity of half a terabyte, and Milton expected that the software would start to overwrite older files once its capacity was reached. He scrolled down the files for all the available dates; there were two weeks' worth, more than long enough for yesterday to still be available.

He opened the folder. Two files were inside: they were labelled 'AM' and 'PM.'

He clicked on the file marked 'AM' and waited for his computer to open its default video player. He saw a static angle from the wall to the side of the doorway. The view included the cage to the left and a square of light that fell from the lamp on the door to the flat that was opposite the brothel.

The time and date were overlaid atop the image. The player had the standard navigation options; Milton clicked play and then set the footage to scroll through at ten times normal speed.

The door opened for the first time at 12.10 a.m. A man emerged, turned away from the camera before Milton could see much of him, did up his coat, and then headed into the lobby and out of the camera's line of sight. A customer.

A man appeared from out of the lobby at 12.25 a.m.: a nervous shrew of a man who glimpsed into the camera long enough for Milton to see his face. He knocked on the door, it opened, and he went inside. Thirty minutes passed before the door opened again and the man hurried out. A second customer.

The view was uninterrupted for the next eight hours.

At 8 a.m., the light from the other side of the hall was interrupted by a line of shadow that was caused, Milton guessed, by the door opposite the brothel being opened and closed. Milton guessed that the occupant of flat number one was going to work.

Another two hours passed before the next visitor came into view. Milton slowed the feed to run in real time. It was a man of reasonably large build, with a shaven head and a broad, flat nose. He knocked on the door, waited, then knocked again. He was impatient. He turned his head and looked over into the lens of the camera. He had small mean eyes, brows that protruded a little, and a stern line to his jaw. Milton could see the resemblance immediately between him and the man that he had killed inside the brothel.

Brothers, then.

The door opened, there was a brief conversation, and the man went inside.

Milton found that he was clenching his fists in anticipation.

The man came out again after eight minutes. He was carrying a leather bag in his right hand. The night's takings, perhaps? He stepped aside to allow a woman to pass through the door. She was black, much shorter than the man, and very pretty. She stood nervously as a third person came out of the doorway. Milton recognised him at once. It was the man he had killed. All three of them were in shot for twenty seconds. The two men conversed, laughed at a joke, pointed at the girl and laughed again. The men were identical. Milton watched. The twins embraced before the man with the bag reached out for the girl, grabbed her by the arm and led her away.

Milton scrubbed backwards through the footage. He added start and stop points, copied the fragment, pasted it into an email and sent it to himself. His phone chimed to confirm that it had been received.

He went back into the hall and peered into the bedroom. Sarah was still on the bed.

"Can I show you something?"

She looked up. "Of course."

He took out his phone and opened the clip that he had sent himself. He put the phone down on the bed so that she could see it.

"Can you tell me who these people are?"

She pressed play.

Milton watched her face as she watched. Her expression changed: she became fearful.

"Who are they?"

"That man is Drago."

"What about the other man?"

"That is Drago's brother. Florin."

"And the girl?"

"That is Nadia."

Chapter Thirteen

MILTON PUT ON HIS COAT and went back into the sitting room. The girl looked settled. She had moved into the sitting room and was sitting on the sofa, wrapped in a blanket that Milton had collected from the bedroom, and was watching junk TV. Milton had cooked a big pot of curry for them both and they had eaten together. Her empty bowl was on the floor by her feet. He stooped down to collect it.

She looked up and saw that he was wearing his jacket. "Where are you going?" she asked, her face betraying a flush of concern.

"I'm going to the shop," he said. "I need to get some bits and pieces. Do you need anything?"

"Do you have any beer?"

"I don't drink."

"Not at all?"

"No. Not for a long time. But it's fine. Buying you a beer isn't going to be a problem. What do you want?"

"I don't mind," she said. "Whatever they have. And some cigarettes."

Milton took his own packet from his pocket and tossed it over to her. His lighter was on the table. "Help yourself," he said. "The landlord doesn't like tenants smoking in the flat, so open a window and blow the smoke outside. What cigarettes do you like?"

"Marlboro Lights."

"The shop's on the main road. I'll be twenty minutes."

Milton went outside, closed the door and, after a moment of thought, very quietly put the key into the lock and turned it. He didn't think that she would try to leave, but it paid to be cautious. She had been through an ordeal, and there was the possibility that it might make her a little unpredictable. Milton wanted her to be there when he came back.

It was a short five-minute walk along Calvert Avenue to get to Shoreditch High Street. The area had long since graduated from edgy to hip and was now so part of the establishment that the bars and eateries looked like they were trying too hard. Men and women were gathering, and the sound of music drifted out onto the street.

There was a twenty-four-hour convenience store on Old Street, and Milton went inside and bought the things that he thought they might need: shower gel, more coffee, a loaf of bread, croissants and jam for breakfast. He found the aisle with the alcohol and paused there uneasily. The hard stuff was with the cigarettes behind the Plexiglas screen that protected the owner, but Milton ran his finger across the bottle tops that stuck out of the cardboard packaging for a six-pack of Corona and knew that he could do plenty of damage to himself without needing gin or vodka. Just one beer would set back all of the progress he had made, all the days of sobriety that he had chalked up. He would be careful. He picked up the six-pack, put it into the basket and took it to the counter. He asked for a packet of Marlboro Lights and requested two fifty-pence pieces in the change.

He checked his watch. He had been out for ten minutes. He had just one more thing to do.

There was an old-fashioned telephone box on the corner of Hackney Road, outside Browns strip club and the Turkish kebab house. Milton went inside. The window had been smothered with calling cards for the prostitutes that worked the area, a panoply of naked flesh and the promised satisfaction of practically any fetish. The booth was foul smelling and had, Milton guessed, most likely been used both as a toilet and a shooting gallery.

He picked up the handset and rested it between his shoulder and ear. He took out his own phone, navigated to the entry in his contacts book that he wanted, and dialled.

#

ALEX HICKS WAS SITTING with his wife, watching television. They were on the sofa, and Rachel was leaning against him. He had his arm around her and, as he squeezed her a little tighter, it seemed again as if she was more substantial than she had been even last week.

"You're putting on weight."

"Thank you, darling," she said, pretending to take offence and jabbing her elbow into his ribs. "Feel free to go and get me another tub of Ben & Jerry's."

"Don't you think so?"

She turned her head so that he could see her smile. "Maybe."

"How much?"

"Four pounds since last week."

He squeezed her. "That's great."

"I haven't been sick for three days."

"I know."

"And I'm sleeping better."

He squeezed her again. He knew how close he had been to losing her. The cancer had been aggressive and virulent, and her doctors had all but given up hope of stopping it. It had started with a melanoma on her back. They had gone to the doctor and she had ordered a biopsy; they had both known, when she was called and asked to make a quick appointment at the surgery, that the news would not be good. It was cancerous, the doctor said. They had to get rid of it. It was removed within a week, but the disease had already spread. The MRI revealed a five-centimetre growth under her left breast that had wormed its way into the wall of her chest. They took that out, too, and the growth on her right lung. They scanned again and found more. It was growing more quickly than they could take it out. The doctors were talking about more surgery and then a course of brutal chemotherapy, but Hicks and his wife had both realised that they were not hopeful of being able to do very much at all.

The news seemed to suck all the fight out of Rachel, but

Hicks was determined that they would not give up. He had researched available treatments and had discovered one that seemed to offer the best chance. It was available at the Memorial Sloan Kettering Cancer Center in New York. They were offering a targeted treatment involving two experimental drugs—Opdivo and Yervoy—that had demonstrated encouraging results in precisely the same kind of cancer that Rachel had developed. They had visited the clinic and started the program. That had been two months ago. The last MRI found no cancer anywhere in her body.

The drugs, while scouring it away, had inflicted the usual panoply of side effects. The Opdivo and Yervoy had caused colitis and pneumonitis. The additional chemotherapy she had undergone had meant that she had lost her hair, and, over the course of the program, a quarter of her body weight. But there was no doubt about it: her hair was regrowing and she was putting weight on again.

His phone was on the arm of the sofa. It started to vibrate.

Rachel looked over at it. "Who's that?"

"I don't know." He picked it up and looked at the screen. "It's a London number."

"You don't recognise it?"

"No."

"Leave it."

"No," he said. "I'd better answer it."

He pressed to accept the call and put the phone to his ear.

"Hello?"

"Hicks?"

"Yes. Who is this?"

"It's Milton."

His wife looked over at him. "Who?"

"Business," he said, a little flustered.

"It's eight o'clock, Alex."

"I know." He disengaged himself from her and stood. "I'll take it in the study."

She nodded, unconcerned, collected the remote control and flicked between the channels. Hicks left the lounge and went into the room that they used as a study. He shut the door behind him and put the phone back against his ear.

"Milton?"

"Hello, Hicks."

"Is everything okay?"

"Everything's fine. How are you?"

"We're good."

"Your wife?"

"She's better, thanks to you. What's going on? I didn't expect to hear from you."

"I need a favour."

Hicks felt a twist of anxiety. Milton was not the sort of man to ask for favours, and Hicks knew that he was in his debt. "What do you need?"

"Don't worry. It's nothing. A surveillance job."

"What? A person? A place?"

"A place. There's a block of flats in Wanstead. East London."

"Okay," he said. "Anything else?"

"It's a brothel. I just want to know if anyone goes in and out."

"That's easy enough."

"And I want to know who runs it."

"That might be more difficult. How will I tell the proprietors and the punters apart?"

"It's run by the Albanian mob. There's a certain look."

"Big? Nasty-looking?"

"Exactly. If you see anyone you think might be involved, I want you to follow them. Find out where they're based."

"I can do that. How long do you want me to watch it?"

"A day should be enough."

"Starting when?"

"Tonight. Can you do it?"

"I'll have to check." He paused, remembering what Milton had done for him and Rachel, and, correcting himself, said, "No, forget it. It's fine. I'll drive down now. Where?"

"You got a pen and paper?"

Hicks reached over for the newspaper he had been reading earlier and took a pen from the table. "Fire away."

Milton gave him an address in East London and Hicks noted it down.

"Anything else I need to know?"

"Yes," he said after a pause. "Be careful. I broke into the flat yesterday. There was a man there. He tried to kill me."

"And?"

"He's not with us anymore."

"Jesus, Milton. Police?"

"I doubt it."

"But they might be looking for you."

"I'm sure they are. I don't know whether they'll have a description of me. But they don't know you."

"Is there anywhere I can lay up and watch?"

"Not really. You might have to be creative."

"Is it too late for me to say no?"

"Too late."

"All right," he said. "It's against my better judgment, but I'm in. Anything else I need to know?"

"Not really." Milton paused, and Hicks could hear the buzz of traffic and voices on the line. "Actually, there is one thing. Your P226?"

The gun was in the garage with the rest of his equipment, hidden in a void beneath the floor. "What about it?"

"Bring it."

Chapter Fourteen

KOSTANTIN PASKO stepped out of his car. It was ten in the evening and raining, the kind of persistent drizzle that was one of the things that he disliked most about London. It wasn't proper rain, the sort that would roll in off the Šar Mountains and soak Ljuboten and Brezovica for days. It was a fine mist that wasn't heavy enough to require an umbrella, but still soaked into clothes and chilled the bones. It was an apologetic kind of rain, and Pasko thought that it suited the country very well. It was a small annoyance, balanced by the opportunities that had been afforded to him since he had arrived in London fifteen years earlier.

Pasko had arrived here after the Yugoslav wars, hidden amongst the tens of thousands of Kosovar and Albanian refugees who had come to London to escape the endless violence back home. He was a veteran of the Kosovo Liberation Army, battle hardened from guerrilla warfare in the mountains and ready to use his experience to make a better life for himself and his family. The Eastern Europeans had flooded London since the nineties, but, of all of them, it was the Albanians who were the most feared. There were hard men among the Poles, for example, but there were stories of Polish builders who had worked for Albanian foremen only to have been beaten to a pulp when they had the temerity to ask for their wages at the end of the week. Pasko's people were strong and proud and fearless.

Pasko had built that kind of reputation for himself. He had been drawn to the underworld like so many of his fellow soldiers. He had initially served under a man named Adem and, when he had been killed in a shoot-out with the Turkish gangsters who controlled the heroin trade, Pasko's reputation made him the obvious replacement. He had not retaliated against the Turks for weeks, waiting until they must have assumed that the threat had passed. But Pasko did not forget. He found the man responsible and shot him to death as he had his beard trimmed in a barber shop on Green Lanes.

But Pasko did not want the drug trade. His genius had been to leave the heroin to the Turks and to take Albanian business in another direction. He had long looked at Soho with hungry eyes. The sex trade appealed to him. It had been the province of the Maltese for decades, but Pasko looked at them and saw them for what they were: soft and arrogant, made fat and lazy by their relationships with the corrupt police officers who ran vice from West End Central. He watched them for months, identifying the leaders and those who would need to be removed so that he could usurp their positions. And then, when the time was right and the pieces were all in play on the board, he had made his move. There were four murders in one night, coordinated and executed with precision, and the Maltese mafia had been decapitated. The Albanians swept in and took the vice trade for themselves.

That had been ten years ago. They had consolidated since then, and, once Soho was secure, Pasko had instigated an aggressive program of expansion. He had properties everywhere now.

Hundreds of girls.

Thousands of customers.

His business made millions.

There were challenges, obstacles that needed to be overcome, but the phone call he had received from Llazar tonight was more worrying than most. He had been in the pub he owned in Maida Vale and had come straight away, driving as quickly as he dared as he made the journey from west to east.

He went to the door of the block of flats. Llazar had texted him the code to unlock it, and he entered it and went inside. He went through the lobby to the hallway. There was a cage blocking the door to his property. He reached through the bars and knocked on the wood.

Llazar opened the door.

"What happened here?"

"Drago," his lieutenant said, swallowing hard and looking away.

"Where is he?"

He swallowed again. "He is dead, boss."

Pasko looked over Llazar's shoulder into the flat. He couldn't remember if he had been to this particular one before. He didn't believe that he had. That wasn't surprising; he had more than fifty flophouses like this in the capital, and the same again in towns and cities as far north as Birmingham and as far south as Portsmouth. He had long since delegated the task of managing their portfolio to Drago. This one looked much like the others that he remembered: plain decor, a little shabby. Pasko wasn't interested in luxury. It was expensive to play at that level, and the return was not as attractive as the amount he could achieve in the budget end of the market. Drago had a head for spread sheets and numbers, and he had explained it all to him.

Pasko corrected himself: he was thinking of his son in the present tense. He felt a flash of anger.

"Get out of my way," he said as he shouldered his way past Llazar and made his way down the corridor.

The first door off the corridor was closed. He went by it, saw the open doors for the bedrooms and the bathroom, glanced inside each of them, and turned back. He walked back to the closed door.

"In here?"

Llazar nodded, seemingly afraid to speak.

Pasko turned the handle and opened the door. He took it in: the narrow kitchen, the counters on both sides of the room. Simple and utilitarian. Everything as he would have expected apart from the body that was laid out on the cheap linoleum floor. The skin of Drago's face had been badly burned: patches of it were red, parts had been scratched away, and his forehead was disfigured by a series of florid boils.

Pasko felt a burst of anger so strong that he had to put out a hand against the counter to steady himself. "What happened to his face?"

Llazar pointed to the bottle of domestic bleach that was standing on the counter. The top had been removed. "He was sprayed with that. Then—" he paused, swallowing again "—then, I think, the bag."

Pasko closed his eyes until the dizziness passed, and then he stood. "Who found him?"

"I did. I came to collect the takings. There was no answer, so I let myself in. The girls were gone and Drago was there."

"The door?"

"Closed."

"The police?"

"No. I've been here ever since I found him. No one has been here."

"Good."

He looked down at Drago and then closed his eyes.

"It is the Maltese?" Llazar asked timidly.

They had had trouble from them over the course of the last few weeks. They had finally found their balls, and now, after all this time, they were trying to take back their business. They had torched two of the flats and had threatened this one. Drago had been here to keep an eye on it.

"Boss?"

It didn't matter who it was. There would be consequences for what they had done.

"Boss?"

"Get Florin."

Chapter Fifteen

ALEX HICKS had made excellent progress. He had left his house in Cambridge at nine thirty, and the roads had been kind. He arrived on the outskirts of London at eleven and finally ran into traffic. There had been a crash earlier beneath the North Circular and the police had closed the outside lane; it had formed a bottleneck, and the cars were beginning to stack up. Hicks drummed his fingers on the wheel, reached up to where he had mounted his phone to the windscreen, and opened the map again. Google was estimating a delay of forty minutes.

As the lines of traffic rolled ahead at fifteen miles an hour, he thought back to the phone call. He had been surprised to hear from Milton again. Two months had passed since Hicks had last visited him in the cabmen's shelter where he had been working. Things had looked very bleak for Hicks and his family before Milton had become involved in their affairs. Hicks had been a soldier, serving with distinction in the SAS before he had quit to try to build a career in private security. He had been desperate for money: the only treatment that offered any hope for Rachel was the experimental program in America that the NHS would not fund. Hicks had had to find one hundred thousand dollars, and his wife's deterioration was a daily reminder that time was not his friend.

Before they had been sucker-punched with the news of her diagnosis, Hicks had been approached by General Richard Higgins, a retired senior officer who had put together a squad of ex-soldiers who were working together on jobs that Higgins sourced. They called themselves the Feather Men on account of their light touch, but they were ruthless killers who took down pimps and criminals and robbed them of their assets. Higgins asked if Hicks wanted in. Hicks had been uncomfortable enough with the idea of it when it had first been pitched to him and had said no. But then the cancer came and his priorities were changed. He had no choice. He said that he had reconsidered, and Higgins welcomed him with open arms.

Hicks had been involved in the operation that had led to the death of a senior Turkish drug baron, but any misgivings he might have had about what he had done were ameliorated by the money that the deaths provided. Thousands and thousands of pounds. He put it toward the money he was saving for the treatment. He had half. He needed the same again.

Hicks might have been able to stomach working with Higgins, but it was when he learned that the general was involved in the protection of senior establishment figures who had been involved in a paedophile ring in the seventies and eighties that he had decided that he had to get out.

Milton, who had been investigating the death of one of the victims of the conspiracy, had helped him to extricate himself. There had been a vicious gunfight on the estate of a grand house in the Cotswolds, during which Milton had pitted the general's men against a small army of underworld goons who were protecting the man whom Milton wanted dead. Hicks had been badly injured during the melee when the general had surprised him, but he had escaped with his life.

Milton's objectives had been settled, and he could have left Hicks to deal with the general alone. He didn't do that. Milton used himself as the bait in a trap to lure the old man out of hiding, and Hicks had taken him out in a drive-by that had been executed cleanly, with no witnesses, and with minimal risk that they might be discovered.

Milton had stolen the general's cash and given Hicks the balance that he needed for his wife's treatment. That was a reason for lifelong gratitude in itself. And then Milton had saved his life, too. He wouldn't—couldn't—forget that.

But there was more, too. Another reason why Hicks was

minded to help. Milton was a quiet man, not prone to outbursts of emotion, not really prone to emotion at all. It was difficult to like him because Milton didn't care whether he was liked. He was solitary and seemingly happy with his solitude; certainly no one would have been able to describe him as a conversationalist. But there was a coldness that lurked beneath the surface, an implacability that Hicks found unsettling. It was expressed in his eyes—icy blue and pitiless—and Hicks had no interest in finding himself in opposition to him. He knew about Milton's history as an assassin, and his reputation, and he had seen, at first hand, what it was like when he allowed the coldness to find its full expression. John Milton was probably the most dangerous man that Hicks had ever met and, while he doubted that Milton would take offence if he turned him down, he had no interest in testing that supposition.

A day or two conducting low-level surveillance was nothing compared to what Hicks owed Milton, and not enough of an imposition that he would risk upsetting him by saying no.

#

EAST LONDON. MIDNIGHT.

The building that Milton wanted Hicks to watch was in Wanstead, an area that Hicks did not know very well at all. But Milton's directions were good, and Hicks was able to find it without trouble. It was at the end of New Wanstead, near to the large Green Man roundabout, and, since it was late and the road was quiet, Hicks reduced his speed and crawled by it so that he could take a good look. It was an average sort of place, and Hicks couldn't see anything out of the ordinary. The windows were all dark. The lobby was dark.

He drove on, found a road that he could turn around in, and came back again on the opposite side of the road. He parked the car when he was still a quarter of a mile away so that he could return on foot.

He strolled along the pavement, slowing his pace as he passed the building and regarding it carefully. There was nothing out of the ordinary that he could see.

He stopped, took out his phone and pretended to take a call. He glanced around again. There was nowhere obvious that he could make discreet observation of the property save the car park of the vet's directly opposite. That wasn't ideal; there were only two other cars in the car park, and a man in a car at this time of night was going to be obvious to anyone who was suspicious enough to be looking. How careful did he have to be? Milton hadn't given him very much in the way of a briefing.

He started off again, back toward his car.

#

HICKS'S PHONE RANG AT TWO IN THE MORNING.

He picked it up and put it to his ear.

"It's me," Milton said. "Anything?"

"I've been outside. There's nothing going on."

"No activity?"

"Nothing. Everything is quiet. What am I looking for?"

"Anything that says the brothel is still open."

"It doesn't look like it."

There was a pause.

"What do you want me to do?" Hicks asked. "It's not easy to put surveillance in right now. There's no one here. I'll stand out if I park outside it."

"Get some sleep and go back tomorrow. I'll call you in the morning."

Chapter Sixteen

THE NIGHTTIME VIGIL had revealed how difficult it would be for Hicks to keep a watch over the property for a whole day. He could park in the car park, but anyone with even the most basic counter-intelligence experience would notice him there. A vacant building to hide inside would have been perfect, but there was none. He could walk up and down the street, but that, too, was less than optimal. He would be noticed.

Milton had been right: he would have to be creative. During his visit to the property the previous night, he had noticed something that would offer him the chance to stand out a little less. He checked out of the cheap hotel where he had spent the night and navigated to the nearest builder's yard. He needed supplies. He loaded a trolley with the things that he needed: a canvas bag, a fluorescent tabard, overalls, a tool belt, steel-capped boots, small plastic CAUTION signs, and a collection of screwdrivers. He paid the clerk, took the trolley to his car, and loaded the goods into the back.

He returned to Wanstead and parked his car farther up the road, out of sight. He collected the bag from the boot and put on the overalls, work boots and tabard. He returned to the telephone junction box that was located on the pavement near the building and set out the warning signs on either side of the box. He knelt down, took out a suitable screwdriver and used it to open the door. There was a tangle of colourful wires, red and yellow and green, a confusing nest that made no sense to him.

It was a tenuous disguise that wouldn't pass even the most cursory of inspections, but he hoped that the ruse would shield him from curiosity.

He pretended to busy himself with work.

#

HICKS SPENT the morning outside the property without incident. It was an excellent position from which to observe. He saw three men and two women emerge from the property. The men and the younger woman were obviously off to work, dressed in smart clothes, some with cases. The other woman, much older, looked as if she was off to the shops when she left at a little past nine. Hicks had seen nothing all day to make him think that there was a brothel there: no obvious customers, no working girls, nothing.

Milton called at midday for an update. Hicks reported and said that he would stay in position through the afternoon.

Milton called again at four and said that if there was still no activity by six, he should leave and come to meet him.

Hicks settled into place again for another stint. Two hours passed and still there was nothing.

That was enough.

He closed the box and secured it again, folded up his warning signs, and took them and the rest of his gear back to his car. He stowed them away, took off the tabard and dropped that in too, and got into the front. He started the engine, glanced across at the building one more time as he went by, and then drove away.

#

HICKS DROVE deeper into East London. He knew London a little, but not Bethnal Green. He knew it by reputation—he had just finished reading a biography of the Kray twins, and he recognised some of the road names as he went by them—but he had never spent any time here. He hadn't given much thought to where Milton was living. The idea of him in any kind of domestic setting was difficult to picture. Hicks didn't know him well enough to say for sure, but Milton didn't strike him as someone who would put down roots. There was something elusive about him, and Hicks had already concluded that he wouldn't have been surprised if he never heard from him again after the business with Higgins was concluded.

Hicks turned onto Arnold Circus and glanced up at the names of the blocks that were fixed to the walls. He checked Milton's address once again: he had said that his flat was in Hurley House. He found the right building, parked and got out of the car. He looked around. There was the circus, the large central space penned in by iron bars, with cars parked in bays around its circumference and a bandstand in the middle. There were the impressive buildings, seven storeys tall and obviously built decades ago, with different coloured courses of bricks so that they reminded Hicks of the layers of a cake. This little patch of East London was still poor and had escaped the relentless process of gentrification that was seemingly pressing out from the centre of the city to swallow the districts to the east. These buildings were solid and well constructed, some of the flats were large, and they were all within walking distance of the Square Mile. Hicks liked tradition and history, but he knew that the benefits of the area meant that it could only be a matter of time before the council sold up to developers and the inhabitants were pushed out.

It was not the sort of place that he would have expected to find a man like Milton, but then he realised that he had never considered the sort of place that a man like Milton might favour. He thought about that now and, as he started towards Hurley House, he could see that it made sense. Each building in this congregation must have held twenty or thirty flats, with perhaps a thousand people washing in and out of the streets that fed into the circus every day. For Milton, who favoured swimming beneath the surface, it must have been ideal.

The entrance to Hurley House was through an old green door with eight opaque glass panels and a covering of gaffer tape where the ninth pane should have been. There was an intercom on the left of the door, but as Hicks pressed the handle with his hand, he saw that the lock had been damaged and the door was standing open. He went inside and followed the adjoining corridor. It was a foul-smelling passage, with litter strewn on the floor and graffiti on the walls. Hicks followed it to a vestibule that had three doors. Milton's flat was in the middle. Hicks knocked. He glanced back into the vestibule as he waited. It, unlike the corridor through which he had passed, had been kept reasonably clean.

The door opened.

"Hello, Hicks."

Hicks turned back. Milton was standing in the doorway.

"Come in."

There was a small hallway, and Milton directed him to the door to the left. Hicks went through into the sitting room. It was a simple, plain room with nothing much to soften the harsh white walls. There was a neatly folded sheet and blanket on the sofa. The furniture was plain and economical, there was a copy of the *Times* on the coffee table, and the only concession to personality was the music playing through the Bluetooth speaker that had been left on the windowsill.

"What are you *wearing*?" Milton asked him.

Hicks looked down at the overalls and boots. "I've been working as a telephone engineer."

"Very inventive."

"My stuff's still in the car. I'll get changed in a minute."

"Do it now if you like. I'll make us a drink. What would you like?"

Hicks said that he would like a coffee, and Milton told him to change in the sitting room while he went to make them. Hicks went back out to the car, grabbed his clothes, went back into the sitting room and changed into them.

The decor was ascetic. A set of Ikea shelves had been arranged against the wall. Milton had stacked a small row of books there; Hicks saw volumes by Dickens, Hardy, Joyce, Orwell and le Carré. A tightly rolled sleeping bag had been left on the floor next to the sofa. There was a small table with two wooden chairs and, atop it, a vase of yellow daffodils. There was a packet of opened cigarettes on the table with a black oxidised Ronson lighter resting atop it. There was also a watch on the table, a silver Rolex Oyster Perpetual that was most likely the most expensive object in the entire flat. It was certainly worth more than the beaten-up laptop on the sofa next to him. Hicks opened the lid and saw a video player on the screen, the image frozen on a man and a woman in a darkened lobby. He closed it.

He looked around. It was small. There was a hallway, with doors leading to the bathroom and the bedroom. He heard the sound of a shower from inside the closed bathroom door. Someone was in there. The bedroom door was closed, but Hicks pushed it open and saw that the bed had been left unmade. Milton and Hicks were both former soldiers, and Hicks suspected that Milton shared the same foible as he did when it came to leaving an unmade bed. Hicks made his as soon as his wife was having her morning shower; the discipline of making up the bed, the same routine every morning, repeated day after day, was the foundation upon which an organised and productive life could be built. Hicks guessed from that and the sleeping bag that Milton had given someone else his room.

"Hicks?"

"Coming," he said.

Milton came out of the kitchen with two mugs. He took them into the sitting room and put them on the table.

"How's your wife?" he asked.

"Good," Hicks said.

"The cancer?"

"It's gone."

"Full remission?"

"They're never going to give us a guarantee, but they can't find any right now. It's better than we could have hoped for. She only had months left. If it wasn't for the money—"

"Forget it," Milton said, interrupting him.

Hicks nodded. "I am grateful, John."

Milton waved it off. "Just means you owe me a few favours. I'll call them in when I need them."

"I can live with that."

"What did you see?"

"Nothing. If there's a brothel there, they didn't have any business going on last night or today. It's like I said: I saw residents going in and out, but that's it. The men visiting places like that have a look about them that's hard to miss. And I didn't see anyone who looked that way."

Milton nodded.

"You want to tell me what's going on?" Hicks said.

Milton took a sip of his coffee and then set the mug down again. He told Hicks about how he had met Samir, and what the young man had told him about his sister and what had happened to her. He explained what had happened in the flat yesterday, about the man he had killed and the woman he had taken out with him.

As Hicks listened, he remembered what Milton had done for Eddie Fabian. The man had been threatened and Milton had helped him, staying the course even when it was obvious that the men who wanted Fabian dead were dangerous. Helping those who had no one else to whom they could turn was evidently something that Milton was focussed upon. Hicks had no idea why that should be so important to him. It was difficult to reconcile with Milton's history in Group Fifteen.

"So the girl—Nadia—she wasn't in the flat?"

"No," Milton said. "That's the problem. They took her away the day before. And the flat was the only lead I had. If they've abandoned it, I'm out of options."

"There must be something else you can do. This other girl?"

"Her name is Sarah," Milton said. "And she doesn't know anything. I've asked."

"What are you going to do, then?"

Milton paused. "There is something. I need another favour."

Hicks parted his hands, inviting Milton to continue.

"The other girl." Milton angled his head and gave a nod. "Sarah. She's in the bathroom."

"You brought her here?"

"She had nowhere else to go."

"You trust her?"

"There's no reason not to trust her," Milton said. "I couldn't leave her on the street. But I need you to look after her."

"Babysitting?" Hicks replied.

Milton said yes.

"Why do you need me to do that?"

"She's a refugee, like Nadia and Samir. Syria. The smugglers who helped her get to Europe sold her to the Albanians, just like they sold Nadia."

"So take her to the police."

"She won't go. She's scared. She thinks they'll just give her back to the pimps."

"So tell her it isn't like that."

"I've been trying. But look at it from her perspective. You ever been to Syria?"

"Never had the pleasure."

"I have. I did a job there. It was bad then, and it's even worse now. The police there are corrupt. She thinks it's the same here. She thinks she'll just get handed over to them again. I get it. She doesn't know any better."

Hicks looked at Milton with scepticism. "This is just business for you?"

"What do you mean?"

Hicks shuffled uncomfortably. "The girl…"

Milton rolled his eyes. "Come on, Hicks."

His irritation was obvious, and Hicks backtracked. "I had to ask."

"It's business," Milton said. "Jesus, what do you take me for? I want to help her."

"Okay," Hicks said. "Sorry."

"I'm not going to be here for the next few days, and I don't want to leave her on her own."

"'The next few days?'"

"Maybe a week. I'm going to Libya."

Hicks looked blankly at him. "What?"

"Nadia is gone. Unless you've got an idea I haven't thought of, I've no way of finding out where she is."

"You could ask around."

Milton frowned and shook his head.

"There are ways of asking," Hicks added. "You know—shake a few trees."

"There are more than a handful of Albanian mafiosi in London, Hicks."

"But maybe you could get something."

"Yes, maybe," Milton said. "Maybe I could find her, but that would take time, and I just don't have that luxury. What if they know I'm after her? There was another girl in the brothel who ran. Maybe she's told them who I was asking about. That might not be the best thing for Nadia. If they hear someone is looking for them… well, it's not going to take a genius to put it all together." He shook his head. "No. I need to be smarter than that."

"Which means?"

"Nadia and her brother came across on a boat from Libya. The smugglers sold her to the pimps. So I'll ask the smugglers to tell me who the pimps are, and then I'll find the pimps."

"You'll *ask* them?"

"You said it yourself. There are ways of asking. I have a contact in Tripoli who can help me. I'll find them; they'll tell me what I need. I can be persuasive, Hicks. You know that."

"And Sarah? Does she know what you're doing?"

"No. And it's best that she doesn't. I've told her that I have something I need to do and that a friend is going to keep an eye out for her. That's you."

"What's she like?"

"Frightened. You'll need to be careful with her. Keep an eye on her. She says she doesn't know how to find the Albanians, and I've got no reason to doubt her, but she's been through a lot. I wouldn't be surprised if she's unpredictable."

"Where does she sleep?"

"My room. I was in here last night. Same goes for you. The sofa's comfortable enough. You've slept in worse places."

Chapter Seventeen

IT WAS TEN when the girl finally came out of the bathroom. Hicks heard the door open and footsteps in the corridor. The door to the sitting room opened, and she was standing there wearing a dressing gown that was much too large for her. Sarah was slender and pretty, with soulful eyes and glossy hair that she wore halfway down her back. Hicks guessed that the bathrobe she was wearing must have belonged to Milton.

She looked into the room, her eyes on Milton first before sliding across to where Hicks was sitting.

"Who's this?" she asked.

"Hicks. The man I told you about."

"You didn't say he was coming today."

"It's fine, Sarah. He's a friend."

"Nice to meet you," Hicks said.

She looked at him with distrustful eyes.

Hicks got up and took a step toward her. As he put out his hand, she took a corresponding step back.

She looked across at Milton. "I don't know anything about him."

Milton smiled, trying to be reassuring; Hicks could see that it wasn't a natural expression for him, and the attempt was only partially successful. "Why don't you sit down and introduce yourself, Hicks?"

Hicks stepped back and regained his seat on the sofa. "Okay," he began. "My name's Hicks, like John says. But you can call me Alex. I used to be a soldier. That's where I met John. I did that for several years until quite recently. Since then, I've been doing private work. Security, that sort of thing."

"When he says security, he means keeping people safe," Milton added. "Bodyguarding. And he's a friend. I'll vouch for him. You'll be just as safe with him as you are with me. I promise."

Hicks could see the slight relaxation in her posture, her shoulders settling down just a little and her arms loosening at her sides. She came fully into the room.

"I'm sorry," she said. "I don't know either of you. And I have reason to distrust men I don't know."

"I understand," Hicks said.

"Has John told you?" she said. "What I used to do?"

"Yes. I know what I need to know."

Milton stood. "I need to go."

Sarah looked alarmed. "Where are you going?"

"I told you, Sarah. I'm going to be travelling for a few days."

"For how long?"

"Just a few days. I promise when I get back, we will sort you out. But you'll be fine until then. Just stay with Alex. He'll look after you."

#

HICKS FOLLOWED MILTON out of the flat and into the vestibule outside.

"You're travelling light," Hicks said, nodding down at the small bag that Milton was carrying over his shoulder.

"I don't need much. A passport and a change of clothes. I'll get the other things I need when I get there."

"Weapon?"

"It's Libya, Hicks. That's not going to be difficult."

"No," Hicks conceded. "I don't suppose it will."

"What about you?"

"I've got my Sig," Hicks said.

Milton took his lighter and cigarettes and put them in his pocket. "I'm not going to be very long."

Hicks put out a hand. "Well, good luck. Don't worry about Sarah. She'll be fine."

Milton clasped his hand. "Thanks," he said. "Be careful.

The Albanians are dangerous."

"Like you said: nothing to worry about as long as they don't know where she is."

"And Sarah's been through a lot. Just keep an eye on her."

"I will."

"The key for the door is in the lock. Help yourself to anything you need. And make yourself at home. I'll be back as soon as this is done."

"Good luck, John."

Milton released his hand, turned, and made his way to the doorway and the street outside. Hicks went back into the flat and closed the door behind him.

Chapter Eighteen

THE ROADS were clear and the drive was easy. Milton plugged his phone into the car's stereo and selected the playlist of eighties songs that reminded him of when he was younger: New Order, Frankie Goes to Hollywood, Tears for Fears, Scritti Politti. He scrolled down until he found the 12" mix of Killing Joke's 'Love Like Blood' and allowed his mind to wander.

He knew that this was the start of a long journey. He had given the situation careful thought, but there was no other obvious way to help Nadia. The pimp was dead. The brothel was abandoned, and it was unlikely that it would ever be visited again. There was no point in finding out who owned it; he expected that he would find a front company, with no way to trace the real ownership behind it. Sarah said that she didn't know anything that would be helpful, and there was no reason to doubt that. Milton couldn't ask the police for help without implicating himself in the death of the pimp. He couldn't ask around in the underworld without putting Nadia in danger.

They were all bad choices. He only had one viable option: he had to follow Nadia's story backwards, all the way back to the start of her voyage. It would involve time and effort on his part, but the memory of that blandly horrible room in the Wanstead apartment block was a difficult one for him to shift.

He was engaged now, committed to helping a girl he had never met on behalf of the brother who only barely trusted him. But Milton didn't care. He wasn't interested in gratitude or a course of action that would make him feel better about himself. He was involved because it was the right thing to do, precisely because he was in a position to make the journey to Libya and call upon favours that would have been beyond the capability of someone like Samir, or just about anyone else.

He was going to do it because he could help, because he had a long ledger of sins for which he had to atone, and because the only way he could atone was by helping others.

#

HE ARRIVED in Dover at midnight. There was a Premier Inn on Marine Parade, overlooking the harbour and the sea beyond. The car park was quiet. Milton found a space, locked the car, and took his bag into the reception. A middle-aged woman was behind the desk.

"Do you have any vacancies?"

"Plenty," she said. "Hotel's half empty. Want one with a sea view?"

"Yes. Thank you."

He filled out the papers, paid in advance, took the key and followed the woman's directions to his room. He unlocked the door and went inside. It was blandly utilitarian, as he had known it would be—the same bed, wardrobe and bureau as he would have found in any other branch of the chain anywhere in the country. The bathroom was similarly simple. He undressed and stood under the shower for fifteen minutes, closing his eyes and letting the hot water run down his face. He took a towel, wrapped it around his waist and went back into the bedroom. He unlocked the window and opened it, pulling it all the way back so that he could light a cigarette and blow the smoke outside without setting off the alarms. He stood there until the cigarette was finished, the net curtain fanning out behind him from the breeze, smelling the salt and looking out over the dark water to the lights on the harbour wall.

He looked at the sea. He thought of Samir and Nadia and the journey that they had undertaken to put their pasts behind them. They had put themselves at great risk in the hope of finding a better future for themselves in Europe, but now Samir was being held in a detention centre, most likely just waiting to be deported back to the country he had fled, and his sister was lost amid the London sex trade with no easy way for Milton to find her. That assumed, of course, that she was even still alive. There was no guarantee of that.

Three drunken men came out of the pub on the corner of the Parade and made their way along the path in front of the hotel. They were loud and rowdy, catcalling the two girls who were passing on the other side of the street, jeering as the women ignored them and increased their pace. Milton tossed the dog-end out of the window, closed it, and went to lie down on the bed. His body was sore, the phantom aches of a thousand injuries pulsing just that little bit more like they always did when he was tired. It had never bothered him before, especially not when he could drink the pain away.

He was getting old.

He fell asleep quickly, dreaming of the sea.

Chapter Nineteen

HICKS WOKE at six the next morning. His sleep had not been particularly refreshing, and he was groggy as he rolled off the sofa and went through into the bathroom. He ran the cold tap until the basin was filled, cupped his hands and filled them with water, and then dunked his face. He pulled back the shower curtain, stepped into the bath and turned the cold tap. He let the cold water play over his body, standing there for a minute until his skin was tingling. He stepped out, wrapped a towel around his midriff, and went back to the sitting room.

Sarah was waiting for him.

"Sorry," he said, gesturing down at the towel. "I didn't know you were up."

She looked at him with an amused cast to her face. "I've been awake for an hour."

Hicks's clothes were on the sofa next to the girl. "Let me just get dressed," he said, stooping to collect them and taking them back to the bathroom to put them on. She certainly seemed to have found some attitude overnight; the anxiety was more difficult to detect now, seemingly replaced by a little sass. Hicks hadn't been expecting that.

She was waiting for him when he returned.

"You want a drink?" he offered. "Coffee?"

"No," she said, drawing her legs up and hugging them to her chest. "How long am I going to have to stay here?"

Hicks had been thinking about that, too. The idea of remaining in Milton's small flat all day wasn't appealing; they would be at each other's throats before long.

"We don't have to stay," he said.

"What do you mean?"

"We could go for a walk?"

"John said I shouldn't go out."

"Not around here. But we can go somewhere it will be safe. No one will see you. Fancy it?"

"I don't know."

"He said you had to stay with me. I know what I'm doing, Sarah. Come on. Get your coat. We'll go for a drive."

#

HICKS'S RANGE ROVER had smoked privacy glass and, once Sarah realised that it was impossible to see into it from the outside, she began to relax. Hicks brought the car right up to the door, reached over to open the passenger side door, and waited for Sarah to hurry inside. She did, closing the door behind her, and Hicks put the vehicle into gear and drove off.

She was quiet until they were heading northeast on the A12.

"Where is John going?"

"He has something he needs to do."

"Where?"

"He didn't tell me," Hicks lied. "But you don't need to worry."

"I'm not worried about him. I don't even know him. I'm worried about me."

"Everything is fine. Nothing is going to happen."

Sarah settled back in the seat and stared out of the window. Hicks reached down to the console, switched over to CarPlay and found a Spotify compilation that he had put together. It was a collection of prog rock classics, with cuts from Steve Hackett, Roxy Music, Spock's Beard, Deep Purple and Marillion. He selected 'Bird Has Flown.'

"What is this?"

Hicks looked across the cabin. Sarah had wrinkled her nose in distaste.

"Deep Purple. You don't like it?"

"Are you kidding? It's horrible."

Hicks smiled and gestured to the console. "Help yourself," he said.

She took a moment to master the Spotify interface, but, when she had, she quickly navigated to Kendrick Lamar and selected 'A.D.H.D.' Hicks did not listen to much current music, but even he recognised the languid, trippy beats that introduced the track.

"Better?" he said.

She smiled at him. "Much."

They passed through Leytonstone, beneath the North Circular and then on through Woodford and Buckhurst Hill. Hicks had lived in Loughton after leaving school and he began to remember the landmarks. He turned onto Epping New Road, turned left at Cross Roads and pulled over into the car park that accommodated the High Beach Tea Hut.

He switched off the engine and the music stopped.

"Where are we?"

"Epping Forest. I used to run in the woods. You don't have to worry out here—no one will see us. Want to go for a walk?"

Hicks blipped the locks and led the way to the kiosk. He bought two coffees in polystyrene cups and led the way into the woods. Sarah was wearing trainers, but the ground was firm and the footing secure; he knew a circular route that was a couple of miles long and figured that would be the most suitable for the purposes of getting a little exercise and fresh air. It was a chance to talk to her, too, and to get her to relax her guard. It would be easier to look after her if she trusted him.

"It is nice here," she said, breathing deeply. "It reminds me of home."

"Where are you from?" Hicks asked her.

"Tartus. There is a mountain range; it catches the water that is blown from the Mediterranean. There are woods and forest, a little like this."

"Tartus is in Syria?"

"Yes. Do you know it?"

"No," he said. "I've never been. The nearest I ever got

to Syria was when I went to Cyprus on holiday." He realised how gauche that sounded the moment the words left his lips. "Sorry," he said.

She waved the apology away. "Why would you want to go there? It was bad enough before, with Assad and his secret police, but it is like hell today. The militias and the government, they don't care about the people. They fight for the city, and if anyone is in their way, they kill them. There is no future for anyone there. I left as soon as I could."

"How?"

She looked down at her feet as she spoke. "My parents were killed and I was left on my own. I sold our house. It was worth one hundred thousand dollars, yet the buyer only offered ten. I had no choice—I had to take it. I took a bus north and paid the bribes to get across the border. I was taken to a people smuggler in a café in the centre of town. He said he would get me to Greece for five thousand dollars. He said I would travel by land via Edirne, but then he changed his mind and said I would sail from Izmir. The boat broke down, but the Greek coast guards came and took us to a refugee camp. I travelled to France, to the Jungle. And that is where I was sold to the Albanians."

"And then brought here?"

"Yes," she said. "A false passport. They say I owe them for that, and I must pay it back by working for them."

They walked in silence for a moment.

"Do you know what you'll do now?" Hicks asked.

"John says he will help me. He seems like he is a good man. I trust him, I think."

"He is," Hicks said. "You can."

"You, too. You have a friendly face."

She looked up from the ground and smiled at him. It changed everything about her face—the austere expression, the distrusting eyes, the lowered brows. They were quickly replaced by sparkle and brightness that underlined her easy, natural beauty.

They reached the halfway point and started to turn back toward the car.

"What about you?"

"There's not much to tell," Hicks said.

"You were a soldier?"

"That's right."

"You have fought?"

"I have."

"You have killed before?"

Hicks turned to look at her. "Why would you want to know something like that?"

She held his eye. "Have you?"

Hicks took a moment to think about what to say. "Yes," he said at last. "That was my job."

"Many men?"

Hicks shook his head. "I don't think we need to talk about that."

"More than one?"

He shook his head again. "If you're asking because you want to know that I can look after you, then you don't need to worry. I can."

"John killed a man. In the flat. Did you know?"

"Yes," Hicks said, a little uncomfortable with her seeming preoccupation with death.

"You are like John?"

Hicks didn't answer that for a moment. He knew that Milton had killed more than just the Albanian. He didn't know how many men and women had been unfortunate enough to have had their files passed to him, but he knew that there would have been plenty. Dozens? Probably. Hicks had undergone the selection procedure that would have seen him admitted into Group Fifteen, the agency that had employed Milton. It had been Milton who had been responsible for rejecting his application. No reason had been given, and Hicks had never asked for an explanation after meeting Milton again. But, seeing what his career had done to Milton—the solitude that he wore like a badge of honour, the conscience that was so obviously tormented—Hicks found that he was glad that he had been turned down.

Sarah was looking at him expectantly.

"Let's change the subject," he said.

Sarah was content to walk in silence and didn't seem interested in asking Hicks anything else about himself. He found himself relaxing in her company, lulled by the steady cadence of their feet on the trail and the chirping of birds as they flitted between the branches overhead.

"Is John paying you?" she said at last.

"For what?"

"Looking after me."

"No."

"So why do you do it?"

"I owe him a favour."

"He seems like that sort of man."

"What sort?"

"The sort who is owed favours. I think he is the sort of man who likes to help people."

"I suppose he does," Hicks said, thinking of his own history with Milton.

"Thank you," she said at last.

"For what?"

"For this. You do not know me. You do not owe me anything, yet you are here. That is kind."

They turned the last, darkened corner and emerged from the vegetation into the open space of the car park again. They made their way across to the Range Rover and Hicks opened the doors. He pressed the engine start button and the console flickered to life. Sarah didn't wait for an invitation: she waited for the apps to appear, scrolled through to Spotify, selected it and browsed through until she found the entry for Eminem.

"I can't tempt you with some Roxy Music?"

"I don't even know what that is."

'The Way I Am' started to play as Hicks fed revs to the engine and rolled out of the car park. Sarah turned her head and gazed out of the window as they picked up speed. He could see her reflection in the mirror. Her eyes were closed and she was gently nodding her head to the beats.

Hicks headed back to the south.

Chapter Twenty

MILTON SHOWERED, dressed in a pair of clean black jeans, a grey crew neck T-shirt and a black bomber jacket. He checked that he had his passport, phone and charger, cigarettes and lighter, car keys and cash, and left his room.

Breakfast was being served in a dining room that was just as bland and functional as the bedroom he had left behind. There were two businessmen sharing a table, and a woman in a skirt and jacket who eyed Milton up as he went to the table and helped himself to a glass of orange juice and a croissant. He ordered a full English breakfast and a pot of coffee and polished it all off while reading the news on his phone.

The businessmen left, and then the woman. Milton finished his third cup of coffee, collected his bag and took it outside. He smoked a cigarette, enjoying the cool breeze that was blowing in off the water and watching as a large ferry moved sluggishly out of the harbour.

He finished the cigarette, ground it underfoot, got into his car and set off.

#

MILTON DROVE to the detention centre, went through the rigmarole of signing in and passed into the reception room again. Two volunteers were waiting inside, setting up their table and fanning out a series of leaflets. Milton went over and took one; it was written in Arabic, and the cover featured a picture of a man and woman who beamed out at the camera with happy smiles. It all seemed very false.

"Hello," said one of the volunteers. "Are you a relative?"

"A friend." He held up the leaflet for her to see. "That happen often?"

"What do you mean?"

"Smiles and laughter. A happy ending."

"More than you might think. But I'd be here even if it didn't. Some of the kids here, they're just boys. They don't speak the language. They're frightened. If we can help them improve things just a little, it's worth it."

Milton nodded and slid the leaflet back into a holder.

The woman smiled at him. "What's your story?"

"Similar," he said. "Just trying to help."

"We could always do with an extra pair of hands."

Milton smiled back at her. "I'm not qualified to give that kind of help."

He turned before she could try to continue the conversation, just as the doors were opened and the detainees were allowed inside.

Samir was at the back of the group. Milton caught his eye and pointed to the same table that they had used before. He went to the table at the back of the room and made two coffees. He turned and saw that Samir was watching him.

Milton went to the table and put the paper cups down.

"I did not think you would come back," Samir said.

"I said that I would."

Samir took the paper cup and put it to his lips. He looked at Milton the whole time, the whites of his eyes standing bright against his black skin.

"I spoke to the lawyer."

"And?"

"She said she will take my case. She says I have a chance. Asylum—she says it is not impossible."

"That's great," Milton said.

"But it might take weeks. There is bureaucracy. I need to be out of here, John. My sister needs me."

"I found the place," Milton said.

"The place?"

"The address you gave me. I visited it."

Samir's expression changed to one that mixed fear and anticipation. "Was she there?"

"No. They moved her. I'm sorry, Samir."

The young man closed his eyes, and Milton saw his larynx bobbing up and down in his throat as he swallowed. "When was this?"

"The day before yesterday."

Samir looked down at the table.

"Has she been in touch again?" Milton asked him.

"No," Samir said. "Nothing. What happened when you were there?"

"I went inside," he said. "I spoke to someone who was there. Another girl. She told me about Nadia. She was there. I was a day too late."

Samir drank again. His hand was shaking.

"I've got a picture I want to show you," Milton said.

He took out his phone and navigated to the still from the security camera that showed the woman and the man as they exited the brothel. He slid the phone across the table. "That's Nadia, isn't it?"

Samir picked up the phone and stared at it. Tears welled in his eyes. "Yes," he said. His voice was husky and he blinked hard, trying to prevent the tears from falling.

"The man she's with—do you recognise him?"

Samir cleared his throat. "No," he said. "I've never seen him before. Do you know who he is?"

"I don't."

"What *do* you know? Do you know anything?"

There was anger in his voice; Milton disregarded it. It was reasonable, and he knew that it wasn't directed at him.

"How will we find her now?" Samir asked when Milton didn't respond.

Milton put the telephone back into his pocket. "I'll find her."

Samir stared hard at him. "But you have no idea, do you? They have taken her somewhere else, and there is no way we will be able to find her."

"Not necessarily. I've been thinking about it. About everything that happened to you. There might be a way we can get to them."

Samir clenched his fists on the table, his knuckles bulging. "How?"

"Tell me about the smugglers."

"Why—"

"Tell me what happened. How you found them. How they operated. Everything."

Samir looked dubious. "We travelled from Eritrea," he began. "I told you."

"Tell me again."

"We travelled for a week to get to Tripoli. We travelled at night, in cages, with no food and no drink. Through the desert. We were near Tripoli when we were captured by Libya Dawn. They are a militia. They fight against the other militias and the government. They buy and sell refugees like us for use as slaves or fighters in their gangs. I did not care about what they did to me. I was worried about Nadia. My sister is pretty." He pointed down to Milton's pocket, where he had put the phone. "You have seen. Very pretty, yes?"

Milton inclined his head.

"And I see how the guards look at her. I know what they are thinking. You understand?"

"Yes," Milton said. "Go on."

"The militia were offered money for us. There were thirty of us. They sold us to a smuggler for one thousand dinars each. The smugglers say that they will get us across the sea, but we must pay them back the one thousand dinars as well as the price of the boat trip, our food, life jackets, and everything else that they say that we need. It was two and a half thousand dinars each. We had been saving our money for months and I paid them. The next morning, they told us we would go. They drove us to Sabratah, where they had their boats. They kept us in houses near the beach and then drove us to the boats in trucks. There were five hundred of us. I thought that they would have many boats, but they did not. Two boats. Two boats for all of us. They told us not to worry, that the ships were new and had a captain and two assistants, but they lied. They guarded us with Kalashnikovs and told us that no one could leave. Then we go, and they followed us in dinghies until we were out at sea. We were lucky, but the other boat broke down. We left it behind. When we arrived on the island, people asked what happened to it. They said we don't know, but then someone on our boat heard that the other boat sank and everyone drowned."

Samir finished and Milton was quiet for a moment.

"I meant what I said," Milton said. "I want to help you, and I want to help your sister, but I don't think I will be able to find her in London now. So I need to work backwards."

"What do you mean?"

"The smugglers. How do they operate?"

Samir shrugged. "It is easy to do. You need a boat and the contacts to find people like me and my sister. A place like Sabratah or Zuwara is like a market. Dozens of smugglers. The passengers are just cargo. If boats leave early, the smugglers with cargo to move will sell them to the smugglers who are ready to go. Say one smuggler has one hundred people. He sells them to another smuggler for one thousand dollars each. He makes a lot of money. The other smuggler, the one who has a boat and is ready to go, he charges the passengers two thousand dollars each. He makes a lot of money, too. I think they are all very rich."

"Which smuggler was responsible for you?"

"He is called Ali. He is in charge of the market at Sabratah. He is the biggest."

"And he arranged your trip?"

Samir nodded. "His boats were ready to leave. He bought us from the militia."

"And how would I find him?"

Samir looked at Milton with wide eyes. "He is in Libya, Mr. Smith."

"I know," Milton said. "You said. How would I find him?"

"You would go to Tripoli."

Part 3

Libya

Chapter Twenty-One

MILTON LOOKED DOWN from the porthole window of the EgyptAir Embraer 170. They were over the coast, the ocean a vivid blue beneath them and the beaches of northern Egypt thin yellow ribbons lapped by the white spume of the incoming waves.

It had been a long day. Milton had driven from Dover to Heathrow and left his car in the long-stay car park. He had gone into the departures lounge, stopped at an ATM to draw out the money that he thought he might need and then changed it into an assortment of currencies: dollars, euros, Egyptian pounds and Lybian dinars. He had given careful thought to the best way to reach Libya. The political instability meant that there was an extremely limited selection of flights into the country, and it wasn't possible to fly direct from the UK.

He had three options.

He could have flown on Air Berlin from Heathrow to Orly and then transferred there to a Tunisair flight to Monastir Habib Bourguiba International Airport. Afriqiyah Airways had just announced a new flight into Tripoli, and Milton could have taken that. But he decided against it. He was travelling under one of his false passports, but his documents were English and he did not want to attract unnecessary attention by being one of the few Europeans with the bravery or stupidity to fly directly into Tripoli.

The second option was to fly Tunisair to Tunis, as before, and then drive the eight hundred kilometres east to Tripoli so that he could avoid drawing unnecessary attention to himself upon his arrival at the airport. It was a ten-hour drive, but still quicker than driving west from Egypt, and it would have been his preference had it not been for the recent gains by ISIS along the northern coast road. He would have to pass through contested territory, and, after careful assessment, he decided that the risks inherent in that route were too severe.

That left him with one other option. He had purchased a flight from Heathrow to Alexandria, flying Aegean to Athens and then EgyptAir to Alexandria. He would make his way across country and cross the border at El Salloum.

"Ladies and gentlemen," the chief steward said over the intercom, "the captain has put on the fasten seat belts sign. Please return to your seats, fasten your seat belts, and put your tray tables in the upright position. We will be commencing our descent into Alexandria shortly."

Milton finished the bottle of sparkling water that he had purchased at Heathrow and dropped it into the black bin liner that was held open by a passing steward. He clipped his belt around him and watched out of the window as they started to descend.

#

MILTON WAITED PATIENTLY before the kiosk while the immigration officer checked his passport. The man looked down at the splayed-open document and then up at Milton. He was travelling under the name of John Smith and was using the false passport that he had used the last time he had travelled into north Africa. He had had no trouble before, and the delay was a little concerning. He had chosen Alexandria rather than Cairo to shave a little time from his onward journey to Tripoli, but he second-guessed himself now. He wondered whether it might have been more prudent to fly into the busier Cairo International than this quieter airport. Alexandria was busy, but it would have been easier to hide within the greater multitudes that would have passed through Egypt's main hub.

Too late for that now, though.

"What's your business in Egypt, Mr. Smith?"

"Pleasure."

"On your own?"

"Yes," he said. "I just want some sun and some peace and quiet."

"Where are you staying?"

"Here—Alexandria."

"Which hotel?"

"The Sheraton Montazah."

Milton had taken the precaution of booking a room. He had no intention of using it, but, since it would be unusual for a tourist to arrive with no accommodation arranged, he knew that his usual thoroughness was important.

The officer considered the information and turned to the computer screen on his desk. Milton wondered whether the Mukhabarat had a record of his reservation. Milton knew that the Egyptian intelligence service was still extant even after the overthrow of the regime that had spawned it.

He had travelled to the country on several occasions before this. The last time was the assignment to Cairo for the joint MI6-Mossad-CIA operation that had sabotaged Iran's nuclear and long-range missile program. He and another Group Fifteen agent had been the British contingent. Milton remembered the meet-up with Avi Bachman, and the thought of the Mossad agent—put out of his mind since the events in Croatia—gave him a moment's pause. He remembered the expedition from Egypt to Iran's Zagros Mountains and the bombs that had degraded the likelihood of there ever being an Islamist nuke.

The border guard looked down at the passport and back to him once again, and then pushed the document through the slot in the Plexiglas screen.

"Welcome to Egypt, Mr. Smith," he said.

Chapter Twenty-Two

MILTON TOOK a taxi from the airport to Misr railway station. Alexandria was teeming with life, its inhabitants going about their daily business under the cosh of a brutal noonday sun. He paid the driver, went into the station concourse and then joined the queue for the ticket office. There were four queues, in fact: three for men and women and one for women alone. It took thirty minutes to get to the head of the line but, as he was about to approach, the clerk pulled down the blind and went for lunch. Milton shook his head with wry recognition, remembering similar experiences of Egyptian customer service, and joined the end of one of the other queues. He waited another twenty minutes, was finally successful in purchasing a ticket, and then made his way to the platforms.

The Egyptian railway network was of variable standard. The line that ran down the spine of the country, connecting Alexandria in the north to Cairo and then Luxor and Aswan in the south, was a prestige line that was provided with lavish funding. Milton remembered it well: the carriages were plush, modern, and air conditioned, and the long journey could be enjoyed in some very decent accommodation.

The other main line, running east to west along the northern coast, was not so pleasant. It connected Alexandria and Sallum, on the border with Libya. Milton had never used it before but, as he boarded and found his way through the busy carriage to his seat, he decided that the accommodation could only be generously described as third class. The carriage was a French design and made from stainless steel, which promised to amplify the heat, and the air conditioning was not particularly impressive.

Milton sat down. The seats were arranged in twos, with

pairs facing each other. He was sitting next to an elderly woman and opposite a younger woman with a young child on the seat next to her. The old woman looked at Milton, said something in Arabic that he took to be derogatory, and then looked away. The mother was too busy keeping her child in line to afford him more than a quick glance.

The journey was almost exactly five hundred kilometres and was timetabled to take six hours. The child promised to be distracting but, on the other hand, her small legs meant that Milton could stretch his out until they were beneath her seat. He took his phone from his pocket, plugged in his earphones, and scrolled through his music until he found the Happy Mondays compilation he wanted. He closed his eyes and waited for the train to leave.

#

MILTON STEPPED DOWN from the train and crossed the platform to the exit. The journey had been long and arduous. Instead of the advertised six hours, the train had been delayed outside El-Agamy and, by the time they reached the end of the line, they had been travelling for closer to nine. It was dusk, and the temperature, although still warm, was more pleasant now than it had been earlier.

The station was basic. A concrete platform was alongside the carriages, a curved wooden roof suspended overhead by a series of wooden pillars. Milton had his ticket ready, but there was no one to show it to. The exit was open and Milton followed the handful of other passengers who had travelled this far until he was outside.

The town of Sallum was a mainly Bedouin community that survived as a regional trading centre. It was rich with Roman history, with wells and the remains of villas nearby, but despite a pleasant beach, it had escaped the relentless tide of commercialism that had changed the rest of the country and did not see many visitors. That was unfortunate. Milton knew that he would be noticed and also that it was unlikely that he would be able to find anywhere to hire a car for his onward journey.

He would be as quick as possible.

The landscape around and about was dominated by the arid countryside. The town was situated on the slopes that led down from higher ground to the sea, with low-slung buildings and a collection of taller hotels by the water. Milton walked away from the station toward the centre of the town and kept going until he reached the collection of cafés down on the dockside. There were a couple of cars parked up against the wall that guarded the drop to the water below. They were both old Ladas, painted black and white in the fashion that marked them out as taxis. The cafés had laid out a row of tables in haphazard fashion, some of them arranged in the road to create an unofficial patio area, and several men were sat around them, smoking from a shisha pipe and drinking *qasab*, the sugarcane drink that was served cold as refreshment against the heat.

Milton approached the men.

"Do any of you speak English?"

The men looked across at him with no attempt to conceal their scorn. One man, swarthy and grizzled, spat down at Milton's feet.

Milton's Arabic was basic, but he could make himself understood. "I'm looking for a taxi."

The man who had spat at him waved a hand dismissively, pushed his chair away from the table and got up. Milton tensed, expecting trouble, but the man shook his head at him, crossed the road and got into one of the taxis. He started the engine and pulled away.

There were three men left around the table and one taxi. Milton turned and pointed to it. "Who drives that car?"

One of the men raised a finger and, to Milton's mild surprise, he spoke in halting English. "What are you?"

"What do you mean?"

"You are not tourist. We get no tourist here."

"I'm a journalist."

"Why would a journalist come here? There is nothing."

Milton took the chair that the first driver had vacated and sat down in it. He looked more carefully at his interlocutor: he was middle-aged, with dark brown eyes and deeply tanned skin. The shisha pipe had four hoses; the man was holding his between the thumb and forefinger of his right hand, the skin stained a dirty yellow from cigarettes.

"Do your friends speak English?"

The man drew on the pipe, inhaled the smoke, and then put the hose down on the table. "No," the man said. "Only me."

Milton would have preferred the conversation to be more private than this. He was miles from Cairo and Alexandria, but close to the border with a volatile neighbour; the Mukhabarat would certainly be present in Sallum. What he was about to say would have interested them if they ever came to hear of it, but trusting that the man was telling the truth was a risk that Milton considered worth taking.

"I'm not here for a story. I want to get over the border."

"Why would you want to do something stupid like that?"

"I've been asked to write a story about what's happening there. I need to get across the border without anyone knowing. Is that your taxi?"

The man didn't answer the question. "It is a dangerous thing you ask," he said instead.

"I know. I'm willing to pay."

The man took up the pipe between his nicotine-stained fingers and inhaled again. "How much?"

"What would you charge?"

"One thousand."

"Egyptian?"

"Dollars."

"Too much. Five hundred."

"Then good luck, sir. I will stay here and you will find another driver."

"Six."

The man inhaled, turned his head a little and blew a jet of smoke just past Milton's head. "Eight."

Milton might be able to find another driver, but every person he spoke to increased the risk that the secret police would hear stories of the Englishman who was asking to be taken across the border into Libya. Milton was confident that there would be no way for the Mukhabarat to tie him back to his previous visits to the country, but risks, however small, had the tendency to accumulate until something really bad happened. There would be the delay, too, and every wasted hour was another for Nadia to spend in the custody of the Albanians.

"Fine," Milton said. "Eight hundred."

The man shook his head, as if surprised that his offer had been accepted, replaced the pipe in its clip and stood. He said goodbye to the two remaining men and nodded that Milton should follow him across the road. He did not walk to the taxi. He carried on, following the road around the corner. Milton saw a few simple food stands on the edge of the road, serving falafel and kebabs, a couple of fuel vendors, and another café with tables equipped with shisha pipes.

There were more cars parked opposite the café, and the man took Milton to one of them. It was a Mercedes-Benz S-Class. It was the old model in which chrome figured prominently: chrome-tipped fins, chrome trim to the left and the right of the radiator, a chrome-plated air intake grid and chrome wheel caps. The car had been badly cared for, with dents in the bodywork and a crack down the middle of the windscreen.

"No," Milton said.

"This is my car. Other drivers available at café."

"How old is this?"

"1959 model," the man said with a flicker of what Milton took to be pride.

"It's older than I am."

"And very reliable. It has never stopped working."

"It's also very conspicuous."

The man looked blankly at him.

"It is obvious. It will stand out."

"No," the man said. "It will not. Lots of old cars in Sallum. Not unusual."

Milton paused and turned back to look at the café. Their conversation was being observed by the men who were smoking at the tables. Milton couldn't very easily go back there now.

"Fine."

"Money."

"In the car," Milton insisted.

The man nodded his assent and went around to the other side of the Mercedes. He opened the door and slid inside and then leaned across to open the passenger door. Milton opened it all the way and settled into his seat.

Chapter Twenty-Three

THE DRIVER HAD stopped before the on-ramp for the International Coastal Road, the reasonably new east–west highway that connected the Arab Mashriq and Maghreb countries. The bulk of the funding for the ambitious project had focussed on the Egyptian span between New Damietta and Alexandria, and the stretch that connected Egypt with Libya through the Gateway Salloum had not been quite so lavishly bestowed. The surface was uneven, and damage caused by daily wear and tear had not been repaired.

"You do not want to be seen crossing border?" the man said.

"No."

"Then you must get in trunk."

Milton did not demur. He got out, waited until the two trucks that had been following behind them had rumbled past, and then opened the trunk and climbed inside. There was a tyre iron and a dirty blanket in the compact space, and Milton put them to the side. He squinted up into the dying light that silhouetted the driver as he came around and slammed the lid of the trunk closed.

The trunk was of a decent size, but it was never going to be comfortable for Milton. He had to lie on his side with his knees drawn right up against his chest. The red of the brake lights shone through holes in the chassis, winking out as the driver put the car into gear and pulled away. The suspension was hard and unforgiving, especially on roads that were as pitted as this.

Milton listened to the sound of the engine and the hum of the tyres across the asphalt. He was aware of the irony of his predicament. Here he was, trying to smuggle himself into Libya, the country that Samir and Nadia had risked their lives trying to leave. Samir had hidden in the back of a lorry to get into the United Kingdom. At least he had had more space than Milton had had in the back of the Mercedes.

The road was straight and, after a distance that he estimated at two miles, the brake lights flickered on and the car started to slow. Milton had done a little research before catching his flight in Athens but still had only a limited idea of what the border crossing was like. He had seen a selection of pictures on Google Images showing a large stone structure with Arabic script and a series of gated openings watched over by brick- and stone-built booths. The crossing had been closed during the worst of the Libyan uprising, and there were suggestions that it would be closed again if the volatility of the situation across the border did not subside. He suspected that more attention was paid to those seeking to leave Libya than those seeking to enter it, but that was just a guess. He had to hope that he was right, because it would be a simple enough thing to find him in the trunk.

What would they do if they did find him? Arrest him? Interrogate him? Deport him? Nothing good could come of it.

He found that he was clenching his fists a little tighter as the car rolled forward.

And then, with no further delay, the engine revved and the car picked up speed.

#

MILTON WAITED until the car slowed to a halt and the engine spluttered into silence.

The lid of the trunk opened and Milton looked up into a darkened sky. The driver was above him, one hand resting on the lid.

"We are here."

Milton levered himself into an upright position, his muscles cramped and aching. They had come to rest in a truck stop. Milton saw three other trucks and, beyond them, the dark shapes of a mountainous landscape, with a series of tall peaks shouldering up against each other to the north. The road continued to the west, where, perhaps a mile away, the lights of a small town could be seen through the gloom. There was a single-storey building behind him and a set of gasoline pumps arranged alongside it.

Milton stepped down from the trunk. A truck pulled out of the stop and rumbled away toward the mountains, and Milton watched it for a moment until the road dipped into a depression and it disappeared.

The only signage was in Arabic, and Milton couldn't read it.

"Where are we?"

"That is Bardiyah," the man said, pointing over at the lights. "This is as far as I take you."

"Fine. Thank you."

The man held out his hand for the rest of his money. Milton took out his dollars and counted out the balance. He took another fifty and held it up. "Don't mention this to anyone," he said. "Understand?"

"Sure."

The man reached across and took the extra fifty. He added it to the other notes, folded them in half, and stuffed them into his pocket. He gave Milton a nod, slammed the lid of the trunk, turned his back and walked around to the front of the car. The engine started and Milton watched for a moment as the car drove away, turning onto the main road and heading to the east, back to the border.

Milton was thirsty and hungry and decided that it was worth the risk of investigating the building. He walked across the lot, looking left and right but seeing no one. A sign pointed around to an entrance that was, judging by the foul smell that emanated from it, the toilets. Milton could hear the sound of running water, and before he could move out of the way, a man emerged from the doorway, wiping his hands against his shirt. Milton guessed that it was the driver of one of the trucks. The man gave him a cursory glance before walking by and heading to the main entrance to the building. A bell rang as he opened the door and went inside.

Milton paused, as if he was considering using the bathroom, and then followed.

Milton glanced through the glass door and saw a row of empty shelves and large gallon water bottles stacked up in a pyramid. Beyond that was an open area with tables and a food service counter beneath an illuminated display that held the menu. The driver had gone through to the café area and was ordering something from the proprietor.

Milton opened the door. The bell rang as he went inside. The store was as badly stocked as it had appeared. The clerk was watching TV and, after looking away from the screen to glance at Milton, he turned his attention back to his football match. Milton collected a bottle of water and a sandwich wrapped in cellophane, paid for the items at the counter and went back outside. He sat down with his back to the wall, took a drink and ate half of the sandwich, and then got up. He estimated that it was a mile to Bardiyah. He took another swig of water, poured a little over his head and scrubbed it into his skin and his scalp, and then started to walk.

Chapter Twenty-Four

MILTON SPENT the night in the Al Burdi Hotel, the only one he could find in Bardiyah. He woke just before dawn. He showered and dressed and then took out a coat hanger from the cupboard. He took a moment to straighten it and then hid it inside the sleeve of his jacket.

The lobby was deserted as Milton passed through it. He went outside into the early morning gloom. Milton went around to the parking lot, his attention focussed on the handful of cars that were parked there. He wanted something unobtrusive, old enough not to draw attention to itself yet still reliable, and he knew that he had found it when he saw the old SEAT Ibiza.

He checked that the lot was unobserved and that it was not covered by CCTV and, satisfied that the way ahead was clear, he made his way to the car. It had an old vertical manual lock, with a button at the top of the door panel just inside the window. He took the coat hanger from his sleeve and peeled back a small portion of the rubber weather-stripping that was fitted to the bottom of the window. He slid the curved end of the hanger between the rubber and the glass, lowering it into the gap with no resistance. He moved the hanger in the gap until it was two inches below the bottom of the window. He felt the locking pin, hooked the hanger around it, and pulled. He felt the locking pin shift and heard the click as the door unlocked.

Milton opened the door and slid inside. He used a coin to prise off the plastic panel on the steering column, and, after finding the wiring harness connector, he stripped the battery wires, wrapped the ends together, and sparked the starter wire. The engine turned over and, as Milton fed in the revs, it caught.

He put the car into drive and pulled out.

He reached across to the glovebox, opened it and emptied it out. There was a copy of the car's handbook and service history, a packet of stale potato chips and an old satnav unit. Milton swept the detritus onto the floor and plugged the satnav into the cigarette lighter. He switched it on and waited for it to acquire a satellite signal. It took a moment, but then it flickered to life and the symbol of a car was placed on the map. Milton scrolled out. The place names were in Arabic. He found the settings, changed the language to English, and switched back to the map. He found Bardiyah. It was small, right up on the northern coast of the country and around twenty kilometres from the crossing at Sallum. He tapped through to the destination entry interface, typed in Tripoli, and waited for a route to be calculated.

Milton rolled up to a crossroads on the western edge of the town and stopped at the red light. There was a loud bang, and Milton turned to look out of the window. An old car was waiting for a green light and its engine had backfired. Milton shook his head with wry amusement. There was no point in pretending otherwise: this was not a friendly place, and it made him nervous.

Milton turned back to the satnav. The route had been calculated: 1400 kilometres, with a driving time of nearly seventeen hours. The directions suggested following route five to the southwest to cut off the peninsula that included Benghazi and Derna, and then following the coast to the northwest until he reached the capital. The route suggested that he pass through Sirte, but Milton knew that town was held by ISIS. He could easily divert around it, though, turning south at As Sultan and picking up the route again at Abugrein. It might add another hour or two to his journey, but it was a compromise that he would be happy to make.

#

THE JOURNEY took all day. He stopped three times: once to relieve himself and twice to fill the car with fuel. He wound down the window and the wind blew in, pleasant ventilation against the searing heat.

He turned to the southwest at Tobruk and then rejoined the coast road again when he reached New Brega. The scenery was stunning. The road followed the line of the coast, often separated from the water by ramshackle-looking barriers. Other times, the barriers were absent and sharp left-hand turns offered a plunge into the Mediterranean for the unwary. He continued to the northwest, the road passing through Bin Jawad, and turned to the south just outside of As Sultan, skirting Sirte and the trouble that had consumed the town since the passing of its most famous son and the ascension of ISIS as the terrorist movement rose up to fill the void.

Milton had an adaptor for his phone in his bag and he plugged it into the lighter and played through all of his Spotify playlists: The Smiths, Morrissey, The Stone Roses, the Mondays, and then a two-hour playlist that was full of alternative music from the eighties.

He reached Misrata, and then Khoms, Msallata and Tajoura.

By the time the outskirts of Tripoli came into view, it was eight in the evening and Milton was struggling to keep his eyes open. He passed through the south-eastern suburbs, driving carefully as the traffic increased in volume. He remembered the buildings constructed in a Western style, the mosques with their domes and minarets, the pedestrians that thronged the pavements. Milton stopped at a red light and watched them as they hurried in front of his car. For a people who had lived through a violent revolution that had still to play all the way out, it was difficult to see any sign that anything had changed. The shops and food shacks on the side of the road were doing brisk evening trade, the streets were busy, and there was an electric buzz in the air.

The light changed and Milton drove by the Corinthia Hotel. It was a four-hundred-foot-high building in the centre of town, with views across the city. It was the hotel preferred by European visitors and diplomats, and offered ease of access to the souk and the cafés. The hotel had been attacked by gunmen a year earlier, and there was a very obvious security presence outside it now. The approach was blocked with concrete berms to prevent suicide bombers from driving up to the building, and armed guards had been positioned outside the main doors. Milton wasn't interested in the hotel. Checking in there would be the best way to announce his arrival to the Mukhabarat.

He had another idea. Milton had stayed in a small hotel the last time he had visited the city, and he preferred the discretion that he knew he would find there. He remembered the location in the medina, near to the Arch of Marcus Aurelius, abandoned the car in a side street and walked the remaining distance.

The hotel was called El Khan and was owned and run by a local couple, Aref and Maya. It had been newly renovated when Milton had last visited, a series of houses within the medina that had been turned into guest accommodation. It was lit up by dozens of small lanterns in the gardens that surrounded it, and Milton heard the musical tinkling of a fountain somewhere within the shroud of vegetation that screened it from the street. The great wooden door with its brass studs was open, and Milton pushed it back and walked inside. He immediately recalled the place: the coolness of the air, the Berber textiles on the wall, the black and white photographs of a time before Gaddafi and the depredations of what had followed his fall. There was a bell on the desk and Milton pressed it. A man appeared from a small antechamber in which an office had been accommodated. He was small and slender, with freckled brown skin and a neat moustache. Milton remembered him: it was Aref, the owner.

"Mr. Smith, it is a pleasure to see you again. How was your journey?"

"It was fine," Milton said.

"When were you here before?"

"Several years ago," Milton said.

"Yes, that's right—before the revolution. Libya has changed, and not always for the better. But we like to think we are the same. How many nights would you like to stay with us?"

"Three, please. I'll pay now."

"Three hundred dinars."

"Are dollars okay?"

"Of course. It will be two hundred."

Milton took out the money and handed it over.

"Thank you, sir. You will be in the Samsara suite. Please—come with me."

Aref led the way to the central courtyard, where chairs with comfortable cushions were arranged around a charcoal brazier that burned frankincense. Milton saw the marble fountain that he had heard from outside, hibiscus blossoms floating in the water. Milton recalled the layout, and the four buildings—each with its own courtyard—that comprised the establishment. They made their way into the rear of the building.

"Are you busy?" Milton asked.

"No, sir. Not at all. Not many people are visiting Tripoli at the moment."

"No, I don't suppose they are."

"What's your business here?"

"I'm meeting a supplier."

"Well, good for you. Libya needs business very badly."

Aref reached a door at the end of a corridor, took out a key and unlocked it. He stepped aside so that Milton could go through. It was the same room that he had stayed in before. Milton didn't know if it was a coincidence or whether the man's records were so precise as to allow him to put him in the same room, but he didn't complain. It was as pleasant as he remembered it. The room was beautifully furnished and spacious, with a modern shower room to the side. There were a number of beautiful touches, including an old Bakelite telephone, which could have graced a museum, sat atop the bureau.

"Is this acceptable, sir?"

"Perfect," Milton said.

"You will remember the swimming pool, perhaps. It is open all day, very nice after a long day of travel."

"I'm afraid I didn't pack for a swim."

"There is a new pair of shorts in the wardrobe. You are welcome to take them. Breakfast is served from six in the dining room. If you need anything at all, please call down to reception and it will be arranged for you."

"Thank you."

"Have a pleasant evening."

The man bowed once and then backed out of the room, shutting the heavy wooden door behind him.

Milton looked around the room. Was it possible that it was bugged? Maybe. The Corinthia most certainly would have been, but this was a little less well known. It didn't matter. Milton was unlikely to speak to anyone, and he could not envisage a conversation where he might compromise himself.

He undressed, opened the cupboard and pulled on the shorts and an extravagantly comfortable dressing gown. He took his key and followed the signs to the pool. It was in another of the courtyards, surrounded by pillars and potted plants, too small to be suitable for swimming but deep enough that he could lower himself into the cold water all the way up to his neck. Milton closed his eyes and submerged his head, the water cold enough to make his skin tingle.

Chapter Twenty-Five

MILTON SLEPT VERY WELL. The room was well appointed and the bed was comfortable. He was bone tired from the previous day's travelling and he had fallen asleep as soon as his head had touched the pillow. He awoke refreshed, showered and shaved, and dressed in clothes that had been laundered for him overnight. He had grown used to the smell of his own sweat, and it was a pleasant change to smell the fresh cleanliness of his shirt. He brewed a cup of instant coffee and drank it as he watched the dawn break over the skyline, the cries of the muezzins audible through the open window.

He ate a light breakfast in the dining room. The chef had prepared *sfinz*. It was an egg dough that had been leavened with baking powder instead of yeast. An egg was cracked into it while it fried for a savoury breakfast, and Milton remembered that it was delicious. There were no other guests at that early hour and he had already been told that the hotel was quiet. Libya was the subject of a travel advisory from the Foreign Office, and most Western companies who had a presence here had already moved their staff out. The El Khan would have been too expensive for most of the locals. Milton wondered whether he might even be the only guest.

Milton left the hotel, squinting up into the bright early sunshine and then surveying the street. There was nothing that caused him any concern, although he knew that he would be making his anonymity more difficult to maintain if he went through with the rendezvous that he had arranged. But there was nothing to be done to avoid that. The meeting was essential if he was to make any progress.

Milton made his way to Caffe Casa, a well-known local coffee shop that was located just off Martyrs' Square. He had emailed his contact before he had left London and arranged to meet him here. Milton approached, paused to tie a lace that did not need to be tied, and checked it over. The establishment was nestled within the walls of the city's Ottoman fort, rubbing up against the gold shops and copper engravers of the old town. The patio was pleasant, the tables shaded by large parasols. The souk was nearby, and the clamour of the stallholders as they called for business filled the air. Milton watched the tables and saw the man he had come to visit. He was sitting with his back to the wall of the café, looking down the street in the opposite direction. He hadn't seen Milton yet.

Milton turned and retraced his steps, walking for a hundred yards before he stopped and entered one of the gold emporia. The owner, a fat man dressed in a poorly fitting suit, looked up and then back down at his newspaper again. Milton made a show of looking at the trays of rings and necklaces in the window, but his attention was through the glass and on the street outside. The regime might well have collapsed since the last time he was here, but Milton was not so naïve as to think that the Libyan Mukhabarat would have been dismantled at the same time as Gaddafi and his cronies had fallen.

"You want anything?" the shopkeeper asked with barely concealed contempt.

"No, thank you," Milton replied. "Just looking."

"Then you can just look outside shop."

Milton took the hint and stepped back into the heat again. He walked back to the café, taking a more circuitous route through the Souk al-Turk, further losing himself among the throng. He emerged directly opposite the tables and saw that his contact was still waiting there. Milton picked a path between the tables and sat down in the vacant chair.

The man looked up from his newspaper. "Mr. Smith," he said.

"Hello, Omar."

The man was wearing dark glasses that hid his eyes; the light was bright, and Milton could see his own reflection in the lenses. He was smartly dressed, wearing a pale linen suit and a duck-egg-blue shirt with two buttons undone. His double cuffs were fastened by silver links, and he wore a silver necklace around his neck. He was self-assured and comfortable.

"It's been a few years."

"It has," Milton agreed.

"It is good to see you again."

Milton doubted that he meant that, but he was happy to play along with the charade. "Good to see you, too."

The waiters at Caffe Casa were notoriously surly. The man who approached their table was no different, almost sneering down at them. "You want coffee?"

"Yes," Milton said. "A double espresso."

The waiter noted it down. "To eat?"

"The brioche is good," Omar said. "They serve it with honey and crushed nuts. Very tasty."

"I'll have that," Milton said.

The waiter scribbled that in his notebook, too, and then left without another word.

"Time flies," Omar said, "but some things never change. My apologies for his manner. I think they are selling their rudeness as part of the 'experience' of coming here. I find it all rather foolish, myself, but their coffee is good, so I keep coming back."

Milton examined the man more closely as they waited for their food and drink. His name was Omar Ben Halim, and he had been an important player in the Jamahiriya, Libya's external intelligence and operational entity. The Libyans had only had a modern intelligence service since the overthrow of the monarchy in 1969, and the regime had modelled the body on the KGB and the Stasi. It had quickly become infamous for its clandestine support of the PLO, the Italian Red Brigades, ETA in Spain, US Black Power groups, and Muslim separatists in the Philippines and

Indonesia. But it was their funding of the Provisional IRA that had aroused the attention of MI6, and, after searching for a suitable turncoat, the agency had settled upon Omar. He had been a colonel in the military until he had been appointed as a commander of the sub-directorate responsible for direct contact with terrorist organisations. What was much less well known about him was that he was a thief. He had been pilfering money from the regime for years and, when MI6 threatened to publicise his crimes, he had been left with little choice but to work for them. Regular cash payments lent the enforced relationship a veneer of civility, and the combination of carrot and stick had ensured his cooperation for thirty years.

The old clock tower was nearby, and it chimed loudly as the waiter returned with a tray bearing Milton's coffee and brioche. He placed the cup and the plate on the table, handed Milton the bill and waited for him to settle it. Omar took out a ten-dollar bill and gave it to the man, dismissing him with a flick of his wrist.

The cup was dirty and chipped. Milton put it to his lips and tried the coffee. It was bitter and not particularly pleasant.

"Good?" Omar asked.

"It's fine."

"And the cake?"

Milton took a bite of the brioche. It was dry, most likely quite old, but he pretended to enjoy it. "Not bad at all."

Omar chuckled. "There is no need to pretend, Mr. Smith. I know that standards have slipped. Tripoli is a different place since the last time you came here. The fall of the regime was supposed to be a new start for my country, but it has not been like that. The colonel had many faults, but he knew how to bind his people together. Now, without him, there is chaos. The militia squabble over who is in command. There is a government here, one in Tobruk and another in Switzerland. The fear of Gaddafi kept things under control. Now, without him, my fear is for the country itself."

"What happened to you?"

"The Jamahiriya was disbanded. The militias claimed credit for it, but the truth is that the staff had long since stopped working for it. Some went abroad. Others left the city and returned to their homes."

"And you?"

Omar reached up and removed his glasses. Milton looked into his olive-coloured eyes; they were flecked with steel. "I stay, Mr. Smith. The Jamahiriya might have gone, but the Mukhabarat still exists. The militias fear it still, as they should. They remember the rooms where they were taken when the colonel wanted to find out the things he needed to know. They remember the things that were done to them to enforce their cooperation. It is a collective memory. And the Mukhabarat's time is coming again. ISIS presents a serious threat. An existential threat. You can find them if you drive for two hours out of Tripoli. And so the militias have allowed the Mukhabarat to reassemble. It has tightened its grip on security across much of the country. It is already back to much of its capacity under the colonel. It is the future of my country's stability. I love Libya, Mr. Smith. And so I work with it now."

The news was welcome. Milton had not known what he would find, but he knew that he would need Omar's help. Without him, he would struggle to find the man he needed to find. That he was still plugged into the security service was a bonus that had not been guaranteed.

"You have come a long way to speak to an old man," Omar said. "How can I help you?"

"I need to find someone."

"Then I would say that person is most unfortunate." Milton knew what he meant: Omar thought that Milton was still involved with Group Fifteen and that the man he was looking for had had his card marked.

Milton saw no point in disabusing him; a little fear could be useful for him, too. "His name is Ali. Do you know him?"

"The smuggler?" Omar said.

"Yes."

He stroked his chin, and Milton could tell that he knew plenty about Ali and that he was assessing why Milton wanted to know about him and how much it would be prudent to reveal. "What do you need to know?"

"Where I can find him. That would be a good start."

"You know these people are dangerous, Mr. Smith? The smugglers are making millions from the migrants. It has made them extremely rich. They will not take kindly to someone—a Westerner—putting his nose in their business."

"I realise that," Milton said. "I'll take my chances. I just need you to help me find him."

"Why?"

"The smugglers are selling girls to pimps in Europe. I want to find the pimps. Ali can tell me what I need to know."

"Or he might shoot you and toss you into the ocean." Omar shook his head with wry amusement. "You are sure?"

"I am."

"Very well. Let me make some enquiries."

"There's something else, too."

Omar spread his hands hospitably. "Name it."

"A weapon."

The suggestion did not faze him. "That can be arranged. What would you like?"

"A small pistol. Something I can conceal."

"That won't be a problem. I should have something for you tomorrow morning. Shall we meet here for breakfast?"

Milton stood. "Of course."

Omar stood, too, reached down for his dark glasses and put them on. "Be careful, Mr. Smith. Tripoli is not a safe place for foreigners."

"I can look after myself."

Omar put out his hand and Milton shook it. "I'll see you tomorrow. Enjoy the rest of your day."

He left. Milton watched him cross the patio and disappear into the crowd before leaving the table himself. He glanced ahead and saw three people who were showing tell-tale signs of interest in him: a man with a bicycle, leaning against the wall of a store; a woman in a red blouse and brown skirt with a small dog on a lead; a man in a purple shirt, smoking a cigarette in the doorway of a bakery. Milton watched them as he set off. The man near the bakery finished his cigarette, tossed it aside and went in through the doorway; Milton dismissed him. The other two watched as Milton walked away from the café and then, with appalling tradecraft, started to follow.

The Mukhabarat might still have been alive, but its new staff were not what Milton remembered.

Milton didn't mind. He wasn't surprised that Omar would have him followed. It was to be expected in a state like this, with a secret service that was so deeply entrenched in the culture that not even the disruption of a coup could shake it loose. Milton had nothing to hide, at least not yet, and, as he ambled into the souk, he made no effort to lose his tails as they drifted into step behind him.

Chapter Twenty-Six

MILTON SPENT THE REST of the day wandering the streets of the city. He visited the Arch of Marcus Aurelius, Martyrs' Square and the fish market, and returned to the café where he had met Omar so that he could spend time at the Al-Majidya mosque. He followed the beach road and looked at the murals that had been painted to celebrate the revolution, more vivid and thoughtful works than the hundreds of graffiti'd images of Gaddafi as a rat that had appeared on almost every street corner.

The secret police followed him throughout the day. The tails were replaced by new operatives every now and again, but they were so green that it was a simple enough thing for Milton to spot the handoffs. After an hour, it was obvious that he was being followed by four agents—three men and a woman—and he put them out of his mind. He had no problem with them following him.

Milton found himself drawn to one particular restaurant on Riad El Solh, opposite the Saint Famille school. It was called Abdul Rahman Hallab & Sons 1881, was reputed as the best in the city, and had even spawned franchises throughout the rest of the region. It was something of a landmark, famed for its *knefe* and baklava and a host of other oriental sweets. The restaurant was housed within a grand building with an imposing doorway and wide windows that let in a plentiful amount of light.

Milton slowed as he walked by the front door. He recalled it well, and the memory took him back to another time that might as well have been a thousand years ago. Hallab was where Milton and Number Five had arranged to meet their target. The man was something of a playboy with a well-known predisposition for European women. Number Five, Lydia Chisholm, was an icy-cold beauty who had been recruited to Group Fifteen after a glittering career in the Special Reconnaissance Unit. Milton hadn't known it at the time, but Chisholm had been involved in the betrayal of Beatrix Rose. That had been the signing of her own death warrant; the agent would eventually be tracked down and murdered for her crimes by Beatrix, Milton's predecessor as Number One of Group Fifteen.

Back then, Chisholm had been the senior agent, and she was responsible for the operation. It had been a classic honey trap, with Chisholm and Milton posing as the representatives of an oil exploration company looking to secure a licence for drilling in the El Sharara area. Their target was a man called Abdullah el-Mizdawi, the brother-in-law of the former dictator and the chairman of the National Oil Company, the entity responsible for the oil business in the country. El-Mizdawi's previous employment was with the intelligence service, and it was this that had brought him to the attention of MI6 and, more particularly, Group Fifteen. A Maltese shopkeeper had provided evidence suggesting that el-Mizdawi had bought the clothes that were later found in the remains of the suitcase bomb that had brought down Pan Am Flight 103 over Lockerbie. Gaddafi had made it clear that his brother-in-law was not about to be extradited for trial, so the prime minister had approved his liquidation. A file had been generated and passed to Control, who had selected Chisholm and Milton.

They had used polonium, a highly radioactive isotope that was one hundred billion times more dangerous than hydrogen cyanide. A microgram—the same amount as a speck of dust—was enough to be a lethal dose. A small amount had been withdrawn from a Cumbrian nuclear reactor, and Group Fifteen had put it to good use in a number of operations around the world. The polonium, while lethal when ingested, was nevertheless very easy to transport. Milton had been responsible for that, bringing it into Libya in the barrel of a modified fountain pen. Chisholm had emptied the container into the sweet tea that al-Mizdawi had ordered. He had come on to her, as they had expected. She had made her excuses and left.

Polonium was an effective and elegant poison. It was an alpha-emitter, and, rather than the gamma-emitters that decayed over years, it decayed in weeks and months. Alpha radiation was absorbed by human tissue, so it would have been impossible for the hospital to detect it using a Geiger counter even if they had known to look. It took three weeks for al-Mizdawi to die, the isotope slowly yet relentlessly attacking the blood cells followed by the liver, kidneys, spleen, bone marrow, gastrointestinal tract and the central nervous system. Milton and Chisholm had been back in London for a week when intelligence from Tripoli Station reported that al-Mizdawi had been admitted to hospital with suspected cancer. Two weeks later, he was dead.

Milton paused on the street, squinting through the bright sunlight at the restaurant. The memory of what they had done there brought back a flood of other memories that Milton had tried hard to suppress. Al-Mizdawi was just one of his victims. He had killed many, many more, and, he knew, he would kill again.

Milton decided that he did not want to be followed back to his hotel, so he went into the restaurant and made as if he was ready to eat. The waiter showed him to a table, and Milton sat down and pretended to look through the menu. One of the tails came into the restaurant, waiting at the maître d's lectern to be seated. Milton waited until the waiter had returned to take his drink order and, then, after he left, got up and made his way to the rear where signs advertised the restrooms.

There were three doors at the end of a short corridor: the men's room, the ladies' room, and a fire exit. Milton pushed the lever to open the door to the exit and went outside, stepping out into an alley where the bins were kept. He walked quickly along the alley to a junction. Left led back to the main street, where he would be picked up again. Right offered a route back to the souk through narrow lanes and alleys, a route where it would be much more difficult to find and track him. He turned right, jogging for the first few hundred metres until he had put several turns between himself and the restaurant, slowing only when he was sure that he was alone.

Chapter Twenty-Seven

MILTON WOKE EARLY the next day, showered and went down to the dining room for breakfast. He enjoyed his *sfinz* and a pot of very strong, syrup-like black tea and wondered what was happening in London. He had agreed with Hicks that he should not contact him unless it was absolutely necessary, and there had been no text messages, emails or any other communication. He knew that Hicks was more than capable of babysitting Sarah for the time he was away, and reminded himself that he would need to give some thought to the best way to make the girl safe as soon as he was able to return.

He had an idea on that score, but his direction would be guided by the resolution that he was able to fashion with the Albanians. He suspected that the resolution would be violent and that it would mean that they no longer posed a threat to Sarah, or to Nadia, but that was in the future.

He had to find them first.

He finished his second round of tea, stood and thanked the waitress, and made his way to the reception.

#

OMAR WAS WAITING for him at the same table at Caffe Casa. Milton pulled out the spare seat and sat down.

"Good morning, Mr. Smith."

"Good morning."

"How are you finding your stay?"

"Weather's nice," Milton said. "But I'm sure you know my itinerary by now."

"What do you mean?"

"Your agents," Milton said, shaking his head. "Where did you get them?"

Omar tried to feign ignorance, but he knew it was pointless and he allowed himself to chuckle. "Are they that obvious?"

Milton turned and pointed to the woman at the other table and, beyond her, the man with the bicycle who was waiting at the mouth of the souk. "They're amateurs, Omar. It took me five minutes to lose them yesterday. It never used to be this bad."

The spook leaned back in his chair and shrugged expansively. "Good men and women are difficult to find these days. The revolution has meant that funding has become precarious. And a career in intelligence does not bear the same cachet as it did under the colonel." He paused to pour out two small glasses of green tea. "But I hope you don't mind. It's not often we have the opportunity to entertain a British spy."

"Not at all."

"Where are you staying?"

"I think I'll keep that to myself."

"I wondered if you would choose the Corinthia?"

"Didn't seem the most private of places the last time I was there."

"You would have been their only guest."

"Business not so good?"

"I hear it will be closing soon unless things change. The proprietors cannot go on funding it indefinitely. A shame."

"Why's that?"

"You are right, of course. It is a friendly place for us. All the rooms are bugged. We were involved before the hotel was even constructed. The rooms were designed to our specifications." He grinned. "Now then, don't tell me that MI6 does not have similar arrangements. I was at the Savoy when I last visited your country. I'm sure everything I said was recorded."

"I wouldn't know," Milton said. "But I'm glad I chose somewhere else." He took a sip of the green tea, thick and sweet, and put the glass back down onto the table. "What do you have for me?"

"Information. The smuggler you are looking for is called Ali Tessema. He is Ethiopian. Everyone knows Ali, but no one will talk about him. He has never been photographed. Police rely upon a picture put together by the people he has trafficked. Here." He took a piece of paper from his bag and slid it across the table. "This is him."

Milton looked at the paper. It was a crude photo fit. The man had a wide face with light brown skin, eyes that were spaced more than the average distance apart, a bulbous nose and full lips. There was an obvious cruelty to him, evident even in the facsimile.

"He looks friendly," Milton said.

"Ali is a most unpleasant man, Mr. Smith. He operates in a dangerous world, and only the most ruthless would last as long as he has."

"What do you know?"

"His name is well known, not just south of the Sahara but also in the Horn of Africa. There was a case, not long ago, where a migrant boat with two hundred and fifty passengers on it capsized and sank. They all drowned."

Milton nodded. Samir had told him about the two boats that had set sail when he made the crossing, and how the other one had not made it to Lampedusa.

"Ali is the kingpin, Mr. Smith. The Italian police have wiretaps with Ali talking to an associate in Khartoum. They discuss the sinking as if it is a minor business problem. He is a very wanted man."

"So where can I find him?"

"That won't be easy. He is an invisible man. The Italians have mandated direct action in Libya. Two months ago, they sent a special forces team here, to Tripoli, and shot dead one of Ali's rivals and eight of his bodyguards. They denied it was them, of course, but the same men returned three weeks ago. They thought that they had located Ali, but, when they stormed the property, he was not there. He is a ghost."

"But you know where he is?"

"Some ideas, yes. He has a series of operating bases within the Sahara." Omar took out a map and laid it over the photograph. "He has a base here." He pointed to a spot on the map. "This is Kufra. It is in the middle of the desert. It has always been a home to smugglers. It is along the trans-Saharan slave route from the Horn of Africa. It is still that way today. They ship everything through Kufra: fuel, weapons, food. And people. Ali transports Eritreans across the Sudanese border and then brings them north to the coast. It has never been safe, but, since the revolution, ISIS has taken the land around it. There is so much chaos now, it is easy for men like Ali to flourish."

"What about Tripoli?"

"His headquarters are in Abu Salim. It is a dangerous area, particularly for a Westerner."

"Where in Abu Salim?"

"Mr. Smith, I am serious: you will have to be very careful. They do not like people looking into their business. And he is very rarely here. He does not stay in the same place."

"I need more than this, Omar."

"I realise that. And I have a contact within his organisation. We placed a man within the uprising before Gaddafi fell. He is a homosexual—they would kill him if they found out, so he has remained loyal to us."

"Very nice."

"*Please.* Are you suggesting that British intelligence wouldn't do such a thing? Come, now—I know you are not that naïve."

Milton shrugged. "Tell me about the contact."

"He has stayed with the militia and provides intelligence to the Mukhabarat. I spoke with this man—he provided me with the information that I have given you. He says that you will not be able to talk to Ali. He would kill you if he knew that you had come here. Even if Ali did agree to meet, it is obvious that he would not willingly discuss his arrangements in Italy with you."

"He doesn't have to be willing," Milton said. "I can be persuasive."

"No, not this time. But there is another way. My contact says that they are filling another boat now. It is due to sail tomorrow. He has agreed to speak with you. He says there are girls on the boat who have been selected for the kind of businesses that you mentioned to me yesterday. It is the pimps you really want, yes?"

Milton nodded.

"So if he can tell you where the boat is due to land, then you could fly out and meet it. The crossing takes two days. You would have plenty of time. My contact tells me that the pimps will be there for an exchange when they land. You could be there to meet them."

Milton considered the suggestion. "When does the boat leave?"

"Tomorrow morning, before dawn."

"I need to speak to your man now, then."

Omar took off his sunglasses and rested them on the table. "He has been reliable so far, but you should think carefully before involving yourself with him. Ali is dangerous. If he was to find out, he would have no hesitation in killing you."

Milton put on his own glasses. "Arrange a meet."

"I have already made the arrangements. He will meet you before evening prayers. He will be outside the Abu Shaala mosque."

"Where is that?"

"Abu Salim."

"And the gun?"

"I'll have it for you tomorrow. We will meet here again."

Chapter Twenty-Eight

MILTON LOOKED AROUND WARILY.

Abu Salim was everything that Omar had warned him it would be. The district was five miles to the south of the coast and dominated by Abu Salim prison. Milton remembered the facility from his last visit to the city. It had become notorious following the massacre of over a thousand prisoners over two days in 1996. They said that the vultures had fed there for days, swooping down and picking at the entrails of the men who had been left in the courtyard to rot. The prison yard itself had now been turned into a vast car market, where locals picked through the hundreds of barely functioning wrecks in the vain hope of finding a bargain. The streets that led away from the prison were beaten down and poor. Precarious apartment blocks stood in need of repair, burned-out cars had been pushed up against the walls, piles of debris spilled out from collapsed buildings, and trash was blown around on the breeze. The locals, too, bore the signs of neglect: there were long queues at the stores that had food, queues of angry cars bullied their way onto gas station forecourts, and pedestrians walked along the side of the road with their eyes downcast, hammered by the sun and the weight of their problems.

The mosque was large, with a particularly tall minaret that Milton was able to see as soon as his taxi entered the district. As they drew closer, he was able to make out more detail: the tall spire with the onion-shaped crown, the gallery from which the muezzin would deliver the call to prayer, the roof-like canopy, the decorative cornices and arches. The mosque itself was surmounted by a large dome, and its walls were topped with decorative crenulations that put Milton in mind of battlements.

The taxi driver pulled up outside the entrance. The area was busy with worshippers who were heeding the call to the Maghrib prayer.

Milton paid the man and asked him to wait. He got out, shut the door and had begun to look around when he heard the sound of the engine and turned back to see the taxi pulling away. There was no point in going after it; it was already too far away and he would just draw attention to himself. He felt vulnerable, though. This was not a friendly neighbourhood, particularly for a Westerner, and he wasn't armed.

The mosque had been built on generous grounds and was surrounded by lawns that were suffering a little in the heat. There was a path that led between two trees to the entrance, and Milton started down it, falling in behind a group of four men who were conversing amiably as they made their way to prayer.

Milton stopped at the entrance, looking left and right for any sign of the man whom he had come here to meet. He didn't see anyone, and, fearful of being spotted as an outsider, he was about to leave when he saw a man step out of the mosque. He was of short stature and slender, and, despite a swagger that looked a little too affected, Milton could see that he was nervous. Milton turned and glanced over at him, then walked away from the entrance until he was in the shade of a tree.

The man followed.

"Mr. Smith?"

"Yes."

"I am Mustafa."

"Where do you want to talk?"

"You must come with me."

He walked on. Milton let him put a little distance between them both and then followed. Mustafa led the way to a car that had been parked in the alleyway behind the mosque.

"Where are we going?" Milton asked.

"We cannot talk here. It's not safe. Ali has eyes everywhere. It is better if we are on the move."

Milton got inside. Mustafa went around to the driver's side, got into the car, started the engine and pulled away.

"Ali is paranoid. But one does not become as successful as he is without caution."

Mustafa drove them away from Abu Salim and onto the modern highway that led to the airport. He glanced up to the rear-view again and again, his fingers drumming against the wheel.

"Relax," Milton said. "We're not being followed."

"Ali is everywhere. How can you be so sure?"

Milton looked in the mirror. "The road is empty. And I'm good at spotting a tail. We don't have one."

Mustafa did not appear to be persuaded, but, as they drove south, he started to relax. Milton took the opportunity to look him over. He was slender, with light brown skin and a narrow face. He was wearing a ball cap that was pulled down low on his forehead, and he had a patchy beard, trimmed around the mouth and beneath the nose, but wispy and unimpressive on his cheeks. Milton guessed that he was young: twenty-five, perhaps, maybe even younger than that.

They drove south in silence for twenty minutes until they reached a large roundabout where the Airport Highway and Qaser Bin Ghashir-Sawani Road met. The traffic grew a little denser, and Mustafa muscled their way around it until they were able to continue to the east. The open spaces of the airport were visible through the wire mesh fence to their right.

They were fifteen miles from Abu Salim now, and Mustafa seemed finally able to relax.

"Are you okay?" Milton asked.

"I'm fine," he said defensively, as if Milton had questioned his bravery. "I'm only here because of Omar."

"I don't care why. You're here, and you're going to help me. Right?"

Mustafa tensed. "Maybe. What do you want?"

"Information."

"About?"

"Ali has an arrangement. He sells women to pimps in Europe. The women go into the sex industry. There was an Eritrean woman, quite young, several weeks ago. Ali put her and her brother on a boat here, and they sailed to Lampedusa. They were split up. The woman was taken to France and then sold to Albanian pimps."

"And?"

"And I want you to tell me everything you know about that."

"I know it happens," Mustafa said. "They pick out the good-looking girls here. Ali has a man; he takes their pictures before they get on the boat. The ones they like, they make sure they are treated very well on the crossing. They are given water and food, life jackets, they stay on the top deck rather than going down below."

"What happens then?"

"When they land? They drive them to wherever they need to go. France, as you say. Italy, Spain, Germany. They are introduced to the purchasers and the deal is done. After that, I cannot tell you."

"There is a boat leaving soon?"

"The day after tomorrow."

"And there will be girls on the boat who will be sold?"

"Yes. There are several."

"I need you to find out where that boat is going to sail to."

"Why?"

"Just find out, Mustafa. That's all I need you to do. Tell me when it is leaving and where it is going. Lampedusa, Malta, Italy, wherever. Find out for me and I'll tell Omar you've done a good job. You won't need to do anything else and you'll never see me again."

"Why are you interested in this?"

"It doesn't matter why."

"Are you a journalist? Writing a story?"

"No."

"Then you are police?"

"I'm not police. It doesn't matter who I am or why I'm interested. You just need to get me that information. Do you understand?"

They passed a slip road that was signposted for the Wadi Alrabie Road. The city was to the west, to the left of the car.

"I will try," Mustafa said. "I will speak to the men and see what I can find. We meet again tomorrow, yes?"

Chapter Twenty-Nine

MUSTAFA HAD DROPPED MILTON outside an abandoned movie theatre on the edge of Abu Salim. He took a bus into the centre of Tripoli and had walked back to his hotel. He turned up the air conditioning and slept. He had an early breakfast, left the hotel at eight and then took a taxi back to the movie theatre.

Mustafa was waiting for him.

Milton got into the car, and Mustafa drove them both away.

"Well?" Milton said.

"There is a problem."

"The boat?"

"It is as I thought. A boat is leaving tomorrow morning. I know what time it is leaving, and where it is leaving from."

"But?"

"I don't know where it is going."

"I need to know, Mustafa."

"I understand that, but I cannot find out. It used to be common knowledge, but Ali has changed things. He is worried, I think, about the boats being intercepted. The Italian navy found the last boat and sent it back. Ali thinks they were warned. Now he only tells a few of the men. And I am not one of them."

Milton gritted his teeth. "So tell me what you do know. Where is it going from?"

"Sabratah. It is a fishing town to the northwest of here. It is fought over by the militia and ISIS. Very dangerous. The government is not there any longer. There are no officials. No police, no army. A lot of chaos. It is very easy to sail a boat out of the harbour. No one cares."

"And from there?"

"There are several possibilities. Many boats go to Malta.

Others to Lampedusa. There are others that will travel to Sicily, and others that will go all the way to the mainland."

"And there's no way of knowing?"

"Ali would know. The captain of the boat, obviously, he knows. Ali's lieutenants, perhaps. I am not a senior man. I do as I am told. I am not given his secrets. I am sorry, Mr. Smith. I tried to find out for you, really, I did. But I do not know what else I can do to help you."

Milton stared out of the dusty windshield as they drove to the south.

There was another way.

"Can you get me to Sabratah?"

Mustafa stared at him with an open mouth.

"Tomorrow morning," Milton said. "Can you get me on the boat?"

He looked over at him. "*What?*"

"I need to know where it is going to end up."

"You're crazy—"

Milton spoke over him. "I need to know where the women will be handed over. If you can't help me, I'll just have to start following them here, rather than when they land."

"You are not listening to me. You cannot go on the boat. Are you crazy? They are dangerous. They sink. You have seen the pictures?"

"If that's the only way I can find the men I need to find, then I don't have any other choice."

Mustafa looked troubled.

Milton pressed, "Can you get me on the boat?"

Mustafa flicked the indicator and pulled over to the side of the road.

"Mustafa?"

"Maybe. It is not an easy thing. Many of the migrants are black. Some of them are Libyans, some Syrian. None of them look like you."

"Can you do it?"

"Maybe. I will need money. The guards will need to be paid."

"How much?"

"I know two of the men. Not much. Two hundred dollars each."

"Fine," Milton said. He reached into his pocket, took out his roll of notes and counted out eight fifties. He folded them and passed them over to Mustafa. The man reached for the notes, but Milton intercepted his hand and held it. "I'm counting on you, Mustafa. You understand that, don't you? It's very important. Don't let me down. Omar would be unhappy if you did. You know what that would mean for you."

"You do not have to threaten me," Mustafa said. "I know very well. That is why I am here."

Milton held Mustafa's hand for a beat and then released it, allowing the Libyan to draw his hand away.

"The boat leaves early tomorrow morning. Very early. Where is your hotel?"

"I'll meet you at the Victory Arch."

"I will be there at half past three." He looked as if he was about to speak again, but he shook his head instead.

"What?" Milton said.

"You should make sure you are well dressed. It can be cold at sea."

Chapter Thirty

MUSTAFA DROVE MILTON back into town and dropped him near the souk.

Milton checked his watch: it was half past nine. He took out his phone and left Omar a message to say that they would need to meet in an hour.

He went back to Caffe Casa and took a seat outside. He attracted the attention of one of the surly waiters, ordered a double espresso and waited for Omar.

He didn't have long to wait. He saw the suave intelligence officer as he approached across Essaa Square, distinctive in his smart pale blue suit, bright white shirt and dark glasses. He was carrying a leather satchel. He saw Milton and picked a route between the tables until he was able to take the seat opposite him.

"Mr. Smith."

"Omar. Would you like a drink?"

"I'll get them. Would you like another?"

"Just a glass of orange juice."

Omar cocked his finger, and the waiter, now considerably less surly than when he had served Milton five minutes earlier, came over and dutifully took the order.

"They try very hard here," Omar said, flicking his fingers to indicate that he meant the café. "They would like us all to think we are in Greece or Italy, sipping a frappe or a Freddo while we watch the world go by. It is a worthy attempt until you hear a car bomb or automatic gunfire and you remember: this is Tripoli, not Paris."

"I've been to worse places."

"Really? You have not been here long enough, Mr. Smith. How was Abu Salim?"

"Yes, that was worse."

"Did you have a profitable meeting with Mustafa?"

"Yes and no."

"You got the information you wanted?"

"Unfortunately not. It seems that Ali is more careful than he used to be. I don't think it was Mustafa's fault. Ali just doesn't advertise the destinations of the boats. And if I don't know where it is going to land, I can't do what needs to be done."

"So what is next?"

"I'm going to go at it from a different angle." Milton didn't trust Omar, and there was no reason to give him more information than was strictly necessary. "You were very helpful. I appreciate it."

Omar raised his hands. "Your gratitude is unnecessary, Mr. Smith. I am happy to help." He started to rise and then paused. "I nearly forgot. You asked me for something. Do you still need it?"

"Yes," Milton said. "I do."

Omar sat down again. He used his foot to push the bag that he had left next to his chair until it was next to Milton's. "Everything you asked for is there. Weapon and ammunition. Can I ask why you need it?"

"I don't like to be unprepared. And, as you say: this is Libya, not Europe." Milton hooked his foot around the bag and dragged it a little closer.

"Will we see each other again?"

"Probably not," Milton said.

"Then goodbye, Mr. Smith. And good luck."

#

MILTON WATCHED OMAR GO AND THEN, when he was out of sight, he stood. He picked up the bag. He knew, of course, that he would be followed again and, when he turned to look, he saw the same agents waiting for him to make his move. They didn't try to conceal themselves this time; Omar must have told them that it was unnecessary. Milton edged between the tables until he was on the square and nodded at the nearest man as he detached himself from his position in the doorway of a shop. The man glared at Milton—Omar must have chided them for their unprofessionalism—and fell into step twenty metres behind him.

Milton went by the clock tower and, as the sun emerged from behind a cloud and shone down on the city, he made his way toward the souk. It was simple to find, and, within moments, he was deep within a maze of narrow streets and alleys that were lined with shops and stalls, their produce and wares spilling out so that it was occasionally necessary to pass between them in single file. The cobbles underfoot were slick with the juice from rotten fruit and animal ordure, racks of ripe vegetables were picked over by discerning locals, fresh fish were laid out on beds of ice, and cheap trinkets were festooned around the necks of battered mannequins that had seen better days.

Milton wandered aimlessly, losing himself in the hubbub until he turned into a narrow alley, passed through an ancient archway and emerged into the part of the market that sold clothes. He bought a new pair of jeans cut from the thickest denim that he could find, a pair of long johns, two T-shirts and a padded jacket. He added a ball cap and a scarf and two packets of cigarettes. His shopping cost a hundred dollars, leaving him with just five hundred. He would have to husband it carefully to make it last.

It took twenty minutes to be sure that he had lost the tail and, once he was sure that he had, he returned to the hotel. He checked his watch as he made his way into the coolness of the lobby: eleven. He was pleased that he had a little extra time. He wasn't going to have long for sleep tonight, and he doubted that there would be much opportunity for relaxation tomorrow.

He went to his room and took the pistol out of the bag to examine it. It was a small handgun, the same size as his open hand. He did not recognise the make and he guessed that it was one of the knock-offs that had started to appear on the local firearms market. It was chambered for .32 ACP, a disappointingly weak handgun calibre, especially when fired from such a short barrel.

He stripped it to ensure that it was clean and that all of the parts were present and working, taking particular care with the firing pin. Omar had provided a box of ammunition. Milton loaded the magazine and ran rounds into and out of the chamber to make sure that it was working as it should. The weakest part on a semi-automatic pistol, especially a cheap one, was the magazine. This one appeared to be satisfactory.

Milton laid the pistol down. He was unimpressed, but it was the best he would have been able to manage on short notice and it would have to suffice.

Milton lay on the bed beneath the overhead fan, and slept.

Chapter Thirty-One

MILTON SET the alarm on his phone for three in the morning, but his sleep had been fitful and he had risen at two thirty. He showered and, still wrapped in the towel, made himself a coffee from the jar of instant granules that had been left on the bureau next to the kettle. He dressed in the warm clothes that he had purchased in the souk yesterday evening. The long johns and the new, thicker jeans felt heavy against his legs. He put on the two long-sleeved T-shirts, his jumper and his boots.

He opened the door and went out into the courtyard. He took out a new packet of cigarettes, tore away the cellophane wrapper, put one between his lips and lit it. He looked into the infinite blackness overhead, listening to the slow sighing of traffic as it passed by outside. It was cold. The night sky was clear, the constellations sparkling. Milton found himself thinking of Samir and Nadia. They would have had a similar view before they set off on the final leg of their journey to bring them to Europe. He wondered what they would have been thinking. They would have been frightened and anxious.

That was not unreasonable.

Milton was anxious, too.

He finished the cigarette, grinding it out against the rough bricks, went back into his room, put on the thick padded jacket that he had bought in the souk, put his pistol, phone and cigarettes into his pocket, and went outside.

\#

MUSTAFA WAS LATE.

They had arranged to meet at three thirty, but it was just before four when Milton saw the car that Mustafa had been driving yesterday. The car slowed and pulled over to the side of the road. Milton opened the door and got inside.

"Is everything okay?"

"Yes," Mustafa said.

"You're late."

"There have been some complications."

"Meaning?"

"Ali is here," he said.

"In Tripoli?"

"Yes. I saw him yesterday. After I left you."

"Is that unusual?"

Mustafa nodded. "He doesn't normally come into the city. I don't know why he would be here. But it makes me nervous."

"You can still get me on the boat?"

"I don't know."

"I need better than that."

"Yes," he said. "Probably. I think so."

They drove west out of Tripoli, following the coast road through Janzour, Az-Zawiyah and Surman. The road was empty at this hour. The landscape was arid and featureless between the towns, but Milton's attention was drawn to the right of the car, to the vast expanse of the sea. The sun was slowly broaching the horizon, and, as it did, the water gradually passed through a spectrum from black to indigo to the darkest of blues. Milton saw the lights of a few other boats far out from shore.

He was preoccupied with the consequences of what he had proposed to do. He was not a man much predisposed to doubt, but he couldn't ignore the unsettled sensation that had lodged in the pit of his stomach. He knew that what he was planning to do was dangerous. That was not the issue; he had lived with danger all of his adult life. The difference this time was that he was trusting his life to smugglers who did not set a high premium upon the safety of their passengers, men whose laxity had already led to many thousands of deaths.

Milton could live with danger when he was in control of the situation, when he could influence events. But he was ceding that control now. So many things could go wrong over which he had no influence. The engine might not be properly maintained so that it broke down miles out at sea. The hull might not be watertight. The boat might be overloaded with passengers. Any of those things were possible, and any one of them might mean that the boat would sink. Milton was an excellent swimmer, but he wasn't going to be able to swim sixty miles back to land.

He would drown, just like everyone else.

"There," Mustafa said, nodding ahead to the lights that were twinkling against the darkness of the sea. "Sabratah."

Chapter Thirty-Two

SABRATAH WAS A SMALL TOWN that had been founded two thousand years earlier as a trading post, serving as a port for products that had been transported north from the African hinterland. It had been an important Roman outpost, and Milton saw traces of the architecture from the period as they passed through the outskirts.

"You like history?" Mustafa said. Milton didn't answer, but Mustafa—who was obviously talking because he was nervous—continued anyway. "There is a Roman theatre here. Very impressive. Villas and temples, too. Tourists used to come here to see them. No one comes now. It is not safe."

They drove down to the seafront. As they drew closer, Milton started to see signs of activity. Men gathered on street corners, shopkeepers began their preparations for the day, stallholders in the marketplace wheeled their carts into place.

Mustafa turned off the road and parked in a vacant lot that overlooked the harbour.

Milton looked out through the windscreen. There were boats docked below, but it was the busy activity around one of the vessels that told of the new direction that its entrepreneurial residents had taken. One of the boats was the centre of a busy scrum of activity. It was at the end of a long jetty, a mooring line tethered to a concrete bollard. It didn't look particularly impressive. It was made of wood, perhaps fifteen metres from bow to stern, with a structure in the middle. Men were aboard it, checking the equipment. One man had removed the inspection hatch and was examining the engine. Other men were on the dock, guarding the way ahead. They were armed with automatic rifles.

Mustafa switched off the engine and sat quietly for a moment.

"Are you sure you want to do this?"

"What do we need to do?" Milton said.

"There will be a bus. Passengers are kept in houses nearby overnight. They will be brought to the boat and then loaded onto it."

"Do I need anything? A ticket?"

"There are no tickets. This is not like taking a train. You just need to be in the group when they are put on the boat."

"How do we do that?"

"I have spoken to one of the guards. I have given him half of the money you gave me. We will join the group with him."

"And then?"

"He will try to help you, but you will be on your own."

"That's not very reassuring." Milton turned and fixed Mustafa in his dead-eyed gaze. "You said you could get me aboard."

Mustafa put up his hands in supplication. "It is the best I can do. Do you have more money?"

"Some," Milton said.

"If anyone stops you, offer them money. Fifty dollars. No more. It will make them forget any questions that they might have."

"That'll be enough?"

"If you give them more, they will think you are rich. Then they will try to take more. No—give them fifty and they will let you go."

"What about Ali?"

Mustafa frowned with anxiety. "If he is there, try not to let him see your face." He took a deep breath and opened the door. "Come on," he said. "We must get to the boat. It leaves soon."

#

A SET of steep stone steps descended the hill down to the harbour. Mustafa led the way with Milton close behind. They were halfway to the bottom when a bus rumbled into view, passing around a bend in the cliff. Mustafa stopped and pointed, but Milton had already seen it. The bus was moving slowly, the engine backfiring as it struggled on. It was too far away for Milton to make out very much in the way of detail, but he could see that every spare seat must have been taken together with the spaces in the aisle. One man, holding an AK-47 aloft, was stood on the sill of the door, hanging on with one hand. The bus slowed as it reached the harbour and the horn sounded.

A second bus appeared around the bend in the cliff, and then a third. They were both as full as the first.

"We must hurry," Mustafa said.

They set off again, descending the steps a little more quickly.

The second and third buses pulled up next to the first. Men with AKs gathered in front of the vehicles, conversing with one another as the passengers were kept inside. Milton could see the men and women more clearly now. He saw dozens of black faces looking out of the windows. As they drew nearer, he started to pick out the faces of children, and then babies in the arms of their mothers.

The men appeared to reach a decision and, with a curt shout, the doors of the buses were opened. The passengers were ordered to disembark, directed into the space that had been formed between the vehicles.

Milton noticed Mustafa was heading towards one of the guards. The man was at the edge of the group, away from his colleagues, marshalling the least-observed edge of the fast-growing crowd. Mustafa gave a low whistle and the guard turned in their direction. The two men exchanged discreet nods of acknowledgement.

"Now," Mustafa said.

Milton overtook Mustafa and hurried to the guard. The man had a scar from his eyebrow down to the corner of his mouth in the shape of a sickle, the edges of the wound twisting as he chewed a wad of gum. He sneered at Milton, cocking an eyebrow, and then took a half turn to face the throng of passengers. That was Milton's invitation to join the crowd. Without a word, he stepped past the guard, not looking at him as he passed.

He pressed into the crowd. There must have been two hundred of them there, and the third bus had not yet started to empty out. The crowd was dense, and Milton was able to hide in the middle of it. He glanced around and saw the faces of the men and women who were waiting to board the boat. There was no talk, just the shuffling of feet and the occasional barked instruction from the guards. Milton made his way to the centre of the crowd. There were some fairer-skinned passengers, the lighter tans and browns of those from north Africa, but most of the others were black, and none of them was as white as he was.

One of the guards raised his voice and barked out an order: "Get on boat!" The man spoke in broken English. There were a lot of different nationalities here; perhaps English was the most commonly understood.

Milton was jostled by the people behind him as the crowd was shepherded away from the buses to the concrete promenade that encircled the harbour. The guards followed them, penning them in tightly and then funnelling them onto the wooden jetty. The sound of their feet changed: the slap of shoes on concrete was joined by the shuffle of shoes across wood. The narrowing of the jetty was a bottleneck that slowed their onward progress, but the guards kept them moving.

There were two guards at the end of the jetty, adjacent to the middle of the boat. They, too, had AK-47s and the passengers were embarking between them.

They were going to get a good look at Milton's white face.

He reached into his jacket pocket for his money, felt for the edge of a note, and pulled it away from the others.

One of the guards was distracted as a man struggled to help his heavily pregnant partner cross the gap between the jetty and the boat and, for a moment, Milton thought he was going to get across without interrogation. But as he waited behind a man with two young boys, the other guard glanced across at him and then performed a quick double take.

"You," he said. "Come here."

The man reached into the queue, grabbed Milton by the elbow and pulled him to the other side of the jetty. Milton looked at him. He was no more than a boy, barely out of his teens. The AK looked big in his hands. Milton would have been able to disarm him in an instant; he could have taken the gun away from him and tossed him into the water, but that would get him nowhere. There were too many guards. He was trapped on the jetty, with nowhere to go but the sea below.

He would have to play this out as best he could.

"You. Where you from?"

"Tripoli."

"Nah," he said. "You are white. You don't come from Tripoli."

"I'm from Qaser Bin Ghashir."

He looked dubious. "You have paid?"

"Yes."

"I do not believe you."

"How would I be here if I hadn't paid?"

"You have more money?"

"Yes."

He put out his hand.

Milton started to speak, feigning indignation, and the man nodded down to the AK. Milton looked suitably fearful, reached into his pocket and handed over the note. The guard looked down at the balled-up note and fingered the end so that he could see the fifty in the corner. He curled his lip, and Milton thought that he was going to ask for more, but, instead, he stood aside and nodded his head toward the boat.

"Move."

Milton did not need to be asked twice. He knew that he had been fortunate. He reached across for the frame of the flying bridge, stretched his leg across the gap between the gunwale and the jetty, and hopped over.

The boat bucked on a swell, the wood creaking ominously.

Milton wondered just *how* fortunate he had been.

Chapter Thirty-Three

THEY LOADED MORE AND MORE passengers onto the boat until there was no more room.

Milton was shepherded to the top deck and found a small slice of space that he could slide into. He was up at the front, near the mizzen mast, and he looked back and assessed the rest of the boat. It had two decks and a flying bridge in the middle, with a hatch that led down to the hold. The entire vessel was made of wood, painted two shades of blue, and with signs of repair where large sections of the hull had been taken out and replaced. What was left was in dreadful condition. The wood was rotten almost everywhere, and Milton was only able to examine it above the waterline; there was no way of predicting what condition it was in below the surface. Milton guessed not very good.

There was a lot of nervous chatter now as the prospect of the voyage became a reality rather than just a vague possibility. The chatter became more animated as the engine started, the diesel unit grumbling ominously before it settled into a more regular chug.

Milton looked back at the harbour and saw that a Mercedes had pulled up next to the jetty. It was a new model, in excellent condition, and it looked out of place next to the three dilapidated buses and the cars that some of the guards had used to reach the waterfront. He watched as the door opened and a man stepped out. The behaviour of the guards changed in an instant: they had been slouching around, smoking cigarettes and sharing jokes, but, at the approach of the newcomer, they stood a little straighter and became a little more alert.

Milton had never seen him before, but Mustafa had been right: he knew Ali Tessema when he saw him. He was taller than most of the guards, at least six feet tall, and dressed in clothes that were clearly expensive. Milton saw the gleam of a gold necklace and gold rings on his fingers that, if they were visible at this distance, must have been significant.

Ali had a strut about him that spoke of confidence and authority. He made his way to the jetty and spoke with the guards. Milton watched anxiously as Ali took the arm of the younger guard whom Milton had bribed and started to ask him questions. Milton had no way of knowing what they were talking about, but, as Ali turned to the boat and gestured toward it, he was worried that they were talking about him. He knew very well that his white skin was an anomaly among the other passengers around him, and he felt as if a spotlight was being shone on him. He pulled his cap down a little, as if that might obscure the obviousness of his difference.

Ali took out and lit a cigarette and then gazed over to the boat. Milton watched him and wondered, as he stood there, if he was calculating how much money the trip was generating for him. If there were three hundred migrants aboard, and they had each paid a thousand dollars—not including the money that they would have paid to be brought across the border and then the desert to the coast—then he must have been looking at least three hundred thousand dollars. The new Mercedes, the sharp clothes and the jewellery were put into context.

Ali Tessema was a rich man.

The smuggler said something to the guards, and two of them hurried down the jetty to the bollards where the mooring lines had been fastened. They unlooped them and tossed the ropes back onto the deck, and one of them barked out an instruction to the man who had taken up position behind the wheel in the flying bridge.

The engine growled loudly and the boat slowly pulled away from the jetty and out into the harbour. Ali had moved over to a group of three guards and, as he pointed to the departing boat, he said something that caused the others to laugh raucously enough for Milton to be able to hear them. They kept laughing, one bent double he was laughing so much. Ali took his cigarette from his mouth, looked at it, and then flicked it into the water. It was difficult to imagine how he might have looked more at ease, starkly at odds with the three hundred passengers he was sending out onto the ocean in a boat that was not fit to make the voyage.

Ali turned and walked back to the Mercedes.

Milton turned, too. He looked out at the shoulders of the harbour as they moved out into the open sea. He inhaled the salty tang of the air, felt the splash of the spume on his face, and tried to ignore the churn of anxiety in his gut.

Chapter Thirty-Four

THE BOAT was slow, and progress was laborious.

After an hour, the coast of Africa had blended into the haze that marked the horizon. It was difficult to judge distances without landmarks to set as waypoints, but Milton knew that a boat like this would travel at around ten knots. They would cover eleven miles an hour at that speed. There were approximately two hundred and fifty miles between them and Malta, and three hundred and fifty between them and the coast of Sicily. It was going to take a day or a day and a half to make land again, and that was if the weather remained kind. If they ran into a storm, they would be looking at a much longer crossing, and that was on the assumption that the boat could make it at all.

The boat's general seaworthiness was of concern. Milton had looked askance at it while it was waiting to be loaded at Sabratah, but, now that they were underway, he was even more worried. It was obvious that it had been loaded down beyond what was reasonable for it to bear. Milton wondered whether he had underestimated the number of migrants aboard, all of them crammed into whatever space they could find. He had not had the opportunity to look down into the area below decks, but he had watched as the smugglers had sent dozens of men and women down through the hatch, and the sound of dozens of voices was audible from beneath him.

Milton counted two hundred men, women and children on the deck with him. Most of them were North African, lighter skinned than those from sub-Saharan Africa who had been sent below. They were pressed up against the side of the boat, like him, or stood up so that they could cling to the metal housing. Others were atop it, some grasping the line that ran between the two masts to aid them in maintaining their balance. The passengers were watched over by two smugglers, each of whom was armed with a pistol. The combined weight of this human cargo meant that the boat had sunk down low in the water, so that the rubber tyres that were roped to the hull sloshed through the surf and clouds of spray occasionally kicked up over the gunwales.

The metal structure in the middle of the deck was badly corroded with rust, and, looking back, Milton saw that the engine was spewing a cloud of fumes and that a slick of oil was trailing behind them. The sea was reasonably calm, but the way the boat pitched and yawed across the gentle waves made Milton fearful of what might happen to them if the wind picked up.

He wondered, again, about the good sense of his plan.

The sun was only three hours above the horizon, yet it was already burning hot. The structure atop the deck would provide a little shade for two or three hours, but, once the sun was above it, there would be no respite. Milton pulled his cap down so that it was low on his head. He took off his jacket, turning it around and hanging it off his head so that it covered his face. It was quickly warm and stuffy, but Milton felt more comfortable. It would be easier when the sun went down, but, for now, the longer he could remain inconspicuous, the better.

The to and fro of the boat as it rolled over the waves became hypnotic and soothing, and, as Milton closed his eyes, he allowed himself to sleep.

Chapter Thirty-Five

MILTON SLEPT FOR SEVERAL HOURS.

He awoke and, as he blinked his eyes and gently came back to his senses, he realised that something was missing. He closed his eyes again and concentrated. He worked out what it was: it was the engine. He couldn't hear it.

He removed the jacket from his head and blinked into the sudden flood of bright light. The migrants around him were looking in the same direction, toward the stern. Milton raised himself up a little so that he could look, too, and saw one of the smugglers signalling to the captain. There came a loud grumble as the captain tried to start the engine, but it spluttered and didn't catch. He tried again, and, after another loud splutter, there came a whine and a groan and then a more insistent chugging.

The passengers cheered and clapped with relief.

Milton turned to the young man to his left. "Do you speak English?"

"A little," he said.

"What happened?"

"The engine stopped."

"For how long?"

"Ten minutes. We have just been drifting. They couldn't fix it."

Milton looked back to the stern. The slick of oil behind them had become wider, the viscous fluid refracting rainbows in the bright sunlight.

"I was worried," the man said. "I have never been on a boat before."

Milton looked at him more carefully. He was in his late teens or early twenties, with clear skin and bright eyes. "What's your name?"

"Kolo."

"I'm John," he said. "Where are you from?"

"Somalia. And you?"

"Libya."

Milton did not want to draw attention to the differences between himself and the others. He changed the subject. "How did you get to Sabratah?"

"They drove us through the Sahara." The boy's English was surprisingly good. "It took one week. They kept us in a house in Tripoli until the boat was ready. Three days. I thought we would never leave."

"What are your plans?"

"I get to Italy; then maybe I try to get to Denmark or Sweden. I have friends there. They have jobs; they can send money home. My parents are old. They have no money. I want to help them. And you?"

Milton had considered a number of cover stories. "I have a friend who works in France. A vineyard." Kolo looked at him blankly. Milton added, "Where they grow grapes for wine."

"Ah, I understand—you help them to harvest the grapes?"

"Yes."

"Hard work, especially if it is hot like this." He pointed up at the clear blue sky and the sun burning down on the sea and the boat.

"Very hard," Milton said. He tugged the brim of his cap so that a little extra shadow fell onto his face. He could feel the heat in the fabric of the cap. It was close to midday and the sun was at its most brutal. The sea shimmered away to infinity on either side of the boat, woozy waves radiating over the surface.

Kolo followed Milton's gaze out over the water.

"Can you swim?" Kolo asked.

"Yes," Milton said.

"I cannot. I have never even seen the sea before." He paused, nodding his head out to the waves. "If we, you know—if we sink, how long do you think we would last in that water?"

"Not long," Milton said honestly. "And being able to swim won't make much difference. We must be a hundred miles from land. And the water is colder than it looks."

"Then we better hope that the boat is better than it looks."

Milton thought Kolo was being morbid, but, when he turned to look over at him, he saw his bright white grin. He was laughing at their predicament.

Milton smiled back at him. "We'll be all right," he said.

#

THE SUN passed its peak and slowly started to descend. Milton stared out at the unchanging vista, the miles of unbroken blue that reached all the way to the horizon, the more vivid colour of the sky merging into the haze so that it became difficult to tell where one stopped and the other began. He looked for other ships, but, save a tiny speck that might have been a fishing vessel, he saw nothing.

They were all alone, miles from assistance, on a boat that was barely seaworthy and manned by a crew who looked as uncomfortable as the passengers.

The sun pounded down onto the deck. Milton's cap offered him some protection, but he could still feel the heat, and it was difficult to stay awake. He put his jacket over his head again and allowed himself to drift off once more.

#

"EXCUSE ME."

Milton awoke. It was Kolo's voice. Milton pulled the jacket off his head and looked over at him. Kolo wasn't talking to him, though; he was calling to one of the smugglers responsible for watching the passengers on their deck.

"Excuse me? Sir?"

The smuggler turned to look at him. "What?"

"I am thirsty."

"What do you want me to do about that?"

"Do you have any water?"

"Yes," the man said, sweeping his arm at the ocean. "I have gallons of it."

"Some water I can drink?"

The man reached into his mouth, took out the wad of gum that he had been chewing and flicked it over the side. He reached up, wiped the sweat away from his forehead and then nodded down at Kolo. "You think this is a pleasure cruise?"

"I am thirsty," Kolo said again. "I need a drink."

The man curled his finger. "Come here."

Kolo got up and, barely able to find the space to bypass the outstretched legs and supine bodies of the others, he made his way across the deck to the smuggler. The man reached around and pulled a pistol out of the waistband of his trousers. He aimed it at the boy, gesturing with his hand that he should hurry over to him.

Milton sat up straight.

"What is it?" Kolo said. "What have I done wrong?"

"You should not be on the top deck."

"I paid for my ticket."

"You are on the boat. That is what you paid for. But the darker your skin, the farther down you go."

The man unlatched the door to the lower deck. A wave of odour washed out of it: petrol fumes, sweat, vomit, excrement and urine. It was so strong that it overwhelmed the saltiness of the sea, and those passengers nearest the door turned away in disgust. Milton looked across and saw a square of gloomy darkness through the open doorway. The Libyan pointed into it with his left hand, his right aiming the gun with a lazy, insouciant confidence.

Milton wanted to intervene, but he knew that there was nothing that he could do. If he spoke out, he would attract attention to himself and the fact that he was so very different from the other passengers. He knew that he was safe only for as long as he kept a low profile, out of sight, avoiding any possibility of attracting attention to himself. He doubted that these men would have any compunction in tossing him over the side.

Kolo looked back at Milton. He held the boy's gaze for a moment and then forced himself to look away. When Milton glanced back again, Kolo had stepped over the sill of the door and was descending the stairs to the lower deck. The Libyan closed the door with a resounding crash and fastened the latch again.

"What about her?" called out one of the passengers.

The smuggler swivelled and looked over at the man who had just spoken. He was Libyan or Syrian, and Milton had noticed that he had been causing trouble over on his side of the boat.

"She is African," the man said. "She is as black as he is."

The smuggler shook his head. "No," he said.

"Come on, man. There's not enough space up here. Put her down with the others, too."

"I paid to—"

The smuggler jabbed the gun in the man's direction; everyone flinched. "Did you hear me? I said she stays here with us. No more talking. If you talk, I shoot you and throw you over the side."

The man raised his hands in surrender, his protest at an end. The smuggler shook his head in disgust, hawked up a wad of phlegm and spat it over the side. He put the gun back into his trousers and turned away.

Milton regarded the girl. She was sitting with her back against the side of the boat. She was tall, with long legs and slender arms. The man who had tried to have her moved looked over at her with a disdain he did not bother to conceal, and she turned her head and looked away. It looked as if she was alone on the boat; her dark skin certainly stood out among the lighter browns of the Libyans and Syrians who sat around her. She turned her head in Milton's direction. She wasn't focussing on anything or anyone, but, for a moment, it felt to him as if she was looking right at him. She was very pretty.

Milton knew why she had been put up on the top deck. He remembered what Mustafa had told him.

She was merchandise.

The Albanians had contracted with Ali for girls, and she was one of them.

He looked around the deck and saw a number of women who bore similarities to the first girl: the teenager sitting with her back to the wheelhouse, surrounded by her family; an older woman, early twenties, gazing out at the ocean; two girls, possibly sisters, talking to each other in nervous whispers. Were they all part of the same consignment? Maybe, maybe not. But Milton was willing to guess that at least some of them had been earmarked for a career that they had not anticipated as soon as they reached their destination.

Milton might not be able to help them while they were on the boat, but things would be different when they reached land. And suspecting who they were would make it easier for him to do what he had planned to do.

They were the bait.

Part 4

London

Chapter Thirty-Six

MILTON HAD been gone for six days.

Hicks and Sarah had settled into a comfortable arrangement that was interspersed with moments of awkwardness. It was a small flat, and the sleeping arrangements were not perfect. Hicks stayed in the living room, and Sarah remained in the bedroom. There had been occasions where they had surprised each other early in the morning or late at night: Hicks going to the bathroom in his shorts as Sarah emerged from her own room in one of Milton's plain white T-shirts barely large enough to reach down to her thighs. The kitchen was tiny, and it was impossible for either of them to pass without brushing up against the other. It had happened twice before Hicks resolved not to try to use the room while Sarah was there. That she was attractive was not in question, and nor was it a problem—Hicks had no interest in her romantically—but the press of her body against his made him feel uncomfortable.

He knew why. He hadn't told Rachel the nature of his business in London. He realised, with a pang of guilt, that he had unconsciously shied away from telling her that he was looking after a young, and unquestionably attractive, woman. There was no reason for his reticence other than the fact that what he was doing made him feel nervous. It was the anticipation that he might make Rachel unhappy, even though, rationally, he knew that she would understand.

That made him question himself more thoroughly, and he started to worry that he had kept quiet because he had a guilty conscience.

Because he did find Sarah physically attractive. Even though he had no intention of acting on that attraction, that

181

knowledge, and the fact that there was still no sign of Milton's return, made him unsettled.

#

THEY RETURNED to Epping Forest for another walk and returned to the car at a little after six. They had walked for three hours, deeper into the forest, and Hicks had found that he had enjoyed the time they spent together. Sarah leaned forward as soon as Hicks started the engine and found Spotify on the console.

"I had a radio in Syria," she said as she scrolled through the curated playlists. "Well—it was my boyfriend's. We listened to it all the time."

"You left it behind?"

"Of course. I could not bring it with me."

"You didn't say you had a boyfriend."

She swiped across the screen. "I did. Not anymore."

"What happened?"

"He was killed."

"I'm sorry—"

She kept swiping.

Hicks proceeded delicately. "Was this before you left?"

"No," she said. "Afterwards. He stayed. The government killed him. He was a porter at the hospital in Zafarana. They dropped a barrel bomb onto the town and then, when the injured were taken to hospital, they dropped two more bombs onto it. He died in the second blast. His parents emailed to tell me."

"I'm sorry. I didn't—"

"Why? It's nothing to do with you, Hicks." She found an old-school hip-hop playlist and Twista started to play. "You can't trust men," she said, lightening her words with a laugh that Hicks could tell was manufactured. "My father. Then Joran. They always leave me, one way or another."

She crossed her legs and drummed her fingers on her knee; save the music, there was silence between them. Hicks didn't know how to respond, so he thought about what she had said as he drove them west to Bethnal Green.

She spoke again as he pulled into a parking space next to Milton's building.

"*You* won't leave me, will you?"

The question caught him askance.

"No," he said. "I won't."

"Really?"

"I promised," Hicks said. "I promised John and I promised you. I'll stay here for as long as I'm needed."

She opened the door, he opened his, and they both stepped out.

"Are you hungry, Hicks?"

He had tried several times to persuade her to call him Alex, but she always reverted back to the more formal address.

"I am," he said. "What do you fancy? A takeout?"

"No. I've had enough pizza and curry to last a lifetime. I thought I would make something. *Dawood basha*. Would you like some?"

"I've no idea what that is."

"Syrian meatballs. The meat is flavoured and cooked in a tomato sauce. It is very good."

"Lovely." He locked the car and walked her to the entrance of the flat. He opened the door and stood aside as she went in. "Do you need anything?"

"I could use some ghee," she said. "I don't have much left."

"I'll get some."

#

HICKS WENT back outside and ambled to the shops on Old Street. He thought about what she had told him. There had been no mention of her boyfriend until then, and, although she had made a joke about it, even Hicks could see that her words were an indication of something that bothered her at a deep level. He was no psychologist, but the diagnosis was, surely, elementary. Her father and then her boyfriend; it wasn't their fault that they had been killed, but their losses had imbued her with a sense of abandonment and an almost constitutional distrust of attachment. It wasn't unreasonable.

Hicks realised how difficult it must have been for her to trust Milton and then, as Milton left, to trust him.

He remembered the comment she had made about the radio and remembered that there was a place that sold cheap electrical goods next to the supermarket. He walked up to it and paused, gazing in through the plate-glass window. There were vacuum cleaners, kitchen appliances, game consoles and, to one side, a digital radio. The proprietor was in the process of closing up. Hicks opened the door and went inside.

\#

SARAH TOLD HIM TO WAIT IN THE SITTING ROOM.

He did as he was told, inhaling the delicious aromas that were spilling out of the open kitchen door. He smelled cooked beef, sautéed onions, tomato and a confection of spices that he couldn't identify but which, nevertheless, smelled appetising.

Hicks left the digital radio on the table.

Sarah came through after ten minutes. She was carrying two bowls, one in her right hand and the other braced between her elbow and wrist, and, in the other hand, she clutched the necks of two bottles of beer. Hicks sat up straight and took the balanced bowl and one of the beers. The meal was appetising: browned meatballs in a thick tomato sauce, served with rice.

"This looks good," he said, slicing through one of the meatballs with his fork.

"What's that?" she said, nodding at the box on the table.

"It's for you," he said.

"What is it?"

"Open it."

She rested her plate of food on the table and took the box out of the plastic bag.

"A radio?"

"You said you missed yours. I thought it might make things a little easier. And, you know, driving with you in the car—I've had enough R&B to last me a lifetime."

She slid her finger inside the box, pulled back the flap and took out the radio. It was a cheap model, a little flimsy, but she made no comment. Instead, she put it back on the table and turned to him. Her face, usually so severe, became bright and open, and a broad smile revealed her white teeth and the sparkle in her eyes.

"Thank you," she said. "You didn't have to do that. You've already done a lot for me."

"Forget it. I thought you'd appreciate it."

"I do," she said. "It's very kind of you."

She held his eye for a moment, long enough for him to feel a twist of awkwardness in his gut. Hicks looked into her dark hazel eyes, noticed that he was holding his breath and, perturbed, looked down at the bowl and started to eat. After another moment, Sarah did the same.

#

THE REST of the evening was very pleasant. Hicks helped Sarah to set up the radio and, after five minutes of frustration trying to interpret a manual that had been put together by someone with only a passing familiarity with the English language, they succeeded. Hicks sat down with a second bottle of beer as Sarah scanned through the channels and, with a grin that underlined that she was choosing for his benefit, settled on Absolute 80s.

"I'm not that old," he complained.

She ignored his protest, waited until the end of the ads

and the start of 'Living on the Ceiling' by Blancmange and then went to sit down in the armchair. She reached out for the packet of cigarettes she had left on the table, took one out and reached back down for her lighter.

"John said—"

"He won't mind," she interrupted, lighting up.

The mood between them was as amiable as it had ever been, and Hicks had no interest in spoiling it over a cigarette or two. He leaned back against the cheap sofa's marked upholstery, took a swig of his beer, and allowed himself to relax.

#

HICKS OPENED HIS EYES. He didn't know what time it was, nor how long he had been asleep, but he realised, quickly, what had awoken him.

Someone was in the room with him. His view was obscured by the armrest of the sofa, but he could see a shadow in the doorway.

He lay still, but slowly reached his hand beneath the cushion that he had been resting his head upon. His fingers touched the stippled grip of his Sig. He closed his hand around it and threaded his finger through the trigger guard.

The shadow stepped toward the sofa. There was a shaft of sodium-yellow street light that cut through a gap in the curtain, and Hicks could see that it was a woman. It was Sarah. She was wrapped in a sheet. She sat on the edge of the sofa, reached down for the edge of his blanket, pulled it aside, and slithered across the cushions and leaned down so that she was pressed up against him. He could feel the softness of her breasts against his chest and the hard angle of her hip as she ground it against his.

Hicks let go of the pistol and sat up.

"Alex?"

It was the first time that she had called him by his first name. He shuffled away from her.

"What's the matter?"

The sheet fell away and Hicks could see the fullness of her body in the silvery light.

"No, Sarah. That's a really bad idea."

"Why not?"

"I can't."

"You don't like me?"

"I didn't say that."

"You don't think I'm pretty?"

"You're very pretty."

"What, then?"

"My wife. I told you—I'm married."

"Why would she need to know?"

Hicks slid farther away and then stood. "You're very beautiful," he said, "and you're very sweet. But I love my wife. I'm faithful to her. I'm not interested in anyone else."

Sarah reached down for the sheet and wrapped it around herself. She stood, but then paused. "Please?" she said. "Can I stay with you? Just for tonight. I'm afraid."

"No," Hicks said. "I can't."

"What about John?"

"I can't speak for him."

"Would he like me?"

"I don't know. But I think he would say the same thing: it's not a very good idea. It's the last thing you need. Work out what you want to do next. You don't need to hurry into a relationship with a man you don't know."

"Who said I wanted a relationship?"

"No." Hicks crossed to her, put his hand on her shoulder and gently impelled her toward the door. "Get some sleep. You must be tired. We'll forget this happened in the morning."

She didn't say another word, but left the room and made her way down the hallway to the bedroom. Hicks waited and watched until she was inside the room and the door had been closed behind her. He shut the door to the reception room, went back to the sofa, lay down again and covered himself with the blanket.

He tried to sleep, but he couldn't. He thought about what had happened. He had done the right thing. He would never have cheated on his wife, and certainly not with a girl who was as plainly vulnerable as Sarah. But that vulnerability worried him. What was it that she wanted? It wasn't about him. He was too old, he wasn't particularly good looking and, most of all, she hardly knew him.

It was the fact that Sarah was vulnerable. She was young, in a country that she didn't know, a country where she had no friends, and she was frightened. She wanted to feel protected, and she was prepared to give herself to a man she didn't know in order to forge a relationship and make that possible.

And Hicks had shunned her.

He got up and went to the front door. The key was still in the lock. He checked again that he had locked it and withdrew the key. He turned and looked down the hallway at the door to her room. It was shut and there was no sound from inside.

Hicks took the key back to the sofa, put it under the cushion next to his pistol, and closed his eyes again.

He could still see her standing naked in the doorway.

Vulnerable.

They would have to talk.

Chapter Thirty-Seven

THE PREVIOUS NIGHT'S EVENTS were on Hicks's mind when he awoke the next morning. He got off the sofa and paused at the door, listening intently. He couldn't hear anything. He reached for the door, almost reluctant to open it, and, when he did, he stepped through with a sheepishness that he knew was ridiculous.

The door to the bedroom was closed. Hicks went to it and listened; he could hear the sound of her breathing.

That, at least, was good. She was still here.

He went into the bathroom, locked the door behind him, and stripped off for a shower.

\#

SARAH WAS waiting for him in the sitting room when he came out.

Hicks looked at her: her eyes were rimmed with red. She had been crying.

"Look—"

She interrupted him. "No," she said.

"About last night—"

"There is no need to talk about it."

"I just don't want you to feel uncomfortable."

She stared at him scornfully. "Why would I feel uncomfortable? I have been selling my body for weeks. Why would I care what you think?"

He felt awkward, unexpectedly put onto the back foot. He knew that he should probably take her invitation and let the matter drop, but he couldn't. "I don't want there to be a bad atmosphere between us. I promised John that I would look after you until he gets back, and I will."

She looked as if she was about to respond, but bit her

lip instead.

"It's going to be fine," Hicks said.

She turned away so that he couldn't see her face. "Is it? How do you know that?"

"John will help you."

"And what is John going to do to do that? You said it yourself—he will tell me to leave, just like you did. And what will I do then?"

"I didn't say that," he said. "I don't know what he'll say. But he's a good man. He'll do whatever he can to fix things for you."

"Enough," she said. "I don't want to talk about it anymore."

Hicks exhaled, a little of the tension dissipating. She went into the kitchen, and, after a moment, he followed. She had filled the kettle and put it back on its stand to boil. Hicks went to the sink and filled it with hot water and detergent. The plates and utensils that they had used last night were stacked on the counter and needed to be washed.

"You want a coffee?" she said.

"Please."

"Don't worry, Hicks. I'm fine."

"Are you sure?"

"Yes."

She scooped a spoonful of coffee granules and poured it into one of the cups.

"Shit," she said.

"What's the matter?"

She held out the jar. It was empty.

"I'll go and get some."

"I need cigarettes, too," she said.

"And I could do with some more beer. Do you want to come?"

"I'd rather stay here," she said. "Do you mind?"

Hicks paused. She was right; there was a risk that she would be seen this close to Wanstead. "No," he said. "Of course not. Will you be all right?"

"I'll be fine," she said. "I'll stay inside."

Hicks decided that it would be good to let her have a little time to herself. They had been together for the better part of a week. They would both benefit from a little time alone to decompress, especially after what had happened the night before. She had said it herself: she would stay inside. She was frightened. She wasn't going anywhere.

"I'll be back at lunch," he said. "No later than that."

"We need some more vegetables for dinner," she said. "I could write you a list."

"Okay." Hicks indicated the pen and the notebook on the counter. "Write down what you need, and I'll go and get it."

He went out into the hallway and put on his jacket and zipped it up so that his shoulder holster and the Sig Sauer were hidden. He went back into the kitchen. Sarah had finished the shopping list. She tore it out of the notebook and handed it to him. "Carrots, green beans, orange juice, yoghurt, cigarettes. Anything else?"

"That's fine."

"What kind of cigarettes?"

"I don't mind."

"Okay." He folded the list and put it in his pocket.

She followed him to the door. "Thank you, Hicks."

"No problem. Lock the door behind me."

He stepped outside into the cool morning air. There was a group of young boys gathered around the bandstand at Arnold Circus, and Hicks could hear the dull thump of music from the open windows of a parked car. He set off, leaving the building behind him and making his way to the convenience store on the main road.

Chapter Thirty-Eight

DRAGO'S WAKE was held at the pub that Pasko owned in Maida Vale. It was a detached, mock-Tudor building of two storeys, standing alone on the corner of Maida Vale and the Kilburn High Road. It had black painted half-timbering and a concreted-over beer garden, where drinkers sheltered beneath mismatched parasols. There was always a barbecue outside, whatever the weather, with men grilling beef and lamb just like they did in the Balkans.

Konstantin Pasko and his wife, together with Florin and the other members of his close family, had lined up at the door and welcomed the other mourners. The men were first, all of them standing in single file, and then the women came next, their heads covered with black scarves. The mourners were taken down the line and introduced to the family by Pasko's grandchildren. Within ten minutes, the room was filled. The children took turns serving everyone with food, raki, and cigarettes.

Pasko sat at the head of the main table. He was supposed to accept the condolences of the other mourners, but each new platitude wound him just a little bit tighter. His jaw began to ache from clenching his teeth, and his knuckles popped as he squeezed his fists. His wife noticed and told him to go outside to get a breath of fresh air.

He didn't argue. With a curt nod, he excused himself from the table and left the room. There was a fine drizzle falling, and he turned up the collar of his coat. Maida Vale was a busy road, and traffic rumbled by in both directions. The strain of keeping a lid on his anger was telling on him. He had a splitting headache and he needed a drink. But that would keep.

"Father."

He turned. It was Florin.

"You know what I want?" Pasko said to him.

"Father—"

"You know Ilya is keeping pigs now? I want to find whoever did that to Drago and feed him to them, inch by inch, until he begs me to stop."

"Father—"

"*What*, Florin?" Pasko snapped.

"That's why I need to speak to you—what happened to Drago. Llazar has one of the girls."

"What?"

"One of the girls from the flat. She's here."

"Which girl?"

"He didn't say."

"She's here now?"

"Yes. Upstairs."

#

THERE WAS a door to the side that gave access to the rear of the pub and the stairs to the upper floors. Pasko and Florin went through into the private hallway next to the armoured door that guarded access to the upper floor. There was an intercom panel next to the door, and Pasko pressed the button.

He heard Hashim's voice. "Yes?"

"It's me. Let me in."

The lock buzzed and Pasko pulled the door back and climbed the stairs. There were several rooms on the first floor: three bedrooms, a relaxation area, a bathroom. A sitting room had been turned into an office. There was a pool table, a small bar and a large flat-screen television that was usually showing football or boxing. Pasko opened the door and went inside. Hashim, one of his deputies, was leaning against the bar. He had fought alongside Pasko at Staro Gracko and Volujak. He was a large man, prone to bouts of depression, but unquestionably loyal.

Pasko stepped inside the room and saw the other

occupant. She was young and pretty, but dressed trashily, like a little tramp. He remembered her from when she had been brought into the country. They had bought her from the smugglers, just like the others they had purchased to swell the staff at their brothels. Syrian, he thought. He remembered her name: Sarah. He recalled it because she was one of the girls who was due to have been in the flat when his son had been killed.

One of the girls who had run.

"It is Sarah, isn't it?" he said.

The girl nodded. She was frightened.

Florin followed his father inside and closed the door behind him.

Pasko turned back to the girl. "Do you know who I am?"

"No."

"I am Konstantin Pasko. You have heard of me, I expect?"

"Yes."

"I understand that you left the flat where we were so kind to let you have a room."

"He took me. He made me go."

"Who?"

"The man who attacked..." The words trailed away.

"The man who murdered my son?"

The girl did not speak, but became even more pale.

"You know I am upset about what happened to him."

"Yes..." she started. "Of course."

"You look thin, Sarah. Have you eaten?"

She shook her head.

There was food on the bar: a platter of smoked meat and pickled preserves. Pasko's attention was drawn to a black pot that had been placed on a serving plate. He took two bowls and a ladle and scooped out two servings. He indicated that the girl should follow him to the table and pulled out a chair for her. She sat, and he put one of the bowls down in front of her. He sat opposite.

"This is paçe," he said. "You know it?"

"No."

"It is an Albanian delicacy, especially popular in the mountains. You take a sheep's head and boil it until the meat comes off easily. Then you stew it with garlic, onion, black pepper and vinegar. You add flour, too, to thicken the stew. It is a hearty meal. Try it. You must eat. You are skin and bones."

She started to eat. It was obvious that the meal was not to her taste, but she dutifully ate the first spoonful, then the second and third.

Pasko ate with her for a moment.

"This man," he said at last. "The man who killed my son. Who is he?"

"His name is John Smith."

"And that is a fake name?"

"I don't know."

"I think so." He took a spoonful and slotted it into his mouth. "Tell me what happened."

"It was a normal day. A client came to see me. I was waiting for him. Drago opened the door, and then Smith forced his way inside. I heard the crash and came out to see what was happening. They were in the kitchen. I don't know what happened, but when I looked inside, Drago was on the floor. He had a bag over his head. He must have suffocated him."

Pasko felt a tremble of anger and concentrated on the stew. He ate two spoonfuls of it, chewing deliberately, looking down into the bowl until he had mastered himself again.

The girl was looking at him nervously when he finally looked up.

"What did he want?"

"He had come for a girl."

"Which girl?"

"She was working in the flat the day before he came. Her name is Nadia. Smith was asking me questions about her. That's who he wanted."

"Why?"

"She has a brother. John said—"

"'John said?'" Florin repeated, interrupting her. "You are on first-name terms with this *nënë-qim*?"

"Be quiet," Pasko snapped at his son. "Go on, Sarah. He said what?"

"He said that she stole a man's phone and contacted her brother. She told him where she was. They're immigrants, like me. The brother came to get her, but he was arrested at the port. Smith was involved somehow, I don't know how, but he is helping the brother. He came to the flat to get her. That's why."

"Do you know the brother's name?" She shook her head, upset that she didn't, and he moved to reassure her. "It doesn't matter. We can just ask Nadia instead."

"Where is Smith now?" Florin asked.

"I don't know. He left to do something. He didn't tell me what."

"So where have you been?"

"At his flat."

"On your own?"

"No. There is another man, a friend of Smith's. He has been guarding me."

"Tell me about him."

"His name is Hicks."

"And?"

"He was a soldier. That's how he knows John Smith. They were both soldiers."

"So why did you take so long to come here?"

She swallowed. "Because they wouldn't let me leave."

Pasko looked at the girl, levelling his gaze at her. She looked down to her hands. Pasko looked at them, too; her nails were chewed. She was lying; her duplicity was as obvious as the nose on her face. He knew what had happened. She had nowhere else to go. She had seen that her rescuers would not be able to offer her what she needed. She wanted to stay in a country that she had worked so hard to reach. She feared that they would abandon her to the authorities, and that would mean that she would be deported. The only man who could offer the certainty of being able to stay was Pasko. She might not like her side of the bargain, but, given the alternatives, it was the best that she would be able to do. There had been runaways before, many of them, but they almost always came back to him. This little *putane* was no different.

Pasko laid down his utensils, took a paper napkin and wiped the corners of his mouth. "So. Mr. Hicks. Where is he now?"

"He went out for the morning—that's when I got away."

"And you came to us."

"I—" She stopped, her throat clotted.

"Hush," Pasko said. "You've done the right thing. I'm pleased you trust me. Do you think he is still out?"

She looked at the clock on the wall. It showed eleven thirty.

"Probably. He said he would be back for lunch."

Pasko took both bowls and stacked them on the table. "You will take us to him now, Sarah."

Pasko stood. Florin was waiting at the edge of the room. He went over to him.

"What will you do?" his son asked.

"This man, this *milosh*—I will talk to him. He will tell me about the man who killed Drago. And then I will kill them both."

Chapter Thirty-Nine

HICKS WALKED for an hour to clear his head.

He went east, all the way to Brick Lane, picking a path through the crowds of people who were in the area for the market. He went south, passing the brightly lit curry houses that made the road famous, ignoring the fast-talking touts who stood outside, encouraging diners to choose their establishment over those of their rivals. He walked all the way down to Quaker Street, turned right and walked on until he reached Commercial Street. He continued to the north, turned onto Shoreditch High Street, and passed shops selling trendy sneakers, art supplies and antiques. He reached Calvert Avenue and turned back to the east, going by the little shack that had been built at the side of the road as a café for taxi drivers. A sign said that it was Syd's Coffee Stall and that it had been there for nearly one hundred years. It reminded Hicks of the shelter where Milton had worked, and that made him think of Milton and how he was determined not to let him down.

He stopped at the convenience store and bought the things on Sarah's list. He checked his watch. It was midday. He had promised her he would be back for lunch. He thanked the man behind the counter, collected the bag of shopping and stepped outside again.

He set off back to the flat.

\#

THE DOOR WAS STILL LOCKED.

Hicks took out his spare key, unlocked it, and went inside.

"I'm back," he called out.

He took off his coat and hung it on one of the spare hooks that were fastened to the wall.

"Sarah?"

Her voice came from the sitting room. "I'm in here."

Hicks stopped in the kitchen and put the plastic bag on the counter. The dirty washing from breakfast was still in the sink. That was unusual, he thought. Sarah had been getting ready to clean them when he had left the flat. He dismissed it. She was waiting until the things from lunch needed to be cleaned. They had got into the habit of doing the washing-up together. He washed, she wiped. They spent the time talking. Hicks enjoyed the little routine.

"You want a drink?" he called out.

"No, thanks," she called back.

Hicks filled the kettle and set it to boil. He took the packet of cigarettes from the bag and went to the sitting room. The door was ajar. He pushed it open and went inside. Sarah was sitting on the sofa, her back to him.

"Are these okay?" he said.

He tossed the cigarettes onto the coffee table. She didn't turn. She didn't move to pick them up.

Hicks stepped into the room.

"Sarah?" he said. "What is it?"

He caught a flash of movement in the corner of his eye, but, before he could react, he felt a sharp pain in the side of his neck. A sensation of coldness spread both up and down his body, and a wave of enervating weakness crippled him. The strength in his legs vanished and he stumbled forward, catching himself on the back of the sofa. Sarah got up quickly, turned to him and then backed away, almost falling over the low table.

She looked up. She wasn't looking at him; she was looking at someone behind him.

Hicks tried to turn. His knees buckled and he fell down, dropping onto his backside. His eyelids felt heavy, as if weighted down, and he had to struggle to keep them from closing. His vision was blurred and, as darkness massed on the edges of his sight and started to swell, he saw a man coming toward him.

Chapter Forty

HICKS COULDN'T OPEN HIS EYES.

He was lying on something uncomfortable, with sharp edges digging into his flesh. He felt so bone tired—why was that?

He lay still for another moment and then forced his eyes open.

He was looking up into the light from two halogen strips that had been fastened to a bare concrete ceiling. The light was bright, and it sent sharp stabs of pain into his brain. He blinked and tried to turn away. He couldn't. He could move his neck, at least a little, but, when he tried to sit, he found that he could not move. Something was restraining him. He tried to raise his hands to cover his face and felt the bonds that were looped around his wrists. He tried to move his legs and felt the same restrictions around his ankles.

He felt the touch of cool air on his body and knew that he was naked.

He started to panic.

He remembered: Milton's flat, Sarah, the man who had been waiting for him behind the door.

He remembered the pain in the side of his neck.

He had been drugged.

His eyes were heavy, but he forced them to stay open. He was in a room. It was a large space, around ten metres square, with bare concrete walls. There were no windows, and the illumination came from the two halogen strips. He saw a metal table on the other side of the room. There was a large item on the table, the length of the table, hidden within a dark plastic bag. There was a metal rack with plastic bottles lined up on the shelves. Wooden coffins were stacked next to the rack, one atop the other.

"Hello, Mr. Hicks."

Hicks followed the voice to his left.

A man was sitting on a chair next to him.

"My name is Pasko," the man said.

Hicks did not answer. The man was big and heavy-set, with an unshaven face and cruel eyes. He was wearing a white shirt and a black tie. Hicks watched as he made a show of taking out the cufflinks. He rolled the sleeves up to his elbows, exposing tattoos that covered both forearms.

"Where am I?"

"You are in one of my businesses. I have several. We have an undertaker's business. It serves the Albanian community in London."

Hicks instinctively turned his head to the metal table. He realised, then, what was in the bag.

"Yes, Mr. Hicks. This room is where the bodies are prepared."

Hicks turned away from the body and raised his head so that he could look down at whatever it was he was lying on. He couldn't see very much, save the edges of metal frame. He could see his wrists; they were secured with leather straps. He glanced back at Pasko. There was a wooden table next to his chair. The table bore a tray and a plain metal box from which Hicks saw two trailing cables.

He slumped down, the back of his head resting against something hard and sharp. "Who are you?"

"I am Sarah's employer."

Hicks raised his head again and looked ahead. He was naked from head to toe. He saw the bottom edge of the frame and, beyond that, three other people. There were two men, one of whom bore a resemblance to Pasko. The third person was behind them. Hicks couldn't see them.

Pasko spoke again. "Are you surprised that she would run straight back to us?"

"A little."

"Did you wonder why?"

"I'd be surprised if it was because of your sparkling personality."

"You are funny, Mr. Hicks. And you are very naïve. It is simple. These girls, they have nothing. They have no one. All they want to do is stay in this country. They know that they cannot go to the police. They will deport them, and all the money that they have spent to get here, all the risks that they have taken—that will all be wasted. The only people who have given them somewhere to stay, who have fed them and given them the chance to earn some money—it is us. We have had girls who have run away before. They always come back. Always. Isn't that right, Sarah?"

Hicks fought the fatigue to glance up again. The two men stood aside so that Hicks could see. Sarah was standing there. She looked at him for a moment, their eyes very briefly connecting, before she looked down.

"No, Sarah," Pasko said. "Look at him."

She did not. Pasko said something in Albanian, and the man next to her grabbed a fistful of her hair and yanked her head up.

"I want you to watch this," Pasko said to her. "It is important."

"Let her go," Hicks said. "She doesn't have anything to do with this."

"I am afraid I must disagree with you," Pasko said. "She most certainly does. Sarah is my property. I paid for her. That means that you and your friend stole from me. And Sarah took a week to come back to me—so that means that she stole from me, too. Sarah understands now that that was wrong. And she is going to watch what happens to those who try to steal from me so that she can tell the other girls."

Hicks struggled to keep his eyes open. "What do you want?"

"I have some questions for you, Mr. Hicks. Are you prepared to cooperate?"

"I'm a little tired. How about we do this later."

"We will do it now. What do you do?"

He closed his eyes. "Security."

"You were a soldier, then? Before?"

"Yes."

"The same. It is easy, isn't it, to identify another soldier? Something gives it away. Something about the way we hold ourselves." He pulled up the chair and sat down. "How was your soldiering?"

"Lots of running around and shouting."

"Have you fought in wars?"

"Yes."

"Ireland?"

"Yes."

"Iraq?"

"Yes."

"Kosovo?"

Hicks could place the accent now. He hadn't heard it for many years, but the suggestion reminded him of the time he had spent in Pristina.

"Yes," he said. "You, too?"

"That was my war. I was born in Prekaz, in Drenica. Central Kosovo. It has many hills, many sheep and cattle, very little money. My father and his father were Kosovo Albanian guerrillas who fought the Serbs. They fought Tito and then Milosevic. I could not read or write, but I listened to their stories when I was young and I remembered them all. They taught me to fight as soon as I could walk. My mother has a picture of me with an AK-47 that was taller than I was. The Serbs were brutal, Hicks. But the Kosovars were strong men. They still are."

Hicks's muscles were cramping, but there was nothing he could do to relieve them.

Pasko continued, ignoring Hicks's discomfort. "I undertook my military training in Labinot-Mal, in Albania. There were one hundred of us. When we returned, we continued the fight for independence. We sabotaged Serbian interests. We killed their soldiers. Eventually, Milosevic paid attention to us. He sent his soldiers to Prekaz. They had tanks and helicopters. They had artillery.

They fired indiscriminately. Women and children were killed. Old men who could not fight. Eventually, there was a siege. They threatened to kill everyone unless we surrendered. They would have done it, Hicks, so we did."

Hicks opened his eyes again. "What does this have to do with me?"

"Be patient. We were taken to the Serbs' police headquarters in Pristina. They beat us for a week before they even asked us what they wanted to know. They used bedposts. They used knives and clubs. Electricity. They injected us with drugs. They starved us. Eventually, I was released. I went back to Albania. We had a staging post in the town of Kukes. There was an old factory there. I was put in charge of interrogating the prisoners that we captured. There were Serbs, Kosovo Albanian collaborators. These men did not have information, Hicks. They had nothing we did not already know. It wasn't about information. It was about creating an example. It was about making them fear us. My superiors wanted to create a myth, someone who would terrify the Serbs. I happened to be very good at what I was asked to do, and they had given me ideas. I was chosen to fulfil that role. My name is still known in Serbia. They called me *kirurg*. It means surgeon."

Hicks strained against the bonds. It was fruitless; they were too strong and, even if he had been able to remove them, what was he going to do? He was weak from whatever sedative they had used to knock him out, and he was badly outnumbered.

"Let me sleep your drugs off," Hicks said. "We can talk about this afterwards."

Pasko shuffled around in the chair so he could get to the box on the table. "My son was killed when the girl was taken from the flat. I know that you did not kill him. I want you to tell me who did."

"I don't know what you're talking about."

Pasko turned back. "Sarah told me what happened. Your friend attacked the flat. Mr. Smith. He was interested in one of our other girls. He took Sarah and promised that he would look after her. But then he left, and he introduced her to you. That is correct, is it not?"

"I don't know anything about that."

"I am not surprised that this would be your attitude," Pasko said. "Let me ask you another question. Do you know what you are lying on?"

"I know it's not very comfortable."

He chuckled. "And we have not even started yet. It is a *parilla*. It means cooking grill. The person answering the questions is placed atop it the same way that meat is placed upon a barbecue. It was introduced in South America during the 1970s and 1980s. Pinochet used it extensively. We built this to his design. If you look to your left, you'll see the wall socket from which the electricity is drawn. It is fed through this control box"—Pasko tapped the box on the table—"and then attached to the victim with electrodes."

Pasko held the box up so that Hicks could look at it. It was a simple design: there was an on-off switch and a rheostat that would control the voltage. Pasko reached down for a wire mesh bag that was attached to the end of one of two wires that led from the box.

He took the bag and leaned down over Hicks's body. "Excuse me," he said as he leaned across and fitted the bag over Hicks's testicles.

Now Hicks did strain, but it was no use.

There was a wooden handle on the table with a metal end. The second wire was attached to the handle, and Pasko picked it up. "The Chileans, in particular, were inventive. For a woman, they would attach the wire to a wetted steel wool pan scrub and insert it into her vagina. For men, they would take a thin metal rod and insert it into the urethra. I have a rod like that in the tray here. Perhaps we will use it later." Pasko took a piece of cloth from the table, folded it into a single strip, and then secured it over Hicks's eyes, knotting it behind his head. "One of the distinguishing features of this equipment is that the shocks are high voltage but low current. You know what that means, of course. The shocks will be excruciating, but they won't kill you. I've used this equipment on people for days at a time."

Hicks couldn't see a thing through the blindfold. He felt a ticklish sensation across his ribs and realised that Pasko was running the metal end across his skin. He couldn't help himself: he instinctively arched his body away from it, but there was nowhere for him to go.

"Let's try again. Who is the man who killed my son?"

Hicks gritted his teeth in anticipation of what he knew was about to come. "I don't know what you're talking about."

He heard the click of the switch and then felt a cold sensation as the metal was held against his knee. A bolt of pain flashed from his groin and then down his leg, sending spasms through the muscle and lighting up every nerve ending. He grunted in pain.

"His name is John Smith. Tell me about him."

Hicks took a moment to regain his composure. "The straps are chafing a bit around my wrists," he managed through the pain. "I don't suppose you could loosen them a bit, could you?"

Pasko laughed. "You are a funny man, Mr. Hicks. Unfortunately for you, I have all day. And I will get the information I need."

Hicks heard the flick of the switch again.

Part 5

Italy and France

Chapter Forty-One

MILTON WATCHED as the faint outline of land became visible through the haze on the horizon. The word was passed back along the boat, and people stood to look. The journey had been long and fraught, and, now that the end was in sight, there was an outpouring of relief.

It was the afternoon of the second day at sea. They had been travelling for thirty-six hours. The worst moments had come during the night. A huge freighter had crossed their path, worryingly close, and their boat had bucked and kicked across the troughs of wake that had been left in the sea. Spray had lashed them and the boat had oscillated to and fro, the captain taking the wrong angle and allowing the waves to strike them side on rather than carving through them. The passengers had exchanged terrified glances, and some of them had started praying. Milton had stayed where he was, his fists clenched, knowing that there was nothing that he could do to affect whether they continued or capsized. The smuggler with the pistol had waved for them all to sit down where they were and, after two or three minutes of uncertainty, the sea calmed down again and they were able to continue. Milton had watched the freighter as it disappeared behind them, visible for another hour until the lights winked out against the horizon and they were alone beneath the stars again.

The pilot nudged the boat to port, the change of direction allowing Milton a better view of the terrain ahead. It was an island; he thought, at first, that it had to be Lampedusa. The island was the first trace of Europe, part of the Pelagie Islands that lay between Italy and Tunisia. As they drew nearer, though, the island grew larger and larger, and Milton realised that it couldn't be Lampedusa.

It must be Sicily.

Details resolved out of the misty haze as they drew closer. Milton saw rocky outcrops of limestone and dolomite, stripped clean and barren thanks to the attention of the wind and the lack of rainfall. He saw buildings and other ships, and then a harbour, the concrete wall of the dock a distinctive grey stripe against the limpid sea.

They drew closer. Milton had expected them to aim for Lampedusa since it was closest, and he had studied the geography of that island before he departed, in preparation for landing there. His knowledge of Sicily was not quite as current. He could be looking at Agrigento or Gela, perhaps. He knew that those towns were on the southern coast of the island. Wherever it was, this particular harbour might have been pleasant at one time, but it was scruffy and down-at-heel now. Most of the businesses that Milton could see were closed, shutters locked down and emblazoned with graffiti.

They sailed into the harbour, the boat approaching a large concrete harbour wall. The tide was low, meaning that there was a climb of six feet from the gunwale to dry land. Milton noticed a wide concrete apron just beyond the dock wall and a steep slope that climbed up sixty or seventy feet to a collection of makeshift buildings and tents that had been erected where the land eventually plateaued. He saw a sign on one of the buildings—LICATA—and assumed that that must be the name of the town. There were several cars parked on the concrete apron, several backed right up to the edge. A crowd of people were waiting on the dockside and the slope. Some of them wore the light blue shirts and dark blue trousers of the Italian police.

The mood had lightened as soon as the passengers had realised that they were going to make it, but now the quick burst of jubilation had been smothered by anxiety. There were immigration officials on the dockside, too, waiting for the boat as it was bumped and buffeted on the rolling waves. The skipper turned the wheel so that they were side on, and men at the fore and aft took the coiled mooring lines and tossed them ashore. They were collected and looped around concrete bollards.

There were a man and woman with two young children ahead of him. The man jumped across first, but, as the woman tried to lift her daughter, the boat jerked on the tide and she lost her balance. She clutched the toddler to her chest as she started to fall ahead, into the suddenly widening gap. Milton reached out and caught her by the shoulder, pulling her back once again. The men on the dock hauled the mooring line and the boat drew closer to the jetty.

"Let me," Milton said and, when she looked at him uncomprehendingly, he pointed at the girl and then to himself. "Let me help."

The woman looked uncertain, but there was a queue of people behind them who were anxious to disembark, and the experience had evidently unsettled her. She nodded and passed the child to Milton. He took the girl and, balancing himself on the gunwale, passed her over the gap to her father. He reached down for the young boy who had been clasping his mother's legs, gently extricated him, and passed him across, too. He waited to help the woman across and then clasped the father's outstretched hand and hopped ashore himself.

"Thank you," the man said.

Milton glanced ahead. Two of the smugglers were approaching a young woman. The boat had been better secured now and passengers were clambering out of the boat more quickly, a stream of them vaulting across to drop to their knees on the concrete. Milton ducked in and out of the crowd, trying to get a better view of the group ahead of him, and, as he clambered up the slope, he was rewarded. The two men had reached the woman and she was protesting, her body language defensive, and, as Milton set off toward her, he saw one of the men grab her by the elbow. She tried to free herself and, failing, she raised her voice and was rewarded with a crisp slap across the cheek. Milton was twenty metres away from her and had to fight the urge to run; instead, he forced himself to slow down, idling at the fringe of the fast-expanding crowd. The man said something, stabbing his finger in the face of the woman and, whatever it was that he said, it subdued her. The fight left her and, with both men on either side of her, putting proprietorial hands on her shoulders, she was angled away from the crowd and started to walk away.

A man in the blue uniform of the Italian police stepped in front of Milton.

"*Scusa*," the man said, holding up his hand and placing it flat against Milton's chest. "What is your name?"

"John Smith. I'm English."

"Your papers, please."

Milton took out his passport and handed it to the man. "I'm English," he repeated.

"But you were on boat?"

"No. Tourist."

The man looked at Milton's fake passport, flipping slowly through the pages as if expecting to find something incriminating. He made a show of it, licking his finger to help him turn the pages, his brow crinkled with deliberate, ponderous concentration. Milton watched over his shoulder as another woman was pulled from the crowd, and then another, and another. He saw three women now, including the woman that the man on the deck had complained about after Kolo had been sent down into the hold. They were being shepherded away from the other migrants, more of the smugglers appearing to prevent the companions of the women from following.

Milton saw a van roll down from a side street up ahead, backing around so that the rear doors were facing the approaching women. They wouldn't wait around; Milton knew that if he didn't act soon, he would lose his opportunity to follow them.

He had to stop himself from sidestepping the policeman. "What's the problem?" he said.

"Why are you at the harbour?"

"I saw the boat," he said. "I know where they've come from. I thought I could help."

"You want to help these *scarafaggios*?" he said. "You tell them to go back where they came from."

Milton's Italian was basic, but he knew the word for cockroach.

The policeman handed the passport back. Milton took it, thanked him, and then set off toward the van. He followed the jetty, passing shuttered huts that offered seaside snacks and moored boats that offered 'sunset aperitivi'.'

The men took the young women to the van. They opened the rear door, put them inside, and shut the door. They shared a joke, the sound of their laughter audible over the noise of the crowd behind them. One of the men got into the driver's seat and the other started around to the other side.

Milton broke into a jog.

The van moved away, slowly negotiating the narrow jetty and then turning onto the road from which it had emerged. It had to slow to turn the corner and Milton was able to close up on it. It was a Mercedes Sprinter and it had been fitted with a rear bumper step. Milton grabbed the door handle with his right hand, stepped up onto the step, and then anchored himself by reaching around the side of the van with his left hand.

The Sprinter struggled up the sloped road away from the harbour. Milton held on.

Chapter Forty-Two

THERE WERE TWO WAYS that they could get off the island and make it to the mainland. They could fly, or they could take the ferry. Milton knew that the latter was the more likely of the two options. The airport was small, and it would be very difficult, if not impossible, for the smugglers to get the women through the administrative rigmarole without arousing suspicion. It was possible that they might have some way of getting through security—a bribed official, perhaps—but it was the least likely of the two choices.

A ferry would be much easier. For them—and for Milton, too.

Milton held on as the Sprinter drove across a wide concrete apron away from the harbour, following a narrow road until they turned onto Via Principe di Napoli. The roads were not busy, and, save a handful of pedestrians who gawped at him as he held onto the back of the van, he was able to stay on the back of the vehicle without incident.

The van drew up to a junction and stopped. Milton glanced around the side of the vehicle and saw that they were about to enter a much busier part of town. There were restaurants on the left, with people eating on the terraces and passing by on the pavements. The harbour was to the right. He saw a parked police car with two officers leaning against it. Milton wouldn't be able to stay on the back of the van without attracting their attention.

He had no choice. He hopped down.

The red light changed to green and the van pulled away. Milton turned and saw a taxi behind him. He waved it down and exhaled with relief as the driver acknowledged him with a flick of his hand and pulled over.

"*Si?*"

"That van," Milton said. "Follow it." The man looked at him uncomprehendingly. Milton searched fruitlessly through his meagre Italian vocabulary. "Follow," he said again.

"Ah," the driver said. "Follow. *Seguire. Sì, signore!*"

\#

THEY DROVE for three hours, following the E931 to the east before turning to the north and bisecting the island. Milton had paid fifty euros and reassured the driver that the rest of the fare would be paid. The man was quiet and, at Milton's direction, kept a reasonable distance behind the Mercedes. Milton was confident that they would not be spotted. There were several destinations that they could have headed for, including Messina for the short ferry hop onto the toe of Italy, but they turned to the west at Campofelice di Roccella and made for Palermo.

\#

THE MERCEDES COULD HAVE TURNED OFF and headed for the airport, but, to Milton's relief, it did not. Instead, it picked a route through the traffic until it reached Banchina Crispi, the long road that served the ferry terminal.

Milton readied himself in the back of the taxi, his limbs stiff from lack of activity. There were three main quays, but only one of them had a ferry tied up alongside. The Mercedes followed the road to the quay and slowed to a stop in the queue of traffic that was waiting to board.

Milton paid the driver and got out. He watched as the cab turned around and drove away.

He ambled forward, walking by the Mercedes and then risking a quick glance inside. The two smugglers he had seen in Licata were in the front, one of them sleeping on a bunched-up jacket that was wedged between his head and the window. Milton could hear a throb of bass from the music that the driver was listening to, his head nodding back and forth.

Milton turned away and kept going. There was a ticket office ahead, and he confirmed with the clerk that the ferry at the quay was the only ship leaving the terminal that day. It was a large vessel, painted white with the name of the operating company—Grandi Navi Veloci—stencilled in blue. The ferry was due to leave for Civitavecchia in two hours, and Milton bought a ticket for it. There were a few other foot passengers waiting to board, and he was able to wait with them as the boat was readied for the voyage.

The Sprinter was quickly surrounded by other cars and commercial vehicles, but Milton was able to keep it under observation without compromising himself. He could see the shape of the two men through the dirty windows, and, after thirty minutes, he observed one of the men as he stepped out to stretch his legs. Milton watched as he stepped between the lines of parked cars and made his way to the portable buildings that served as the facility's restrooms.

Milton considered whether now was the time to make his move.

He decided against it. He had another idea that he liked better.

The ferry was equipped with a bow door and the rattle of its chains announced that it was about to be lowered so that embarkation could begin. A gangplank was lowered and the foot passengers were encouraged to embark. Milton dawdled, hanging at the back of the crowd, waiting until the traffic started to move. An official in an orange tabard waved the first car forward. The Sprinter was near the front and, as Milton took his first step onto the gangplank, it bumped over the lip of the ramp and was swallowed into the darkened maw of the ferry.

Chapter Forty-Three

THE CROSSING TO CIVITAVECCHIA was scheduled to take fourteen hours. Milton made his way to the upper deck and stood by the rail as the engine was started, the mooring lines untied and the ship slid away from the dock. They passed out of the harbour and turned to the north, the captain marking their departure with a long blast of the horn.

Milton turned away from the rail.

Fourteen hours.

Plenty of time for what he proposed to do.

Milton was thorough. He took an hour to scout the ferry. It was a medium-sized vessel. There was a car deck and then two decks above that for the passengers. Green Deck was at the top of the boat, and Milton started there. There was a restaurant and a café, bathrooms, and lounges with rows of chairs that were fixed to the floor. There were a handful of passengers stretched out on the hard plastic seats in the common areas, a few tourists eating in the restaurant, but not much else besides. The ship was basic, with minimal amenities, and had not been decorated for years. It was shabby and cheap, with peeling paint, doors that were sticky and difficult to open, and dirty windows. There was an open deck at the stern which was, rather optimistically, labelled as a sun deck. Milton walked the deck from bow to stern and didn't see the two smugglers or the girls that they had put into the back of the van.

He methodically repeated the exercise for Blue Deck. It accommodated cabins for the passengers, with no real communal spaces. There was no sign of the smugglers.

Drivers were supposed to leave their vehicles on the car deck once the ship was underway, but the men would not easily be able to take the women into a public space without

217

the risk of discovery. Milton suspected that they must have an arrangement with corrupt members of the ferry staff that meant that they could stay with their vehicle.

The car deck was the last place to check. Milton opened the door to the stairs and, bracing himself against the gentle rocking of the ship, he made his way down.

He opened the door and breathed in the smell of motor oil and fumes. The deck was only half full, and he saw the Sprinter immediately. It was up at the front of the deck, surrounded by cars and another, similar van. He saw the shapes of the two men in the front of the vehicle. He looked deeper into the deck and saw the orange tabard that denoted one of the load operators; the man was heading his way, and Milton had no interest in a conversation that might draw attention to him.

It didn't matter. He was satisfied: the men were aboard, and they would need to take breaks for the bathroom and refreshments. He would just have to wait.

#

MILTON CLIMBED TO THE TOP OF THE SHIP.

He retraced his steps back to the larger of the two cafés. There were tables with plastic coverings, wooden partitions topped with smoked-glass panels marked with the ferry operator's logo, and half-domed fittings that spilled out harsh ultraviolet light. He went up to the counter and ordered a cup of black coffee and a bowl of reheated pasta and then took a table in the main café from where he could see both doors that opened into it. He was famished; he finished the pasta and then went back for a second bowl, together with a limp salad that was soggy with balsamic dressing. He had another coffee and then smoked a cigarette on the deck, the smoke torn into shreds by the stiff breeze as soon as it left his lips.

He went back inside, took his seat again, took off his watch and laid it on the table. He watched as the hands turned about the dial, counting off the hours.

Ten o'clock.

Eleven.

Midnight.

One.

The ferry had been at sea for six hours. Milton was about to go down to the car deck again when he recognised one of the smugglers. It was the young man who had sent Kolo down to the hold. Milton caught only a glimpse of him as he went by, but it was enough: he recognised the same sneer, the unpleasant upturn to his lips, and the glitter of cruelty in his eyes.

There were only a handful of other passengers in the café, and the man had his pick of vacant tables. He chose one near the door to the sun deck, draped his jacket over the back of a chair, and followed the signs to the restroom.

Milton stayed where he was and watched. It was obvious what the smugglers were doing: they were taking it in shifts to relieve themselves and eat.

The man came back out, collected a tray, and came back with a plate of chips, a burger and a can of Coke.

The smuggler had his back to him; Milton could watch with impunity.

Chapter Forty-Four

THE SMUGGLER ate his dinner, drained his can of Coke, and then went outside onto the deck.

Milton gave him a moment and then followed.

They were at the stern of the ship. It was cold and there was no one else with them outside. Milton looked back. They were well out at sea by now. Milton glanced up, but he couldn't see any cameras that might record what he had decided to do.

The smuggler was looking back at the wake that patterned the sea behind them, a ghostly trail that stretched away in the ferry's lights. He had his hand to his mouth, and Milton saw a cloud of smoke above his head as he exhaled.

"Excuse me," Milton said.

The man turned, the cigarette in his mouth flaring as he inhaled. He reached up with his thumb and forefinger to remove the cigarette. "What?"

The man was relaxed. He was inclined at a slight angle, leaning back so that the top railing was just below the points of his shoulder blades. His left arm was out straight, resting on the railing, and his legs were crossed, his right ankle resting across the left. Milton took it all in, assessed it all, considered it.

Milton took out his own cigarettes. He withdrew one and held it up.

"Do you have a light?"

The man looked ready to deliver a rebuke, but, instead, sighed with ostentatious irritation and put his left hand into the hip pocket of his jeans. That was exactly what Milton hoped he might do; he might have been able to hold on with his left hand but, now, his hand restrained within the tight pocket, that would be impossible.

"You don't recognise me, do you?"

"No," the man said, although Milton fancied that a flicker of fear crossed over his face.

"I was on the boat from Sabratah with you."

Milton dropped the cigarette and reached out with his right hand, grabbing the man's belt and sliding his fingers around the leather. He stepped in close, reaching his left hand up to the smuggler's sternum and pushing down even as he heaved up on the belt. The man realised, too late, what Milton was doing, and tried to struggle. It was futile. Milton had raised him up enough so that the railing was halfway down his back, a useful fulcrum for him to pivot the man over. The man struggled, but he had no purchase, no anchor, no way of resisting Milton's impetus.

Milton leaned closer so that his voice was the last thing the man heard. "Can you swim?" he said.

He released his grip on the belt, looped his right arm beneath the man's knees, and gave one final heave.

The smuggler toppled over the railing and fell down into the storm of wash below.

Milton saw the splash, but the sound of it was inaudible. He could see the young man struggling against the frothy spume. The ferry was moving quickly, and the man was already twenty metres away. Milton could see his arms waving. He might have been calling out, but that would have been pointless; the engines were loud, and the sound of the rushing water added to the noise.

Milton turned his back and straightened the sleeves of his jacket.

A man and his teenage son emerged from the restaurant.

"Evening," Milton said.

"Hello."

Milton smiled and went back into the warmth.

Chapter Forty-Five

MILTON WENT back down to the car deck again. He could see the dark shape of the second man in the passenger seat of the Sprinter. He followed the side of the deck until he was out of sight of the van and then returned to it on the other side, staying down low and keeping out of sight of the mirrors as best he could. There were two members of the crew at the far end of the deck, but they were turned away and engaged in conversation; Milton was not concerned that he would be seen.

He advanced one car at a time until he was at the back of the Mercedes. The windows were tinted and he couldn't see through them, but he crouched down low enough that he wouldn't be visible from the interior and took out the small pistol that Omar had given him in Tripoli. He checked that it was ready to fire and, holding it in his right hand, he stayed low and skirted the van until he was just behind the passenger door. He glanced up: the handle needed to be squeezed in order to activate the operating levers inside the door cavity. He checked that the crew members were distracted, and was pleased to see that they had moved farther away. The noise of the engines seemed to be a little louder, too, which was doubly fortunate. He would not be observed.

He reached up with his left hand, shuffling a little closer to reach the handle more easily, squeezed the handle and yanked the door open.

The second smuggler was watching a film on an old iPad. He was older than the man Milton had tossed overboard, but still young. He had his feet propped up against the dash, both hands laced behind his head and the iPad resting in his lap. He turned at the sound of the door opening, the sudden movement dislodging the iPad so that it fell onto the seat and then into the footwell. The man put his feet down and unclasped his hands so that he could start to reach for the glovebox, but there was no way that he would be able to get there before Milton jammed the pistol into his ribs.

"Shush," Milton said, putting his finger to his lips. "Put your hands on the dashboard and spread your legs."

The man hesitated, unsure of what to do.

"Now."

Milton frisked him. In his inside pocket were a passport and a wallet that was thick with banknotes; he tossed them onto the seat. He patted the front pockets of his black jeans and took out a butterfly knife. The man had a Samsung phone in the opposite pocket and nothing else of note.

"Get into the other seat."

Milton trained the gun on him as the smuggler shuffled across the seats. The man caught the hem of his trousers on the handbrake, jerking his leg until he could free it, and then raised his hands before his chest as he half-turned in the driver's seat. "What do you want?"

"I'd like to talk to you."

"About?"

"We'll get to that."

"And then?"

"Depends on what you tell me."

Milton quietly closed the door and settled into the seat. The gun was still in his right hand, his elbow resting against his ribs, his arm held steady and his aim true. The smuggler looked down at the ugly pistol and then up again at Milton. He could see that he was uncertain, but not yet cowed; he would have liked to crack him across the scalp with the butt of the pistol, but that would have left a mark and Milton couldn't be sure that he mightn't still need him. An obvious wound would risk giving the game away.

"What's your name?"

"Hamza."

"Very good, Hamza. Next question: the girls in the

back," he said, giving a small nod of his head to indicate them. "Where are you taking them?"

"Italy."

Milton switched the gun to his left hand, resting it in his lap. "And then?"

"I don't know."

Milton slapped the man in the face. He struck him with an open hand, not hard enough to leave a mark, and, when the man looked back again, his eyes burning with fresh anger, Milton cuffed him again.

"Try again, Hamza."

"Or what? You will slap me?"

Milton shuffled closer, grabbed the man by the hair and dragged his head back. He pushed the muzzle of the gun into his mouth.

"No," Milton said. "I'll shoot you."

Hamza's eyes bulged fearfully.

"Aren't you curious why your friend hasn't come back?"

Hamza couldn't speak with the gun in his mouth.

"He's not coming back," Milton said. "He's dead. I threw him overboard. And unless you start doing what you're told, I'll kill you too."

Hamza couldn't swallow, and a trail of saliva ran out of the side of his mouth.

"Shall we try again?"

He nodded.

Milton withdrew the gun and aimed it at him again. "Good. So, like I said, I have some questions for you. Shall we start with that easy one? The girls. Where are you taking them?"

"France."

"Go on."

"There is a place where the immigrants go, where they try to get into Britain."

"Outside Calais? The Jungle?"

"The Jungle, yes—the camp. There is a meeting there."

"What happens?"

"They will be sold."

"Who are you meeting?"

"A man from London. The Albanian. I do not know his name. He looks at the girls. Checks them out. Perhaps he sees one he likes. He buys her. Perhaps he does not. He pays me or he does not pay me, and I leave."

"The girls?"

"Any girl he does not buy, she is free to go."

"And if he does buy?"

"They go with him. That is not my concern."

Milton tightened his grip around the butt of the pistol; Hamza noticed the increased tension.

"How do they get them out of the country?"

"They have a business. I do not know the word. It is for when you are dead."

"An undertaker's?"

"The boxes that bodies go into before they are put in the ground."

"They put them in coffins?"

"Coffins, yes. I have not seen them. But that is what I have been told."

Milton allowed that thought to sink in a little. It was morbid and unpleasant, but it was clever. Coffins? Surely immigration would wave a coffin through. Who would open a coffin?

"Why do you want to know this?" Hamza said fretfully.

Milton ignored him. "This is what we're going to do," he said instead, putting a little iron certainty in his voice and underlining it by reaching out until the gun's muzzle was pressed up against the man's temple. "We're going to drive to Calais. You and me, our own little road trip. The girls in the back don't need to come—we'll let them out as soon as we get to Italy. You're going to take me to meet the Albanian. If anything happens that means we don't make it all the way there—and I mean anything, whether it's your fault or just dumb luck—I'll shoot you and then I'll disappear. That clear enough for you?"

Hamza nodded.

Milton looked at his watch. "We've got another seven hours before we dock. Have you got a contact on the ferry? Someone who lets you stay with the vehicle?"

"Yes," the man said. "We always use this crossing. There are three crewmen. They are paid not to bother us."

Milton had guessed as much, but it was fortunate. There was an opening in the partition that divided the cab from the rest of the van; it was covered with a slat that could be pulled back.

Milton kept the gun trained on Hamza and pulled the slat back.

"Hello?" he said. "Can you hear me?"

There was no response.

"My name is John. I'm here to help you. Can you hear me?"

"Yes," came a quiet voice in reply.

"Can you speak English?"

"A little."

"How many of you are there?"

"Three."

"Do you have food and water?"

"Yes," the woman said.

"And you are okay?"

"Yes."

There was a pause, and the sound of hushed conversation. Milton spared a quick glance into the rear. It was dark, but the light from the cab meant that he could see the dim shapes of people behind him.

"What is happening?" the woman asked.

"I need you to be patient," Milton said. "We're on a ferry, crossing to Italy. We have another seven hours to go. I need you to stay in the back until we land. As soon as we do, I'll find somewhere safe for you to get out and you'll be free to go. Is that okay?"

"What about the men who took us?"

"You don't need to worry about them anymore. Okay?"

"Yes," she said.

"If you need anything, just knock."

"I understand."

Milton closed the slide.

Hamza eyed the pistol. "You will just let them go?"

"That's right," Milton said.

"You know who I work for?"

"Yes. I know all about Ali."

"He will find out what you have done."

"I'm sure he will."

"And he will find you."

"Perhaps I'll find him first," Milton said. "But you don't need to worry about him. Think about yourself. You've got a little under seven hours to make sure you don't give me a reason to get rid of you before we get off the ship. If I were you, I'd be a good boy and shut my mouth."

Chapter Forty-Six

MILTON KEPT the gun on Hamza for the duration of the crossing. He sat sideways, his back resting against the door and his legs bent with his feet on the seat. He held the pistol down low and hidden behind his right leg so that it wouldn't be obvious to any of the stewards should they decide to check the vehicles. But his caution was unnecessary; no one came to check. Hamza was no trouble, either. He was obviously frightened by him and sat quietly in the driver's seat, occasionally glancing down at the gun, his hands alternating between his lap and the wheel, his fingers fretting.

Eventually, Hamza closed his eyes and slept. Milton did not. He waited and watched.

He thought about the women in the back. He wanted to go around to check on them, but he knew that he would either have to leave Hamza or take him out of the van at gunpoint, and he couldn't safely do either of those things. He wanted to let the women out, but there was no telling what might happen if he did that. What if a member of the crew was suspicious? What if they were asked to show their papers? It could all unravel very quickly.

He tried to alleviate his disquiet by reminding himself that the three women would be free to go as soon as he could find somewhere safe for them to be left. He had checked the glovebox and found a reasonable number of euros in a clear plastic folder; he would divide the money among them so that they could buy tickets to wherever they wanted to go.

The deck started to become busier. Milton checked his watch: an hour to go.

Another ten minutes passed and then he heard the sound of a klaxon from above. The noise of the engine changed as the ferry started to slow.

The remainder of the hour passed and then he heard the sound of chains rattling as the bow door was lowered. Bright morning light flooded into the deck and, when Milton glanced into the wing mirrors, he could see buildings and vehicles on the dock. It was the port of Civitavecchia. Passengers returned to their cars and the vehicles nearest to the door began to disembark.

"You're driving," Milton told Hamza. "Nice and careful. Remember what I said. Any mistakes, and you get shot."

Milton trained his gun on the smuggler as he slotted the van into the small queue of traffic waiting to drive off the ramp. The load operator disembarked the cars one by one, and soon it was their turn. They rattled over the ramp and rolled onto the dock, picking up speed as they aimed toward the facility's exit gates.

"Drive," Milton said.

Chapter Forty-Seven

CIVITAVECCHIA WAS on the western coast of the Italian mainland, in the central region of Lazio and eighty kilometres west-north-west of Rome.

Milton told Hamza to drive them north, reminding him that he was still very much at his mercy by prodding him in the ribs with the muzzle of the pistol.

They followed the E80 for half an hour until they approached the smaller town of Tarquinia. The terrain was flat and the grass in the fields on either side of the road was scrubby and sparse from the salt in the air and the battering that it received from the sun. They came to a bus stop and then to a food truck that was parked at the side of the road. Milton told Hamza to turn off. The food truck was advertised as 'Mario's Paninis,' but the metal shutters were down and it was closed. Milton indicated a space away from the truck and the portable toilet beside it and waited until they came to a stop.

"Turn around," Milton said.

"What?"

"Turn around and face the window."

Hamza did as he was told.

"Put your hands together behind your back."

The man paused, turning his head to look back in confusion. Milton reached across, took a handful of the man's thick black hair, and banged his forehead against the glass.

"Now, Hamza. Don't make me ask you again."

The smuggler did as he was told.

Milton laid the pistol on the seat and took the butterfly knife that he had confiscated from Hamza in the ferry. He flicked his wrist and fanned the knife, the blade emerging from the grooves in the handles. They called them balisongs in the Philippines, and Milton had been on the wrong end of one while he was on an assignment in Manila; he had a scar on his wrist to remind him of it. There was a roll of gaffer tape in the glovebox and he lashed a good length of it around Hamza's wrists, severing it with the knife. He arranged the smuggler so that he was facing forward, pinning his arms behind him.

"It is painful," Hamza complained. "My arms—"

"Tough shit," Milton said. "Wait there."

He flicked his wrist again to close the blade, put it and the pistol into his pocket, opened the door and stepped out. It was a bright morning, clear and fresh, and he took a welcome lungful of air. He felt that he was making progress. It had been two weeks since he had met Samir. Perhaps he would be able to bring the matter to a head.

He went around to the back of the van and opened the doors. Light flooded onto the faces of three women. They blinked in the sudden brightness and then, when their vision cleared and they saw him, they shuffled away into the back of the van. Milton looked: he saw empty food wrappers, empty plastic bottles and piled blankets. The women had been cared for, to a point, but he knew that was only because they were merchandise, and that they would fetch the best price only if they arrived at their destination in good health. The pitiful sight of an empty banana skin discarded at the door next to a bucket that had obviously been used as a toilet filled him with a new jolt of fury.

"It's okay," he said, stripping the anger from his voice. "I'm John."

The women stayed where they were.

"You don't need to be afraid of me. I'm sorry you've had to stay in here, but it's safe now. You can come out."

They stayed where they were.

"You're free to go."

It was obvious that the women were frightened. There was good reason for that: they had taken a dangerous voyage to a country they didn't know; they had been hauled away from their friends and family and put in the back of a van and driven away. They had been in the van for the better part of the day and now, after all of that, here he was telling them that they were free to go? Suspicion was natural. Fear was natural.

"Which one of you was I speaking to?"

One of the women, the one on the right of the van and nearest to him, very timidly raised her hand.

"Thank you. I know you're scared. But the men who took you from the boat can't hurt you anymore."

The woman in the middle stared at him. Milton recognised her: it was the girl who had been seated near him on the top deck of the smugglers' boat. She spoke in Arabic to the woman who spoke English. "She says you were on the boat."

"I was."

"You are working with them? With the smugglers?"

"No. I want to help you."

The woman in the middle stared at him and said something else in Arabic.

"She says why should we believe you?"

"I understand that. I wouldn't trust me if I was in your shoes, either. But I promise: no tricks. You can leave. We're in Italy. I have money for you, too. You can go wherever you like. Here."

He kept enough of the smuggler's money to pay for fuel and sundries and left the rest just inside the compartment. He stepped away from the door and went around to the side. He didn't have to wait long. The woman who spoke English was the first to get down. The second and third women followed immediately afterwards. The three of them stayed close together, as if it might be safer that way. The first woman had the money; the other two were each carrying large bottles of water.

"Where are we?" she said.

"Tarquinia. Rome is just over an hour to the south. There's a bus stop five minutes down the road. You've got more than enough money to go wherever you want. Just be careful."

She glanced around Milton to the front of the Sprinter, as if trying to look inside. "The men who took us?"

"They aren't interested in you anymore. They won't try to stop you. They won't come after you, either. Really, I promise—you're safe. You should go."

Milton could only do so much to persuade them, but he hoped that it was enough. The three of them stood out gathered here like this. Their darker skin made it obvious that they didn't belong there. Cars were passing on both sides of the road, and it would have been a simple enough thing for a passing police patrol to spot them and come back for a second look. Milton would have preferred to offer more assistance, but he could not. He was here for Nadia, he reminded himself, and he needed to get going.

The women conversed in quick, hushed Arabic before the one who spoke English turned back to Milton and held up the money. "Thank you," she said.

Milton nodded. They turned away from the van and set off to the south, heading in the direction of the bus stop that Milton had seen a mile before the food truck.

Milton waited until they were five hundred yards away and then, after checking that the road was quiet in both directions, he opened the driver's door. Hamza turned to look, but was unable to prevent Milton from slipping his hands beneath his shoulders and hauling him out onto the dusty verge. Milton dragged him around to the back of the Sprinter and bundled him into the compartment.

"Where are we going?"

"I told you. Calais."

"That's a day's drive."

"Fifteen hours. Sixteen with a couple of stops."

"You want me to be back here for sixteen hours?"

Milton laughed. "Are you serious? You're complaining?" Milton levelled the pistol at his head. "Put your legs together."

Hamza did as he was told, and Milton wrapped tape around his ankles and then up to his knees. He stepped back and admired his handiwork. The man was secure. Milton grabbed Hamza and hauled him into a sitting position, then watched as he shuffled backwards until his back was against the compartment wall.

Hamza nodded down at his crotch. "I need a piss."

"You'll work it out."

Milton took one final length of tape and hopped inside. The smell was unpleasant: hot and fetid, with the unmistakeable odour of stale urine. He knelt down next to Hamza and pressed the tape over his mouth, wrapping it all the way around his head.

He cupped the man's chin in his hand and held his face up so that he could look down at him. He put his finger to his lips and then got out, slamming the door behind him.

Milton went around to the front and slid into the seat. He would follow the coastal road to the north, cross into France near Geneva and then take the Autoroute to Bourg-en-Bresse. He would turn to the north and head for Dijon and Reims and then, finally, Calais. All in all, he would have to drive for a thousand miles.

Milton turned the ignition and pulled out onto the empty road. He followed it to the north.

Chapter Forty-Eight

MILTON DROVE NORTH. The Sprinter had a twenty-gallon tank, and it was half full. He guessed that an older model like this would top out at around thirty miles a gallon, and that meant that he would most likely manage around three hundred miles before he had to stop.

He crossed the border into France at Entrèves, with the hulking mass of Mount Blanc to his left. He continued to the northwest, following the T1 and then the A40 through the mountains. He had underestimated the additional fuel that would be consumed in ascending the Alps, and he made it as far as the ski resort of Chamonix before he had to stop and fill up.

He checked on Hamza before setting off again, removing the tape from his mouth and allowing him a moment to take a drink. The smuggler had wet himself at some point during the journey, his faded jeans a little darker around the crotch. Milton made no comment, taking the bottle away from him and wrapping a fresh length of tape around his mouth.

He got back into the front and set off again, following the A40 towards Geneva.

#

MILTON KEPT GOING.

He followed the route that Google suggested, following the A40 along the southern border of Switzerland, turning north at Bourg-en-Bresse and then continuing to Lons-le-Saunier, Dijon, Troyes, Reims, Arras and, finally, Calais.

It was one in the morning. Hamza had explained that his rendezvous with the Albanian was scheduled for nine. Milton was tired and he wanted to have had the benefit of at least a little sleep before then. He found a quiet lay-by on the A26 outside Saint-Omer and pulled over.

He went around and got into the back of the van.

Hamza was sitting with his back against the wall, propping his weight against one of the rear wheel arches.

Milton took the tape from his mouth and put the bottle of water to his lips.

"Where are we?" Hamza asked.

"Twenty miles from Calais."

"What are you going to do with me?"

"You're going to help me find the Albanian. You're going to tell me where I need to go to meet him, and then I'm going to leave you somewhere you won't be found."

"And then?"

"If I find him, I'll call the police and tell them where you are. If I don't, and I have to come back—" Milton let the sentence die. "That wouldn't be the best outcome for you."

"I will tell you," Hamza said.

"I know you will."

Milton was disgusted by him. He fastened a fresh length of tape across his mouth, wrapping it around his head, and then wound another length of tape around his wrists. Once Milton was satisfied that the smuggler was secure, he went back into the front and lay across the seats.

He set his alarm for six and fell asleep within moments of closing his eyes.

Chapter Forty-Nine

THEY CALLED IT THE JUNGLE, and it was with good reason. The camp had taken over twenty or thirty acres of rough scrubland on the eastern edge of Calais. It was not static, and, over the time it had first coalesced, the tents and structures had been cleared and the inhabitants had moved on. The men and women and children had gathered again around a new location, pitched their tents and built their ramshackle hovels and, before long, the camp had reformed once more. This latest iteration of the camp had found a home in a former landfill site three miles from the centre of the town. Satellites had sprung up in other spots around the perimeter of the town, but this was the principal gathering.

Milton had left the Sprinter on a quiet road that led up to a derelict quarry. He had interrogated Hamza one final time, and the smuggler had given him clear directions and a description of the tent within which the meeting would take place. Milton had gagged him again and left him trussed up in the back of the van. He made sure that the odds were against anyone coming across the van, that if he did nothing, then Hamza would die there. It was a tempting proposition, but Milton knew that that way of thinking was the influence of his old self. It would be the satisfaction of his own selfish desire to punish, and giving in to the temptation would bring him closer to the bottle. The man that he had tossed over the side of the ferry had been different: then, there had been a need to thin out the numbers against him. He knew, though, of course, that retribution had been a contributing motivation. He remembered the way that Kolo had been treated, and the smuggler had personified all of the cruelties that Milton saw in Ali's operation.

Bad luck for him.

But Milton would play this one straight. He would call the police and alert them once he was out of harm's way. The authorities could deal with Hamza.

#

THERE WAS A MILE between the van and the camp and now, as Milton crested a hill, he saw the sprawling site laid out below him. There were no obvious boundaries, with tents being pitched wherever there were suitable spaces, growing denser and denser as they drew nearer to the middle of the camp. He saw the flicker of campfires and the tendrils of smoke that curled into the gloomy early morning; artificial lights shone steadily near to electrical generators. It was impossible to judge how many people were stuffed into the camp, but Milton guessed that it was in the thousands.

There was little order to the way the camp had grown, but spaces had been left between tents that resembled roads or paths. Milton started down into the fringe of the camp and followed the paths deeper inside. Whole families were crammed into tents, pale faces staring out of the openings at the comings and goings. Milton saw children gazing out at him with sad eyes, and their parents, recognising him as European, put out their hands for change.

Hamza's instructions were good, and Milton made his way via a series of waypoints that matched the descriptions that he had been given: a cargo container that had been set down on bricks to serve as a legal advice centre; an open kitchen where volunteers served free meals; a lean-to that had been fashioned out of concrete blocks and sheets of corrugated metal, a sign on that sheeting announcing that this was a shop. Milton glanced in through the doorway and saw rows of shelving illuminated by a single naked bulb, each shelf holding tins of food, bags of rice and bottled water. He passed a similar structure, but larger, this one equipped with picnic tables and chairs and advertised as a café. There were two tables outside the entrance, too, and the men who sat around them, smoking and drinking tea, watched Milton pass with surly interest.

Milton found a tent that was being used as a clothes shop. He went inside and, for a few euros, he was able to buy a second hand jacket that was stained and threadbare, a garment that would blend in much better than the jacket he was wearing. He changed, discreetly transferred his pistol to the inside pocket, gave his jacket to a coatless man who was browsing the rails, and went outside again.

Milton continued to the middle of the camp. The scrum of people grew denser, with crowds gathering around a caravan that was marked with the logos of Médecins Sans Frontières and another that was staffed by volunteers offering immigration advice. Milton had to shoulder his way through the sudden tide of people who surged toward another caravan where bags of rice were being given out. It was hot and smelly, the air freighted with the odour of unwashed human bodies and raw sewage. It was difficult to understand how people could live like this.

Milton paused. Hamza had said that the rendezvous was in a tent here. He had described the tent, but now, as Milton searched, he couldn't see it.

Milton looked left and right and saw a man with two pretty young girls approaching from behind. He waited until they passed. The man was behind the girls, leading them ahead with hands on their shoulders. They looked frightened, and the man was impatient and self-important.

Milton recognised them for what they were: another smuggler bringing more merchandise for sale.

Milton followed and watched. The man led the girls to a tent, stopped them with a hand on each shoulder, and spoke to them.

Milton stopped, too, stepping inside another semi-permanent structure that had been given over to another shop.

The proprietor glared up at him. "What you want?"

Milton spared a quick glimpse at him and his store. The man had built a set of rickety shelves to display the sum total of his goods: a dozen boxed mobile phones, with a sign behind the counter announcing that he also had SIM cards to sell.

He looked back outside. The tent was as Hamza had described it: large, the canvas patched and stitched and marked with a stencil that identified it as property of the UN. The tent flap had been opened and folded back against the side of the tent, and the two girls were being ushered inside.

"You can't just stand there," the shopkeeper complained.

"That tent over there," Milton said, pointing as the man who had shepherded the two girls went inside and pulled the tent flap closed behind him. "Who's inside?"

The proprietor came out from behind the counter. "You buy, or go."

Milton ignored his complaint. Instead, he took a note from his pocket and gave it to the man. "That tent," he said. "Tell me about it."

The man held out his hand with the note laid flat across it. "Another."

Milton took another ten and laid it atop the first.

"I don't know who they are," the man said. "I have seen them before. Two times. The last time was one week ago. The men are not from the camp."

"Describe them."

"There are three. One is big—this big." The proprietor was a touch under six feet tall, and he raised his hand four or five inches above his head. "Shaved head, tattoos on his neck. The other two come with him. All white. Not from camp."

"And?"

"Girls come to see them. Most girls come out again, go back to camp. Others stay. They take them away. It is like a bazaar. A souk. You know these words?"

"I do. Thank you."

Milton stepped away from the proprietor and turned away. He reached into his pocket for the little pistol. His fingers found the grip, and he pressed down until the butt was pressed in his palm and his finger was around the outside of the trigger guard. He pulled it out a little, freeing it so that it would be easier to pull, and crossed the path to the tent into which the man had led the two women.

He could hear the sounds of conversation emanating from inside: laughter, a timorous voice, a harsh word, more laughter. He walked on for a little while, turning through the chaotic lanes and alleys until he was at the other side of the tent. He couldn't see anything that gave him any cause for concern. The people went about their business, none of them sparing the tent any more attention than the other tents nearby.

Milton continued around it until he was back at the front again.

He took the gun out, holding it against his body so that it would be hidden from the crowds that eddied along the thoroughfare behind him.

He knew what he was going to do. His plan had been successful, so far at least; this was where the Albanians came to do their recruitment. This was the place they came to stock their brothels.

He held the gun in his right hand; he reached out with his left for the flap of the tent.

"Excuse me, sir."

Milton turned his head. There was a man next to him.

Milton realised what was about to happen, but by then it was too late for him to do anything about it. He was aware of a second person behind him, but, before he could turn or step away, he felt a sharp scratching against the skin on the back of his neck. He felt a sensation of cold deep inside his muscles. His arm, held up so that he could probe his neck with his fingers, became weak. He was dazed by sudden wooziness, and the strength drained out of his legs as if at the press of a switch.

He stumbled forward, his fall arrested by hands that slipped beneath his shoulders.

The tent flaps were opened, and Milton caught a glimpse of the men and women inside, lit by the flickering light of a hurricane lamp, before he was dropped inside. He fell to his knees. He looked up into the frightened faces of the women he had seen outside, and, behind them, a large man with a shaven head and tattoos on his neck.

He was identical to the man Milton had suffocated in the brothel.

Milton lost his balance and toppled over onto his side, the plasticky smell of the groundsheet filling his nostrils.

A curtain of darkness fell. His eyes closed, and the darkness was complete.

Part 6

London

Chapter Fifty

MILTON OPENED HIS EYES. It was dark; no, he corrected, not just dark, but *dark* in that there was a complete absence of light. He closed his eyes again, aware of the migraine that was pounding against the inside of his skull. His thoughts moved slowly, and it was a struggle to put words together. He breathed in and out, trying to compose himself, trying to remember what had happened. For a moment he was certain that he had been drinking. It felt the same as he remembered it, waking up in a room that he didn't remember, his memories gone. A classic alcoholic blackout. But no. He could taste something in his mouth. Not alcohol. It was metallic. Unpleasant.

He hadn't been drinking. It was anaesthetic.

The memories rushed up at him.

The camp.

The tent.

The man who had distracted him and the accomplice who had injected him in the neck.

The men and the women inside the tent.

He tried to move his arms, but he couldn't. They were behind his back, his wrists shackled together. His shoulders throbbed with cramp. He concentrated on his legs. They, at least, were free. He opened his eyes again. Nothing. No light. He was on his back, lying on something firm. Not a mattress. Something solid. The floor, perhaps.

He moved his legs to the side and found that he had only a few inches of space before his feet bumped up against something solid. He lifted his right leg and found that his toes quickly touched up against another obstruction. He shuffled his body to the right and then the left, his shoulders bumping against what he now was sure were the sides to something.

As consciousness returned more fully, he became aware of a rising and falling, up and down, again and again. As he became more aware of it, he felt a throb of nausea. He managed to turn his head in time, and, his mouth to the side, he voided his guts. The vomit kept coming, obliterating the metallic aftertaste of the anaesthetic with its overpowering acrid tang. He felt the warmth of it against his shoulder and the top of his arm, and, as he moved, he felt it sliding beneath his back.

He kicked up, and the sound of his boot as it crashed into the obstruction left him with no doubts at all.

He had been sealed inside a wooden box.

He remembered what Hamza had told him.

How the smugglers moved the women over the border.

He was in a coffin.

He let his head fall back. He felt hollowed out. A numbing wave of lassitude rolled over him and, helpless to resist it, he closed his eyes.

Chapter Fifty-One

MILTON CAME AROUND AGAIN.

Something had jolted him awake.

He opened his eyes, saw the darkness again, and remembered: he was in a box.

No, not a box.

A coffin.

He blinked, trying to clear the gunk from his eyes.

He heard the sound of voices, a language that he couldn't place—guttural, harsh—and, as he tried to move his arms, remembered from the pain that they were fixed behind his back. He struggled with the bonds. There was no play there, and no prospect that he would be able to break free. The muscles in his shoulders and the top of his back throbbed with a fearsome ache, locked into an unnatural position for who knew how long, and his hands were numb from where his weight had been pressed down against them.

The voices continued. There were two, one of them more strident than the other. He tried to listen, to understand what was being said, but he didn't recognise the language. The voices were muffled, and he was still stupefied from whatever it was that had been used to knock him out.

He heard the creak of splintering wood. A patch of light appeared above his head, widening as the groaning continued and the nails that secured the lid to the rest of the coffin were prised out. Milton tried to rouse himself. The lid closed again, but now with narrow lines of light limning the joins between the box and the lid, and then there came the sound of breaking wood as the crowbar was jammed into the opposite corner and that nail forced out. More light, and then still more as the nails at the corners of the box nearest Milton's feet were removed.

The lid was lifted up and tossed aside, and bright, painful, artificial light flooded down.

Milton was blinded by it.

He heard voices, louder now that they were no longer muffled by the box, and felt hands on his shoulders and around his ankles. He was hauled out of the box, his legs lifted over the edge and dropped to the floor.

He opened his eyes, wincing at the stabbing pain from the light, forcing the lids apart so that he could start to understand the mess he was in.

He was in a room, lying against a cold, undressed concrete floor. To his right was a coffin. Wooden, a little longer than him. Cheap. There were other coffins in the room, a whole line of them stacked up against the opposite wall.

The voices spoke again. They were behind him. Milton tried to turn his head so that he could see who was speaking. He twisted around and saw a pair of booted feet stride through his field of vision. He looked up and saw a big man with a shaven head and tattoos on his neck.

He remembered him. The man in the tent. The twin of the man Milton had killed.

The Albanian?

The man gestured down at him, spat out an instruction, and left the room through a plain wooden door.

Milton felt hands beneath his shoulders and he was dragged away in the opposite direction. He looked up at the ceiling, then at the top of a door frame, and then he was in a more dimly lit corridor with a single bulb that fizzed and hissed, the light flickering on and off.

The man who was dragging him dropped him to the floor. Milton heard the sound of a key turning inside a lock, a door opening, and then he was hauled through a second door into a darker room that was only barely illuminated from the glow that leaked in from the bulb in the corridor.

"You stay here," came a voice, in heavily accented

English. "No noise. No trouble. Understand?"

"My arms," Milton said. "Please. I can't feel my hands."

There was no response. The door slammed.

Chapter Fifty-Two

MILTON HEARD the key turn in the lock and then the sound of footsteps fading away as the man made his way back along the corridor.

He looked around the room. It wasn't quite as dark as he had first thought—there was a little dim light filtering through a gap between the bottom of the door and the floor—but it was too dark to make out much of anything. The floor was bare concrete. Milton could smell urine and excrement.

"Who's there?"

Milton jumped. "Hicks?"

"Milton? Is that you?"

Milton turned and located the voice: it was coming from the corner of the room.

He sat up and used his legs to shuffle across.

"Milton?"

"I'm here."

Milton could see the shape of a man and, as his eyes adjusted, he could make out a little detail.

It *was* Hicks. He had been badly beaten. His face was covered in bruises, and both eyes were partially closed thanks to contusions that had swollen the flesh around his brows. His nose was stoppered with plugs of dried blood, and it looked as if he had lost a tooth. He was dressed in what Milton thought was a dressing gown, his legs and feet naked.

"What do I look like?" Hicks asked.

"Can't see much."

"That's probably for the best."

"Are you okay?"

"Been better."

"Anything broken?"

"Lost a tooth. Nothing else. They were working up to that."

"Are you cuffed?"

Hicks held up his right hand. A metal bracelet had been fitted to his wrist, and a chain led from the cuff to a ring that had been fitted to the wall. He jangled the chain and then let his head hang down.

"Do you know where we are?" Milton asked him.

"I think it's an undertaker's."

"Yes," Milton said. "It is."

"What happened?"

"I was in France. Calais. They jumped me. I think they brought me over in a coffin. It's clever—bringing people into the country in boxes. Who's going to open a coffin to check?"

Hicks tried to shift his position and groaned in pain.

"What about you?" Milton asked him.

"They knocked me out. Injected me with something."

"How did they find you?"

"Sarah."

"What do you mean?"

"She fucked us over," Hicks said.

"What are you talking about?"

Hicks sighed. "She ran off and told them where to find me."

"Why would she do that?"

"She came onto me—"

"Oh, Hicks…"

"Piss off, John, *please*. I turned her down. But I've been thinking about it—why she'd do it. She was scared. She was looking for someone to guarantee she'd be safe. The way she was thinking, maybe if she got together with me—or you—then we'd make sure she'd be okay. But I told her no; I said I loved my wife. She panicked, she didn't know what else to do, so she went back to what she knew. That's the only way they could have found us. She told them what happened and where I was, and then they came after me."

"When was this?"

"I'm not sure. It's difficult to keep track of time. A couple of days ago. They worked me over. It's not just a beating. They did that for shits and giggles. They've got a torture table. They strap you onto it and then run electricity through you. I held out for as long as I could, but he knows what he's doing."

"Who?"

"The main man. His name is Pasko."

"What did you tell him?"

He delivered the word in a blank voice. "Everything."

"About me?"

"Everything."

"Nadia?"

"*Everything,* John. About her, her brother, you topping the bloke in the brothel, you going to Libya… everything."

Milton had been blaming himself for being taken, but they had been ready for him. There was nothing to suggest that might even have been a possibility. Milton had been beating himself up for allowing it to happen, and the knowledge that it was a trap should have made him feel better. It didn't. He just felt angry.

"I'm sorry, John," Hicks said.

"Forget it."

"The Regiment trained me how to withstand torture. Name, rank, regiment. That's what you give them—that, and nothing else. I tried. I reckon I lasted a day before I buckled."

Milton had received the same training, and then another course—degrees of magnitude more intense—when he joined the Group. Theory was one thing. Practical experience during training was another, but it could only approximate what it was like to be in the control of a trained interrogator with no ethical limits on the means available to him. Milton had been with soldiers who boasted that they would never buckle under torture. That was bullshit. All you could do was delay the inevitable. It wasn't a question of will. It was a question of biology. The torturer would always get what he wanted: it was just a question of when.

"I told you," Milton said. "Forget it. It's not your fault. I don't blame you."

"Wish I could say that made me feel better."

"Enough self-pity. It's not going to get us anywhere. We need to work out how to get away from here. What do you know about them?"

He paused.

"Hicks?"

"They're bad guys. Albanian mafia. Ex-Kosovo Liberation. I served in Kosovo, and those boys were fucking maniacs. And this guy…" Hicks paused. "Pasko? He's beyond that. He's a fucking psychopath."

"How many others?"

"I've seen three. One of them is called Llazar. There's another, a big one—shaved head, tattoos."

"I've had the pleasure of his acquaintance," Milton said. "That's the brother of the man I killed. His twin. He brought me over, I think. Anyone else?"

"I'm not sure. But I haven't been conscious the whole time."

"All right," Milton said. He shuffled around so that he could lean his back against the wall next to Hicks. "What about Sarah?"

"I haven't seen her. But I doubt this was the best move she ever made."

Milton didn't answer, and they both let the silence go unchecked.

"We're in a hole," Hicks finally said after a long moment.

"Look on the bright side," Milton said. "I found them. The bad guys. That's what I wanted. I'm where I want to be."

"Are you having a laugh?"

"It's not exactly how I would have liked it."

"What are you going to do?"

"Make trouble."

#

IT WAS DIFFICULT to judge the passage of time, but Milton guessed that no more than a couple of hours had passed when the key was turned in the lock and the door opened.

Light from the single bulb bled inside, framing the man in the doorway in silhouette. It was enough for Milton to see that he was holding a knife in his hand.

The man took a step into the room. It was the big man, the twin of the man Milton had killed.

"Get up."

Milton stayed where he was. "What are you doing?"

"You come with me."

"Not until you tell me what's going on."

A second man came inside. The first man stepped closer and held the knife against Milton's throat. He pressed the point against his larynx and then down to his chest. Milton was defenceless; he remained stock-still, his attention focussed on the scratch of the blade as it traced across his skin all the way down to his sternum.

"You will get up," the man said.

The second man stepped forward and grabbed Milton's shoulders. He allowed himself to be hauled to his feet.

"So you're the brother?" Milton said.

"The brother?"

"Of the man I killed."

It was dark, but Milton thought he saw a flash of white teeth. "Yes," the man said. "I am Florin. My brother was Drago."

Florin stabbed a finger at Hicks and said something else that Milton didn't understand. The second man stooped down, grabbed Hicks by the lapels of the gown he was wearing, and tugged him to his feet. He took a key from his pocket and released the chain from the hook on the wall. The man put Hicks's arms behind his back and hooked the newly free cuff around his spare wrist. He locked it and led Hicks out of the room.

Florin stepped around Milton until he was behind him

and then shoved him in the back. Milton stumbled, bounced off the wall, but managed to maintain his balance.

"Out," Florin said. "Or I cut your throat."

Milton did as he was told.

Chapter Fifty-Three

THE FIRST THING that Milton saw as he was pushed into the room was the bed frame with no mattress. He knew what it was: a *parilla*. He had seen them before, in South America and Africa. He had seen how effective they were, too, how men who had been strong and insolent had been reduced to pathetic facsimiles of themselves after just a few minutes at the hands of a skilled torturer. He had stood over a bed in Baghdad and watched as an al-Qaeda functionary had buckled and then broke, revealing a few more breadcrumbs along the trail that eventually led to Osama. But he had never experienced one for himself. The prospect was not appealing.

Milton took everything in. The room was large. There was a metal table, a row of shelves and coffins stacked up against the wall. There was a single wooden chair next to the *parilla* and a wooden table next to it. Metal rings had been fixed along one of the walls. Milton watched as Hicks was dragged across the room, the cuff around his right wrist unfastened and then locked around one of the rings. Hicks slumped down, his back against the brick. There were no windows. Two doors: one through which they had entered and another in the opposite wall. The light came from halogen strips overhead.

There were three men in the room with them. Florin was behind him, his hand grasping the bunched-up fabric of Milton's shirt. The second man was next to Hicks, a pistol in his hand. A third man, one whom Milton had not seen before, was adjusting the dials on an electricity box on a table next to the *parilla*.

Milton flexed his arms a little, but the shackles were still taut. He was going to have to get them off before he could do anything.

The second door opened and a fourth man came into the room. He was big and brawny, with a shaven head and a pitiless mien. He was rolling up the sleeves of a denim shirt, folding them back to reveal thick forearms that had been decorated with ink. Milton could see the family resemblance: this must be Pasko, the father of Florin and Drago.

He spoke in English. "Is this him? Milton?"

"Yes, Father."

Pasko approached Milton, stopping when he was a foot or two away, and then coolly appraised him. "You are unimpressive," he said with a derisive curl of his lip.

"I'm sorry," Milton said.

"Sorry?"

"About everything that's happened."

"He is pathetic," Pasko said. "How does a man like this kill a man like Drago?"

"It was an accident," Milton said. "Please. I'm sorry."

Pasko turned away from him. "Undress him."

The man next to Hicks tapped his finger against his gun. Milton knew better than to struggle. Florin freed his arms, then pulled off his sweatshirt and the T-shirt underneath it.

"Everything," Pasko said, nodding down to Milton's trousers.

Florin undid his belt, pulled his trousers down and then his shorts. He removed his shoes and socks. All of Milton's tattoos were visible now, including the Roman 'IX' that he had had stencilled over his heart to remind him of the lessons that he was trying to learn from the program and, more particularly, Eddie Fabian's example. The ninth step. The making of amends. This was Milton's way of paying back the men and women that he had killed.

Pasko regarded him. "As God intended."

There was something about nakedness that implied vulnerability. Milton was happy to let them draw that conclusion. He covered his crotch with his cupped hands.

"I'm sorry," Milton said again.

Pasko laughed humourlessly. "It is too late to apologise. You have to pay for what you did."

"I'm sorry."

"You came for the girl, didn't you? Nadia. Would you like to see her? Would you like to see the cause of all your troubles?"

Milton looked down.

Pasko grunted in disgust. He turned to the man by the control box. "Bring her in. She should see the kind of man who came to rescue her. Sarah, too. Both of them."

The man said something in Albanian and left the room through the door that Milton and Hicks had been brought in through.

"Shall we let the girls watch, John?"

"I said I was sorry—"

Pasko nodded and Florin drilled Milton with a right hook that thudded against his liver. He didn't have to pretend to be hurt; Florin was big and he threw a stiff punch. Milton reflexively bent down, dropped to his knees and covered up. He coughed, making it last a little longer for more effect.

"Here," Pasko said. "Sarah. And here is Nadia, too. You are the cause of a lot of unfortunate trouble, my dear. Pick him up."

Florin reached down and grabbed Milton underneath the shoulders. He allowed himself to be hauled up and turned around. The fourth man had brought two young women into the room. Sarah wouldn't look at him. The other girl was dark skinned, tall and slender, with expressive eyes. She had been fixating on the *parilla* and, when she turned to look at Milton, her face was full of terror at the prospect of what she might see or, perhaps, what might happen to her.

"Stand straight, like a man," Pasko ordered. "Put your hands down. Let them see you."

Milton did as he was told.

"This is John Milton, Nadia. This is the white knight

who has come to save you."

Pasko grinned and then nodded again. Florin hit Milton again, the same right-handed swing that landed in almost the exact same place. Milton groaned out loud and dropped to his knees again.

"Up."

Florin hauled Milton upright again.

"Tell me, John. Do you think she is worth it?"

Milton feigned a hacking cough instead of answering. His liver ached, but the pain was helpful. He could focus on it, concentrate on the pulse and throb until the last wisps of the anaesthetic were blown away. He was alert. A reflexive part of himself was instinctively maintaining a mental map of the room and the places of the eight people within it.

Pasko, three steps behind Milton and one step to the left, next to the *parilla*.

Florin, next to Milton.

Hicks, fastened to the wall.

The gunman, leaning against the wall next to Hicks.

Nadia and Sarah, standing in front of the door.

The man who had collected the women, standing behind them with his hands on their shoulders.

Pasko gestured to Sarah. "You have done well. She brought us to your friend, John. Did you know that?"

"Yes," Milton said. "He told me."

"Sarah, come here."

Milton looked up. Sarah had turned to face Pasko, and now Milton could see the fear on her face. She was terrified. Pasko gestured that she should come closer.

"I did what you asked," Sarah said. "I took you to them."

"You did. And you did very well. Please—closer."

Sarah did as she was told, stepping away from Nadia and taking four steps across the room. She had to pass right by Milton to get to where Pasko was standing. She came close enough for him to see the wideness of her eyes, to hear the shallow breaths that passed in and out between cracked lips.

Pasko stepped forward to meet her, looping his left arm around her shoulders, drawing her into his embrace. Sarah's body was tense and the embrace was awkward.

Milton saw Pasko's right hand slide into his pocket and emerge with a small knife.

"No, Pasko—"

The words died in his mouth. Pasko drew back his right hand and stabbed her in the stomach.

He saw Sarah's eyes widen and her mouth fall open.

Pasko held Sarah close to him, the knife pressed into her gut.

Hicks swore and yanked against his restraints.

Pasko released Sarah and stepped away from her.

Sarah gasped. She dropped to the floor, her hands pressed to the wound in her gut.

Pasko's shirt was stained with the fresh bloom of her blood. He reached up and pressed the palm of his hand into the middle of it. He stepped closer to Milton, laid his palm on his chest, and then dragged it down. It left scarlet tracks across Milton's flesh.

"She betrayed me, John. A week away from us? She could have left much sooner than she did. How could I trust her after that? I had no choice, and that is your fault. Her blood is on your conscience."

Chapter Fifty-Four

MILTON'S MUSCLES burned with adrenaline, but he forced himself to wait. The man next to Hicks had raised the gun and aimed it at him. There was nothing he could do.

Sarah was curled up on the floor, blood pooling around her body.

Pasko ignored her as if she wasn't even there. He gestured across to Nadia with the bloodied knife. "Your brother found Mr. Milton, Nadia. Did you know that? He was driving the lorry that Samir used to get into the country. I am going to punish John this afternoon, and then I am going to kill him and his friend. You are going to watch. And then you are going to persuade me that you will never try to contact your brother again. Because we know where he is, don't we, John? Mr. Hicks told me. He is in Dover. The detention facility. Applying for asylum. It would be very easy for me to pay someone to put a knife in his heart. I could kill you, just like that silly bitch on the floor, and then I could kill your brother, too. You need to persuade me that I don't need to do that."

"I won't," she said.

"Pasko—" Milton started.

Pasko gestured to Florin. "Get him ready. Help him, Llazar."

The last few moments had been a surprise—to everyone, not just to Milton. He turned his head to look back at Florin and the man with the gun, who must have been Llazar. They hesitated; not because they were frightened of Milton—and why would they be, with him naked and pathetic?—but because they were frightened of Pasko.

"Now!" Pasko spat.

Florin grabbed Milton's shoulders.

Milton struggled.

Milton allowed Florin to wrap his arms around his chest.

Pasko took a quarter turn and laid a finger against the charge box. "You know what this is, Nadia?"

Llazar put the gun away and stepped closer to Milton and Florin.

Nadia did not answer.

"It is a *parilla*," Pasko said. "I normally use it when I want to extract information. Not today, though. I am going to use it to torture him. And when I have inflicted enough pain, I will kill him." Pasko laid the bloody knife down on the table. "Come over here," he said to Nadia. "You can help me. I'll show you how to use it."

Nadia turned and tried to run for the door. It was pointless—the fourth man was still standing before it, blocking it with his bulk, but it was a distraction. Llazar turned his head a fraction toward the sudden commotion as the fourth man caught Nadia with a backhanded slap across the face. Llazar was directly in front of Hicks, and he wasn't concentrating. Hicks sprang up, wrapped his right arm around Llazar's neck and fell back, his weight bringing them both down to the floor.

It was the chance that Milton had been waiting for. He jerked his head backwards, his skull cracking into Florin's face. His grip was released, and Milton threw the hardest punch that he could muster. His right hand connected; Florin stumbled back, lost his footing, and fell onto his backside.

Milton turned and barged into the man next to Nadia, driving him all the way across the room until they crashed into the door. Milton had his arms around the man's torso, holding his arms in place even as he tried to free them. The goon butted Milton, his brow clashing against Milton's left eyebrow and immediately cutting it open. Milton felt the blood well up before it bubbled over and ran down into his eye. He butted back, clashing his forehead into the man's nose, and then reached up and rested both hands so that they were spread around the side of the man's head, his fingers splayed and his thumbs pressing against his eyes. He pushed hard. The pads of his thumbs dug into the man's eye sockets and he felt the aqueous fluid within the cavities as it bulged and spread around the pressure. The man screamed, reaching his hands up until they fastened around Milton's wrists, but it was too late. Milton pushed harder and was rewarded with a popping sensation and then a gushing of blood that burst around his thumbs and ran down his wrists.

Nadia screamed.

Milton turned and quickly located the others.

Llazar had freed himself from Hicks and was rising to his feet. His gun was on the floor, dislodged during the struggle.

Florin was getting up, too, a knife in his fist.

Pasko went for the blade on the table.

Three on one.

Florin squared up to him. He had blood running out of his nose from where Milton had struck him. Milton could see that the man was a comfortable and adept fighter: his weight was evenly balanced, and his arms were loose and moving freely as he passed the knife from hand to hand.

Milton sensed movement and turned as Llazar swung the wooden chair at him. Milton had just long enough to raise his arms to cover his head, and the chair broke across his right shoulder and the top of his arm.

Florin sprang forward and slashed down. Milton sprang away into the middle of the room, the knife nicking his shoulder. Pain flashed. Milton ignored it.

Florin had overstretched and unbalanced himself. Milton stepped up, wrapped his arms around the bigger man's waist, and heaved up, lifting him off the floor and bringing him across the room until they both clattered into the *parilla*. Milton slammed Florin down onto it, the sudden impact enough to send them both through the metal grid and onto the floor between the frame.

Llazar grabbed Milton from behind and yanked him up. Florin disengaged himself from the wrecked frame as Milton put his feet on the metal and pushed back, toppling Llazar.

Florin stabbed again at Milton's gut just as Hicks arched his back and kicked out at the big man. The top of his foot cracked into Florin's elbow. His thrust was redirected, the tip of the knife flashing across Milton's skin, scoring a narrow trench from his breast down to his navel.

Milton was lying atop Llazar.

"Milton!" Hicks warned.

Florin drew back with the knife and stabbed down. Milton intercepted the downward thrust and redirected it, the six-inch blade disappearing into Llazar's shoulder. Milton held the blade there as Florin tried to free it and then drilled the point of his elbow into the bigger man's face. Florin's nose exploded, even more blood spilling out to mingle with the flow that had already been discharged. He slumped to the side, the back of his head bouncing against the concrete.

Florin fell flat and then lay still.

Milton quickly looked up.

Pasko had grabbed Nadia and now he was backing away, the smashed *parilla* standing between them.

Milton twisted the knife in Llazar's shoulder and then yanked it out.

Llazar screamed in pain.

Milton put the blade to Llazar's throat, pushed down and swept it to the right in a firm, fluid motion. The blade cut deep enough to sever the windpipe. Blood pulsed out of the wide incision, spraying up and splashing over Milton's skin.

Milton spun at the sound of a slamming door. The door through which Pasko had entered was closed; the older man had fled. He turned. Nadia wasn't there. Milton gasped for breath and looked down at his body. He was covered in blood: some of it his own, most of it from the men that he had disabled.

He turned to Hicks. "You okay?"

"Fine. Go and get her."

Milton ran for the door.

Chapter Fifty-Five

THE DOOR WAS LOCKED.

Shit.

Pasko had abandoned his son to buy himself a little extra time.

"Milton."

He turned back into the room. Hicks nodded to Florin. He was starting to stir.

Milton went to Llazar's body. The blood was still bubbling out of his neck, the force stilled now that his heart had stopped pumping. Milton frisked the body quickly and expertly and pulled out a ring of keys from his pocket. There was only one key on the ring that could fit the bracelet around Hicks's wrist, and, when Milton tried it, the cuff popped open.

"Nadia," Hicks said.

"They'll be long gone by now." Milton angled his chin in Florin's direction. "But he's left us with him."

Milton unlocked the bracelet that was still attached to the wall and went over to Florin. The big man was coming around. Milton turned him over onto his stomach and cuffed his hands behind his back.

Hicks was kneeling over Sarah's body.

"Dead?"

Hicks nodded.

"Don't worry. He'll pay. But we've got to get out of here."

"I know."

"Florin, too. Take his legs."

Hicks grabbed Florin by the ankles and Milton grasped him beneath the shoulders. Between them, they carried him through the door through which they had entered the room.

\#

THEY WERE IN THE BASEMENT OF THE
BUILDING.

The floor was used for storage; Milton found a room
full of empty coffins and another with bottles of chemicals.
A third room was equipped with another stainless steel table
that was gently cambered toward a drain in the middle. The
table, and the other equipment around it, was self-evidently
used for the preparation of bodies. The more Milton
considered it, the more he was impressed with what Pasko
had built. The business would be useful for washing the
dirty money from his illicit operations and would offer
additional side benefits, too: it made the importation of new
workers for the brothels both simple and reliable.

And, he suspected, access to cremation would be a
useful way to dispose of bodies.

Hicks found his clothes in a storage cupboard and
dressed.

Milton collected his own clothes from the room with
the *parilla* and took them to a small bathroom at the end of
the corridor. There was a cracked mirror on the wall and
Milton regarded himself: he was a mess. There was a cut in
his eyebrow from where he had been butted; his shoulder
was discoloured with a darkening bruise from where the
chair had been broken over him; he had bloody wounds on
his shoulder and chest where Florin's knife had scored him.
Beyond his own wounds, he had more blood on his face
and down his body from the three men he had taken out.

He took a handful of toilet paper and mopped off as
much of the blood as he could. It wasn't ideal, and plenty
was left smeared across his skin, but there was no time to
be more thorough.

There was one more room to check. Milton forced the
door and found his pistol and the flick knife that he had
confiscated from Hamza.

He pocketed both and went back to the preparation
room.

Florin was sitting on the floor with his back against the

wall and his chin resting on his chest. Hicks had thrown water in Florin's face; the blood from his crushed nose had been diluted and smeared, staining his shirt, but he was finally coming around. He opened his eyes, closed them again, and then tried to move his arms. The cuffs rattled behind his back, and his eyes opened for a second time, his face switching from confusion to anger.

"Wake up," Milton said.

Florin looked up at him with no attempt to disguise the hatred in his eyes.

"Where are we?"

Florin spat at Milton; the gobbet landed at his feet.

Milton took out the balisong and snapped the blade open. He reached down with his left hand, grabbed Florin by the chin, and raised his head so that his neck was exposed. "I've killed one of your friends this evening," Milton said, laying the edge of the blade against his larynx. "Don't think you're a special snowflake. Answer the question."

Florin paused, weighing up how much trouble he was in—and deciding, perhaps, that it was rather a lot—and cleared his throat. "North London."

"Where?"

"Kilburn."

"Do you have a car?"

"Outside."

Milton nodded to Hicks and they both reached down to bring Florin up to his feet.

"Which way is out?" Milton asked. "Up?"

Florin nodded.

#

MILTON LEFT HICKS to help Florin up the stairs and went on ahead. He drew the pistol and held it ready as he emerged into a small lobby. There were three doors: the door to his right led to a chapel of rest, the door directly ahead opened into a tastefully decorated office where the undertaker could meet prospective clients, and the door to the left led outside. It was ajar. Milton was reluctant to use it.

"Is there another way out?"

"Through the office," Florin said. "There's a fire door."

"Where's your car?"

"In the car park."

"Keys?"

"In my jacket pocket. Hanging up over there."

There was a large padded leather jacket on a hat stand in the corner of the lobby. Milton took it and emptied the pockets: he found a bunch of keys, a wallet and a mobile phone.

He held the phone out. "Passcode?"

Florin recited a six-figure combination and, when Milton entered it, the phone unlocked.

"Your father's number?"

"The last number I called."

Milton scrolled to the relevant page and saw an outgoing call from earlier that day. The call was credited to BABA.

He put the items back into the pockets, slipped the jacket on, opened the door, and made his way into the office. The room was dark. There was a single window, but it was covered by a blind and it was dusk outside. There was a single desk with a PC, a keyboard and a mouse, together with a neatly arranged tray of stationery. Milton paused, collected a stapler and slid it into his pocket. He crossed to a door that was opened with a panic bar. Milton edged up to the door and, with the pistol in his right hand, he reached out with his left and pushed down on the bar.

The door swung open. There was a car park outside. A black BMW 750 was parked ten feet away. It was the only vehicle that he could see. He waited for a moment, looking up and down the street beyond the car park. The undertaker's was screened by a wall and several neatly trimmed trees, and he could see a row of illuminated awnings and the occasional car that passed by. He didn't recognise the location.

Hicks brought Florin to the door.

There was no sign of anyone outside. No sign that anyone was observing him. No sign that Pasko was still here.

Milton reached for the keys and blipped the lock. The BMW's lights flashed and, with a second press, the powered tailgate began to rise.

Milton ducked down and hurried outside. He made it to the car without incident. Pasko was long gone.

He looked into the trunk. It was spacious and offered more than enough room for Florin.

He turned back and gestured that Hicks should bring Florin outside. Milton helped him to manoeuvre the bigger man inside, arranging him so that he was lying on his side with his knees up against his chest and his wrists behind his back. Milton closed the boot and got into the front of the car. Hicks slid in next to him.

"We need to set up an exchange," Milton said. "Nadia for Florin."

"You trust Pasko?"

"No. But he's lost one son. You think he wants to lose the other?"

"I doubt it. Are you going to call him?"

"His number's in Florin's phone."

"Where are you going to suggest?"

"I've got an idea."

Chapter Fifty-Six

MILTON DROVE for ten minutes until he was well away from the undertaker's. He parked at the side of the road and took out Florin's phone. He entered the passcode, navigated to the phone menu, and flicked through until he had the number for BABA. He pressed dial.

The call rang three times before it was answered.

"Florin?"

"Milton."

Pasko paused before he responded. "It appears that I owe you an apology, Mr. Milton. You are a resourceful man. I underestimated you."

"You wouldn't be the first."

"Perhaps. But I have something that you want. The girl. She is here, with me. It will be a simple thing to punish her for the inconvenience that she has caused."

"Florin might have a different view about that."

There was no response. Milton could hear the hush of traffic on the other end of the line. Milton waited for Pasko to speak.

"What do you propose?"

"An exchange."

"My son for the whore?"

"That's right."

There was another pause as Pasko considered the offer. "I need to speak to Florin," he said.

"No," Milton said. "He's alive. You'll have to trust me."

"Then there will be no exchange."

"I'm not a fool, Pasko. I don't speak Albanian. I don't want him telling you something that might be unhelpful to me. You know I want the girl. I know you want him. I don't have a hand to play if he's dead."

There was no response. He heard the muffled sound of

a car horn and then the sound of voices.

"Fine," Pasko said. "We will meet. Florin for the whore. Where?"

"The Golden Jubilee Bridge. You know it?"

"Yes."

"The side nearest to the Houses of Parliament." He looked at the clock in the dashboard. "I'll meet you in the middle of the bridge. One hour. Bring the girl. I'll bring your boy."

Chapter Fifty-Seven

MILTON FOUND A QUIET SPOT on the way to the rendezvous. He parked up and went around to the trunk. Hicks joined him.

"Ready?"

Hicks nodded.

"On three. One, two, three."

They lifted Florin out of the trunk and marched him around to the back of the car. He slid onto the seat, his arms still pressed awkwardly behind his back. Milton gave Hicks the key to the cuffs and his pistol.

"Get in next to him," he said. "Put a bullet in his knee if he causes any trouble."

"With pleasure."

"Take the cuffs off when we get close."

Hicks indicated that Florin should shuffle across to the other side and got into the back with him. Milton closed the door and went around to the trunk. He shrugged off Florin's heavy leather jacket and took the flick knife and stapler from his pocket. He spread the jacket out so that he could get to the lining and, working carefully, inserted the blade of the knife between it and the leather. He sliced open a small incision, just big enough for him to slide three fingers inside, took his phone from his pocket and slid it inside. He took the stapler, fed both sides of the sliced-open liner into its mouth, and stapled them together. He repeated the procedure two more times. He was happy with his handiwork when he was done.

He got back into the car and continued into the centre of the city.

\#

MILTON PARKED the BMW on Embankment Place. It was an arcade of shops beneath the mass of the Hungerford railway bridge. Embankment underground station was behind them, with a Costa Coffee on the corner. The car was alongside Action Bikes and opposite a business that specialised in commercial scuba gear. The area was lit by harsh artificial lights that were fitted to the underside of the bridge. There was a stream of pedestrians disappearing into the underground station and emerging from it. A man and a woman staggered by the car, both of them obviously drunk, arm in arm to lend each other support.

"Ready?" Milton said.

"You sure about this?"

"I am."

Milton stepped out of the car and went back to the door next to Florin. He took the knife from his pocket, held it to the window so that Florin could see it, and then opened the door. The Albanian slid out.

"Take it easy," Milton said.

He reached into the car, collected Florin's heavy leather jacket, and handed it to him. The big man put it on. Milton put his hand on Florin's shoulder and guided him to the front of the car. Hicks stepped out, the small gun hidden within the folds of his open jacket.

"This way," Milton said, nudging Florin in the back.

They set off to the south, between the pillars that supported the bridge. Florin was in the front with Milton within touching distance and Hicks just behind him and to the side. Milton didn't expect trouble from Florin. He had seen a demonstration of what Milton was capable of, and he knew that Hicks was armed and had very good reason to bear a grudge. And he knew that he was about to be handed over to his father. The trouble—and there would be trouble—would come later.

They emerged onto the pavement at Northumberland Avenue. There was a green cabmen's shelter on the corner, and Milton thought of the similar shelter in Russell Square where he had worked until recently. They passed the shelter and reached the double flight of steps that led up to the bridge. Milton guided Florin to the steps.

"Up."

They ascended. There were two pedestrian bridges across the river, one each side of the old Hungerford railway bridge that ferried trains between Charing Cross and Waterloo. The bridges were both deceptively light, contrasting with the bulk of the old concrete and iron railway bridge that they enclosed. There were more people on the bridge, men and women crossing to and from the South Bank. It was busy; that was good. There were CCTV cameras, too; that was also good. The potential witnesses and the fact that everything was recorded increased the odds that the exchange would go down without incident.

They continued out across the dark waters of the Thames, looking down as a squat tug muscled three garbage-filled barges to the north, running against the tide. The Houses of Parliament were to the right and, opposite them on the other side of the river, was the floodlit wheel of the London Eye and the vast hulk of the old city hall.

Milton was alert. Florin walked with a slouch, an arm's breadth away from him. Hicks stayed just behind.

They were a quarter of the way across when Milton saw Pasko. He was approaching them from the South Bank. His right hand was in his pocket. There was a woman ahead of him.

Nadia.

Florin straightened up and walked a little faster.

Milton reached out and took his shoulder. "Nice and easy," he said.

They met in the middle, between two of the seven pylons that suspended the bridge.

Milton took Florin's shoulder again. "Stop."

Florin did as he was told. A train rumbled out of the station and headed out across the river, the lights from the carriage flickering between the metal struts of the railway bridge.

Milton looked at Nadia. She looked frightened, staring at him with a mixture of confusion and trepidation. The first time she had laid eyes on him, he had been naked, yet he had killed one man and blinded another. She knew nothing about him beyond that he was capable of moments of extreme brutality; it was reasonable that he made her anxious.

Pasko grabbed Nadia by the elbow and told her to stop. He kept his right hand in his pocket. Milton knew that he was hiding his own weapon there.

There were six feet between the two groups.

"Nadia," Milton said, "are you okay?"

The young woman nodded.

Milton looked over at Pasko. "Let's make this quick. And no drama. Hicks has a weapon. You have a weapon. We're surrounded by witnesses, and there's a camera above you."

Pasko smiled coldly. "There will be no drama."

"Simultaneous, then."

"Fine."

Pasko released Nadia.

Milton released Florin.

He stepped across the space until he was next to his father, and then he turned back and glared at Milton.

Nadia took a step and then froze, caught between Milton and Pasko.

"It's all right," Milton said. "You're safe now."

Another train thundered into the station, its brakes screeching. Milton looked back, beyond Nadia, to Pasko and Florin. He wanted this to be done. The longer they all stood here, the better the chance that something might go wrong.

"Please, Nadia. Trust me."

She swallowed and, after another moment, she stepped toward him.

Milton reached out and gently took Nadia's hand.

"We are not finished," Pasko said. "This is not over."

Milton fished into his pocket and took out Florin's phone. "Here," he said, holding it up so that they could see it and then tossing it over at them. Florin caught it.

"Give it to me," Pasko said.

His son did as he was told. Pasko stepped over to the rail and dropped the phone over the side.

"Father—"

Pasko turned back to Milton. "Do you think I am a fool?" he said, his face twisted with scorn. "What was it? A tracking app?"

Milton didn't answer.

"You do not find us. We find *you*."

Pasko started to back away. Florin followed and, when the distance between them and Milton was sufficient, they turned and walked away.

"Come on," Milton said to Nadia. "Let's go."

Chapter Fifty-Eight

THEY MADE their way back to Florin's BMW.

"You drive," he said to Hicks.

He opened the door for Nadia, waited for her to get in, then went around to the other side. He lowered himself into the back so that he was next to her. She was quiet, sitting with her legs pressed together and her hands folded in her lap.

"Are you okay?" Milton asked as Hicks turned the car around and pulled away.

"Yes," she said in a soft, careful voice. "You mentioned my brother. Is he here?"

"He's in the country. He came to find you."

"He said Dover. Is that right?"

Milton explained. He told her everything: about how Samir had tried to get into the country, how he had been caught and detained, and how Milton had promised to help. There was no need to mention Libya or the crossing or the drive through France to Calais. All that was important was that he was helping Samir, and that, now he had her, he would do everything he could to get them back together.

"I want to see him," she said. "Is it possible?"

"We need to think about that," Milton said. "You're here illegally. I'm not sure going to an immigration centre is the best thing to do right now."

"So what *do* I do?"

"You need to claim asylum."

"How can I do that?"

"There's someone I want you to meet. She's helping your brother. She'll be able to help you, too."

The light at the junction of Villiers Street and the Strand went to red. Hicks stopped and immediately stretched across to the glove compartment and started to empty it out onto the passenger seat. There were papers, a folder with the RAC logo stamped on it, a bottle of Diet Coke. Hicks emptied everything out and then cursed under his breath.

"What is it?" Milton asked.

"Pasko. We can't leave him out there."

"We're not going to."

"And he's not going to forget what you did."

"I know."

"You…" He didn't finish the sentence, remembering that Nadia was in the back. "What you did to his son, Milton."

"I don't want him to forget."

"But we don't know where they are." He gestured to the mess of papers and other debris on the passenger seat. "There must be something. Registration documents. Insurance. *Something.* Have you looked?"

"I don't need to."

"Why not? What do you mean?"

"Give me your phone."

"What—"

"Give it to me."

Hicks reached into his pocket, took out his phone, and passed it back. Milton opened up the browser and navigated to the page for iCloud. He logged into his account and opened the Find My Phone app. A map appeared. It showed the grid of roads to the south of the South Bank Centre. After a moment, a red dot was placed in the middle of the map. The dot jerked along Belvedere Road toward Waterloo Bridge.

Milton handed the phone back to Hicks.

He looked at the screen. "You're kidding?"

The car behind them tooted its horn. The light was green.

"Best I could do on short notice. Let's get to work."

Chapter Fifty-Nine

MILTON SAT in the front seat of the car he had stolen and looked across the road at the pub.

It was a large building on the corner of Maida Vale and Kilburn Park Road. It was detached, with a decent amount of space between it and the nearest buildings on either side. The building was set across two storeys and was deep, running back a fair distance from the street. There was a small beer garden behind railings at the front and a larger space for cars and the wheeled industrial bins to the rear. Tables were pushed up against the building along Kilburn Park Road with an A-frame that promised food and live Albanian music. Banners for BT and Sky Sports had been lashed to the railings at the Maida Vale side of the building, and a line of cars separated the wide pavement from the street. The pub had been whitewashed and the awnings painted black in an effort, perhaps, to evoke Tudor design and make it look a little older than it was; in reality, Milton guessed the building had been put up forty years ago at the longest.

Milton had parked opposite the twenty-four-hour Milad Supermarket, partially obscured by a white van that had been double-parked on the yellow lines. He had followed the GPS signal here and, as he checked his phone again, he saw that the signal was still registering from the inside of the building.

The pub was busy. Milton watched the comings and goings for an hour. There was a small group of men in the space at the front of the garden, using a fixed brick oven to barbecue meat that they ate with their beers. It wasn't warm, yet they were outside wearing T-shirts and laughing raucously as they ate and drank and smoked.

Hicks had given Milton his phone to use, and now it rang. It was Hicks.

"It's me," Milton said. "How is she?"

"She's fine."

"Where are you?"

"On the road. There's a place up ahead. You?"

"I'm here. Let's leave it at that."

"Good luck, John."

"And you. I'll speak to you afterwards."

He ended the call and scrolled across to the Find My Phone app again. The red dot was where it had been before, pulsing in and out at the junction of Kilburn High Road and Maida Vale. He put the phone down on the dash and maintained his vigil, watching as the men extinguished the flame in the oven, covered the grille with a metal cloche, and then went inside.

He checked the time.

Eleven.

Last orders.

#

PASKO AND FLORIN climbed the stairs to the room at the back of the pub. The window was open, and they could hear the conversation of the drinkers at the tables along the side of the building and the sound of the traffic as it turned off and onto Maida Vale. Pasko went across to the window and glanced outside; he could see the edge of the large satellite dish that they used to get the TV channels from Eastern Europe, the back of the apartment block that faced the pub and, overhead, the blinking lights of a passenger jet as it passed below the plump moon.

Pasko hated frustration. He had lived his life with the aim of always moving forward, never stopping, like a shark. And this man—Milton—had stymied him. That could not be allowed to go uncorrected.

He clenched his fists and rested them on the sill as he looked outside, allowing the breeze to play over his face.

"Are you all right?" Florin said.

Pasko didn't answer.

"How are we going to find him?" Florin said. "He is not an amateur, Father. You saw what he did. He blinded Hashim. He killed Llazar. He could've killed me."

"It doesn't matter. There are two of them. Only two. We have men everywhere. Someone knows who they are. And we still have leverage. The brother—they are holding him at Dover. I have a friend there. Very corrupt. We can pay to have him released into our care. If Milton cares for the girl so much, he will care that we have the brother. We will use him to flush him out."

"When?"

"Tomorrow. I will drive there tomorrow." Pasko turned back from the window. "We were lazy. We underestimated him. We will not do that again. He is my priority now. I will find him, and I will make him suffer for what he has done."

Chapter Sixty

MIDNIGHT.

Milton checked the app one more time. The signal was where it had been for the last two hours, at the junction of Maida Vale and the Kilburn High Road.

His cellphone was still inside the pub.

The pub had emptied out over the course of the last forty minutes. Milton wondered whether it might be the sort of place where a drinker would stay after hours, but it was on a main road, and unlicensed drinking would be easy to spot by anyone who happened to be passing by.

Twenty and then thirty men, together with the occasional woman, came outside and dispersed in taxis and on foot.

The lights inside the building were switched off and the doors were closed.

Milton decided to take a closer look.

He got out of the car and stopped in the supermarket. He bought a roll of duct tape for a pound, walked down Maida Vale and turned left onto Kilburn High Road. The building to his immediate left was a five-storey Victorian block, since turned into office space. There was a line of cars parked next to the pavement, and Milton stayed behind them as he continued down the road and observed the pub from this new angle. The empty glasses had been removed from the picnic tables, the rubbish removed and the ashtrays taken inside to be emptied. The pub's name was stencilled on the wall between two large bay windows; shutters had been pulled across the windows, with just a sliver of light visible down the point where they came together.

He walked until he was at the end of the property. The pub was next to a modern three-storey apartment block.

There were cars parked in the parking space, next to the bins. There was a window above the bins, next to a large satellite dish. The window was open, and the room inside was lit.

Milton stood next to a Nissan SUV and watched the window for a moment. He saw movement, a man passing across it, then nothing, then a man looking up into the sky.

Pasko.

He was unmistakeable.

Milton was level with the window, and Pasko would only have been able to see him if he looked sharply to his left. He didn't, and Milton didn't wait long enough for him to get a second chance. He turned back until he was shielded by the edge of the building and then crossed the road between a Jaguar and a Mercedes. He paused at each of the bay windows, but the blinds were drawn too closely together and it was too dark inside for him to see anything. But it was quiet, and he was satisfied from what he had observed that the room was empty.

As far as he was able to tell, the only room that was occupied was the one on the first floor where he had seen Pasko.

The front door was substantial and almost certainly locked. It was also plainly visible from the road, and there would be innumerable witnesses if he tried to force it to get inside.

He would try the back, instead.

#

HICKS GLANCED over at Nadia.

"You sure you're all right?" he asked, for at least the fourth time since they had started off.

"I am." She nodded.

"You hungry?"

"Yes."

"There are services up ahead. We'll get something to eat

and a couple of rooms for the night."

She didn't respond, and, as Hicks saw the signage for Medway Services up ahead, he flicked the indicator and pulled into the slow lane, then onto the slip road.

He thought about Milton. He should have been there with him. He was still sore from the beatings that he had taken from the Albanians, but every time he felt the tender bruises on his legs and buttocks or the weals across his back, it reminded him of the liberties that Pasko had taken. He would have liked to have been able to pay that back himself. More than that, and his selfish reasons aside, he didn't like the idea that Milton was going after the Albanians alone. He knew that Milton was more than able to take care of himself, but the odds would have been better with the two of them.

But Milton had insisted and, eventually, Hicks had conceded.

He approached the entrance to the car park and slowed down to twenty. Milton had been clear. The girl was the priority. Hicks was to get her out of harm's way. He looked across the cabin to Nadia sitting with her hands clasped in her lap, her face betraying the anxiety that she was so obviously feeling.

It was late and the car park for the Travelodge was almost empty. Hicks turned into a vacant space and rolled to a stop.

"Come on," he said. "I'm exhausted. Let's get inside."

Chapter Sixty-One

THE BACK DOOR TO THE PUB was shielded from the street by one of the large industrial bins. Milton approached it and, after confirming that he couldn't be seen from the pavement, he paused there and listened. He filtered out the buzz of the city, the steady hum of traffic passing by on Maida Vale, and focussed on the interior of the building beyond the door. Nothing. He thought he could hear the sound of a television from the open window above him, and, as he took a step back and looked up at it, he saw the flickering light playing against the thin sliver of whitewashed ceiling that he could see.

He tried the handle.

It was locked.

The door had a glass panel above the handle. Milton took the duct tape and covered the entire sheet with a lattice of interlocking strips. There was no glass visible when he was finished. A heavy glass ashtray had been left out on one of the tables; Milton collected it and used it to gently tap against the covered glass. He increased the force until he was rewarded with a cracking noise. He pushed at the corner of the panel with his fingers, pressing the weakened part until it broke away from the rest of the glass, the tape preventing all but the smallest pieces from falling to the floor inside. The opening was wide enough for Milton to reach through and turn the key from the inside.

He took out his pistol and opened the door. It opened into a small lobby. He closed the door behind him. There were no windows and it was dark. He waited until his eyes had adjusted to the gloom and then examined the space more carefully.

The lobby was around two metres wide and three metres long. There were three doors leading off it: two were normal, and looked plain. The third, to Milton's left, was much more significant. He approached it. It was made of metal, fitting snugly into the frame. There was an eye-slit two-thirds of the way to the top, the handle looked sturdy and the hinge areas looked to have been reinforced. There was an intercom unit to the right of the frame.

Milton laid his fingers against the cold steel. Pasko had provided himself with a secure area on the upper floors of the building. There was no way that Milton was going to be able to open it.

He stood still and held his breath. He listened. He could hear the muffled sound of a TV from behind the heavy door, but nothing else.

He checked the remaining two doors. He crept forward, the pistol held in a loose two-handed grip. He paused when he reached the door to the right of the door through which he had entered, listening intently, his breath reduced to a shallow in and out. He still couldn't hear anything. The door was slightly ajar, and Milton took his left hand off the pistol and reached down to give it a gentle push with the tips of his fingers.

The door opened and Milton stepped through into the main room of the pub. There was a standard lamp in the corner of the room and, as Milton watched, it switched itself off. Amber light from the streetlamp outside the windows leaked in through a gap in the curtains, and there was still enough brightness for Milton to be able to make out the details of the room. The chairs had been turned over and rested on the tables. The floor had been mopped, the dim light glittering against streaks of moisture that had still to dry.

Milton stood quietly in the doorway, confident that the room was empty but waiting until he was sure.

Milton backed up, stepped into the corridor again, and pushed the door almost closed, leaving it just slightly ajar once more.

He went to the third door. There was a key in the lock,

but it, too, had been left ajar. He opened it fully. There was a small commercial kitchen inside. A sash window overlooked the street and there was plenty of light for Milton to look around. He saw a gas cooker and combi oven, a large dishwasher and racks of glasses and plates that had been left out to dry.

He had an idea.

He returned to the main room and crossed over to the standard lamp. It was connected to the power via a digital timer plug. Milton unplugged the plug from the socket. He took it, and the lamp, back into the kitchen.

He put the lamp down and laid his fingertips on the light bulb; it was still hot. There was a stack of dishcloths on the counter and he took one, wrapped it around the bulb and very carefully unscrewed it. He put the bulb on the counter, covered it with the cloth, and used the end of a knife to tap firmly against it until he heard the glass crack. He removed the cloth and examined his handiwork: the bulb was shattered, but the filament was still intact.

Milton screwed the bulb back into the lamp and connected the timer plug to the mains.

He took another four dishcloths and ran them under the tap until they were sopping wet. He pressed the damp cloths against the join where the sash window met the sill so that it was as airtight as he could make it.

He went to the refrigerator and unplugged it. Next, he turned to the cooker and disconnected the electronic ignition. He needed to reduce the chance of a premature detonation.

Finally, he opened all of the gas taps, listening as the hiss of the escaping gas grew louder with every new tap that he opened.

The kitchen was a small space, and, as far as he could make it, sealed. Some of the gas might leak out, but not too much. The pressure in the gas lines would be low, perhaps 0.3 psi, not much stronger than a child blowing bubbles through a straw. But there were six taps, including one larger central burner, and they were all open. Now he just had to judge how long it would take to fill the kitchen with enough gas so that the air would be combustible.

How long?

Three or four hours.

He looked at his watch.

Twelve thirty.

He crouched next to the timer plug and set it to come on at five in the morning.

He left the kitchen and locked the door. The bottom edge was flush to the floor. The gas was lighter than air and would rise to the top of the room; not much would be able to get out this way. He pocketed the key and paused in the lobby, listening intently. He could hear muffled conversation from upstairs, but the sound of the open gas taps inside the kitchen was inaudible.

Milton considered the situation for one final time.

He had watched the building for long enough to be as confident as he could be that it was empty save for Pasko and Florin.

He had heard nothing to suggest otherwise since he had been inside.

It was detached, with space between it and the neighbouring properties.

And it was late.

Milton went back to the car to wait.

Chapter Sixty-Two

PASKO WENT TO THE WINDOW AGAIN. He gazed out. It was ten minutes to five and he could see the faintest signs of the approaching dawn on the horizon. It was cool and fresh. Neither he nor Florin had been able to sleep, and now he was beginning to feel the start of a headache. The air was pleasant on his face. Florin had put on the television. There was a highlights show from the week's Champions' League, and he was staring at it dumbly. Pasko would normally have been happy to watch it, too, but he was distracted and frustrated.

The sound from the television stopped. Pasko turned to see that Florin had the remote in his hand.

"What is it?"

He was quiet for a moment, his head cocked as if he was listening for something. "I thought I heard something."

"I didn't hear anything."

"I heard something."

They both paused to listen.

"It's a phone," Florin said.

"What?"

"It must be yours. I don't have mine."

"It's not mine. What the fuck? Where is it?"

Florin frowned. He closed his eyes until he could place the location of the noise. "It's coming from my jacket."

He reached into his pockets, the two at the front and then the two inside, but found nothing. The phone was definitely inside. It kept ringing.

"Give it here," Pasko snapped, snatching the jacket and spreading it out on the floor. He looked down at it and saw a line of three staples just above the bottom of the garment. He took a knife from the table and pressed the tip so that it pierced the material. Florin made as if to complain, but, before he could say anything, Pasko dragged the knife down and ripped the lining straight down the middle. He dropped the knife, took the lining in both hands, and tore it open.

The phone had been hidden between the lining and the rest of the jacket.

It kept ringing.

Pasko glared at his son as he pressed the button to answer the call and put it to his ear.

"Hello, Pasko."

"Milton, where are you?"

"Come to the window."

"I don't think so."

"I'm not going to shoot you."

"I won't take the chance."

"Relax, Pasko. I'm just outside. I've been here all night. I saw you at the window. You're wearing the same jacket you were wearing on the bridge. If I was going to shoot you, I could have done it ten times over by now."

Pasko moved slowly to the window, unable to resist. He pressed himself flat against the wall, and then, very carefully, he glanced outside.

"That's it," Milton said. "I'm on the other side of the street. I'm waving."

Pasko looked and saw him. Milton was standing beneath a streetlamp, his arm raised.

"You should have been more careful," Milton said.

"Very inventive. But it won't do you any good. There's only one of you. Two if your friend is here, too. What do you propose to do? Are you going to force your way inside? It is impossible."

"I've already been inside."

"No, Milton, you have not." He tried to find his usual bluster, but he felt a twist of anxiety in his gut as he said it.

"You're behind a locked door. I saw it. I had a good look downstairs."

"You should have stayed. I would have come and had a drink with you."

"I didn't have time for that. I was a little busy."

"Really?"

"The kitchen is directly below you, isn't it?"

Pasko frowned. He turned his head and looked back at Florin; his son was watching him, confusion on his face. "What?" he mouthed.

"You don't need to answer, Pasko. I know it is. I could hear you moving about upstairs when I was in it."

"Doing what?"

"I sealed the room and opened the gas taps. They've been on for four hours. I'm not an expert, Pasko, but that's a small room and the pressure out of those gas lines was reasonable. I'm thinking that there's enough gas in there now for it to make for a healthy explosion."

Pasko put his hand over the phone. He stepped closer to Florin and hissed, "Go downstairs and check the kitchen."

"Why?"

"See if anyone has been inside."

Florin took Pasko's pistol from the table and hurried out of the room. Pasko heard him clatter down the stairs.

"Still there, Pasko?"

"You're bluffing."

"Am I? I suppose we'll find out in a minute."

"What do you want?"

"You've caused a lot of misery and unhappiness. I want you to pay for what you've done."

Florin lumbered up the stairs again. Pasko covered the phone. "Well?"

Florin's face was white. "The door's locked and the key is gone. And I can smell gas."

"Pasko," Milton said. "Have you checked?"

"What do you want?" Pasko said. "You want me to apologise?"

"No. It's too late for that. Let me explain something for you. I look at life like I'm running a ledger. You've got the things you're proud of on one side, things you're ashamed of on the other. For a long time, all I did was bad. Everything on the one side of the ledger. Like you, really. I'm trying to find some balance now."

Pasko looked out of the window again. Milton was nowhere to be seen.

"Where are you?" he said.

There was no answer.

"I'm not scared of you, Milton!"

Milton spoke again. "Goodbye, Pasko."

The line went dead.

Chapter Sixty-Three

MILTON CHECKED HIS WATCH.

Two minutes to five.

He walked away and headed south along Kilburn High Road.

The explosion was powerful. Milton turned. The pressure wave rushed out, picking up the large bin and tossing it into the street, shoving the parked cars across the road and blowing in the windows of the office block. A large cloud of grey smoke and debris billowed out of the freshly opened space, fragments of brick and debris from inside clattering down onto the street. The dust cloud rose up and wreathed the building, so thick that it was impossible to see inside.

Milton got into his car as alarms started to blare, a frantic cacophony as a dozen different sounds clamoured in a discordant harmony. The dust and smoke started to clear and, as he glanced back in his mirrors, Milton was able to see the extent of the damage. The naked filament would have combusted without the inert gas to protect it, and that, in turn, would have caused the gas in the air to ignite. The building had been torn in two. Half of it was still standing, albeit with severe damage, but the other half was simply not there anymore. There were small stretches of the walls on the ground floor that remained, but everything else had been reduced to a smoking pile of debris. Timbers had collapsed on top of one another, and piles of bricks were strewn all the way across the road. The seat of the explosion had been the kitchen. It was gone. The rooms above it—the rooms where Milton knew Pasko and Florin had been waiting—were gone, too.

Milton started the engine and, carefully and deliberately, pulled out into the empty road and drove away to the south.

He was three minutes away when he heard the sirens of the first emergency vehicles.

He drove on.

Chapter Sixty-Four

THE WAITING ROOM was as quiet as it had been the last time Milton had visited the holding facility. He waited patiently, the sharp edges of the plastic chair digging into his ribs and aggravating the bruises that had developed following the fight with the Albanians two days earlier. He had gingerly examined his body in the mirror after he had showered this morning. The cuts from Florin's knife were superficial and had not required stitches, but they had left lurid purple scores across his skin. His knuckles were bruised, and he had a prominent black eye from where he had been butted in the face. His brow had been cut, too, and a raised sickle, with crusted blood scabbed across the wound, reached down to just above his eyelid. The receptionist had looked at him with a wariness that she wasn't able to suppress, and, for a moment, Milton thought that she was going to ask him to leave. Cynthia Whitchurch had stepped forward, telling the woman—who evidently recognised her—that Milton was her guest and that she would vouch for him. That had done the trick, and the woman had invited them—a little reluctantly, perhaps—to take their seats and wait for the doors to open.

Milton glanced over to his right. Whitchurch was sitting next to Nadia. She was taking down the details that she would need in order to represent her as a client in the application for asylum that they were going to make this afternoon. Nadia had already explained what had happened to her; she had started the story with the commencement of their journey in Eritrea, followed with the crossing to Lampedusa, described her abduction, and then what the Albanians had made her do.

Milton had counselled her not to mention any of the events that had led to her freedom; instead, they had settled on a version of events that had seen her simply walk away from the brothel in which she had been held, with Samir sending Milton to collect her after the siblings had made contact once again. If Cynthia harboured any suspicion that she was being fed an abbreviated version of the truth, it wasn't obvious. Milton doubted that she would dig too deep. Her motivation, written plainly on her face, was to secure the safety of her clients. Samir and Nadia were fortunate to have her.

The doors opened. "You can go through now," the guard called out.

"Ready, Nadia?" Cynthia said.

"Just a moment, please."

"Of course. I'll see you inside when you're ready." Cynthia got to her feet and made her way over to the entrance.

Nadia paused, seemingly reluctant to follow.

Milton went to her. "It's all right," he said. "Your brother will be there in a minute. He'll be glad to see you."

She held his gaze for a moment, and Milton thought that he could see the pain and fear of the last few months in her deep brown eyes. She blinked and found a shy smile, and the moment passed.

"Thank you," she said, placing her hands on his shoulders and laying a cool kiss on his cheek.

Milton found himself smiling.

She turned away from him and joined the lawyer at the door. Milton stayed a few steps away, reluctant to share in a moment that he thought best to be private. He could see through the door, though, and he noticed Samir as he came in through the doors at the other side of the visiting room. The young man stood in the doorway for a moment, the other inmates passing on either side of him, and then he saw his sister. He grinned, beaming out his happiness, and hurried ahead. Nadia went inside, too, and the siblings met in the middle of the room, embracing fiercely, their sobs loud enough for Milton to hear.

He watched them for a moment. They were so swept up in themselves that they did not notice him, and, as Samir showed his sister to the table that he and Milton had sat at just over a fortnight ago, Milton turned and made his way quietly towards the exit.

#

"MR. SMITH!"

Milton stopped at the exit. He turned. Cynthia Whitchurch was hurrying toward him.

"Are you going?"

"Yes," he said. "They haven't seen one another for months. They don't need me around to get in the way."

"But you've done so much for them. For both of them."

"There'll be another time for that," Milton said. "I'll wait until you get them asylum."

"That might be a few months."

"But you think you can?"

She paused. "It's possible. I mean, on a compassionate level, there's no question that they should get it. What's happened to them—everyone can see they deserve it. But what's right and what's legally possible are not the same thing."

"But?"

"I'm quite confident."

Milton put out his hand. "I have to go," he said.

"You have my number," she said. "Give me a call in a couple of weeks. I think this will all be sorted out by then." The lawyer shook his hand. "What are you doing now?" she asked him. "I was going to buy you a coffee."

"It's kind of you, but I can't—I've got a plane to catch."

"Somewhere nice?"

"Not that kind of trip, I'm afraid."

"Business?"

"That's right," Milton said. "Business."

He shook her hand again, told her to call him if there

was anything that he could do to help, and pushed the exit door open. He passed through security, nodded to the guard standing by the X-ray machine, and went outside into the cold, bright morning.

EPILOGUE

Libya

Chapter Sixty-Five

ALI TESSEMA OPENED HIS EYES. His bedroom was dark. The window was open, and he could hear the soft susurration of the sea as it rolled against the beach below.

He thought that he had heard something.

He lay still, damp sheets clinging to his sweaty body, and listened. There was nothing. No sound. He must have been dreaming. He had been drinking all night, expensive Russian vodka that he had smuggled into the country to beat the ban on alcohol. There had been rather a lot of it, and he had been drunk when he had finally stumbled into bed. He still felt a little drunk, and now he was hearing things.

He exhaled, allowing his shoulders to sink back against the mattress, and closed his eyes again.

"Wake up, Ali."

He stopped breathing; his heart felt as if it had stopped beating in his chest. He put down his right arm and levered himself to a half-sitting position. The gentle wind parted the curtains, with just enough moonlight admitted for him to see the man sitting in the armchair on the other side of the room. He was dressed all in black: black combat trousers, a black tactical jacket and black boots. He was wearing a black balaclava that obscured everything save for his eyes and mouth. His left leg was crossed over his right knee and his hands were in his lap. Ali glanced down and saw a pistol in his right hand, the metal sparkling in the dim light.

"Wake up."

Ali had a pistol of his own in the drawer next to the bed. "Who are you?"

The man turned his head so that a little more light fell down onto him. His lips were pressed together in a tight line.

Ali's left hand was still beneath the covers. He carefully, slowly, started to slide it toward the drawer. "What is your name?"

"Milton."

"My guards?"

"Dead, Ali." The man stood and indicated the room with a flick of the pistol. "This is a very nice place. It must have been very expensive."

Ali's throat was suddenly very dry. He swallowed.

"How much did it cost?"

He found that he couldn't answer.

"You can't remember?"

His hand was at the edge of the mattress. "Yes. It was expensive."

The man gestured down at him. "Don't bother," he said. "Your gun's over there."

Ali looked. His pistol and the box of ammunition that he kept with it were on the table next to the armchair.

The breeze died down and the curtains closed. The light disappeared. The man was a shadow now, a darker shape amid the gloom. Ali could feel his presence, close, but he dared not move.

"How many people had to die so you could have a house like this?"

He tried to swallow. "I run a business. I help people. I give them a chance to find a better life."

"No, you don't. You profit from the pain and misery of desperate men and women. Men and women and children. I've seen how you do business. I've been on one of your boats. I've seen the others that didn't make it to port because they were unfit for the voyage. You are a parasite. You're *worse* than a parasite. Did you really think that there would never be a reckoning for what you've done?"

The shadow was at the foot of the bed. The curtains parted again and the light glinted off the barrel of a pistol that had been raised and aimed at him.

"Please. What do you want? Money? *Please*. I give you

more money than you have ever seen before."

"Your money can't help you now."

The bullet hit him in the forehead. He was dead before he could hear the sound of the gun.

#

MILTON LEFT THE SPENT round on the floor of the bedroom. He was armed with a Beretta 92FS 9x19mm pistol, the sidearm favoured by the COMSUBIN—the *Comando Subacquei ed Incursori*—the special forces unit of the Italian navy. The weapons were reasonably exotic, and Hicks had secured them from a dealer who asked no questions in exchange for a significant mark-up on the purchase price. He had purchased their ammunition from Fiocchi Munizioni, the manufacturer from Lecco that had long been favoured by the Italian military. Milton had no idea how vigorous the investigation into the murders at Ali Tessema's property would be, but, in the event that it was thorough, it would be a simple enough thing to track the rounds that had killed the men back to Italy, and then to connect the murders with the COMSUBIN's previous assassinations of smugglers in Tripoli and Zuwara. The dots would be easy to join. The investigation would be shelved.

He went back through the house. It was a large place on the outskirts of Tripoli that Ali had been given by the militia that had confiscated it after the fall of Gaddafi. It had belonged to one of the colonel's playboy sons and still bore the signs of the opulence that was once a family trademark. The main reception room was a mess, with smashed bottles of Moet and Dom Perignon on the floor and a large pile of cocaine on a white Pearl River baby grand. Milton's boots crunched fragments of a shattered vodka bottle into the thick carpet. There were six men and two women in the room. All of them were still asleep. Milton had passed through the room without disturbing them, and none of them had stirred while he had attended to his business. His

Beretta had been fitted with a silencer, and the cylinder had flattened the noise of the gunshot. The revellers would wake up in the morning none the wiser to the execution that had happened just a few feet from where they had been sleeping off the excesses of the night before. Then they would find Ali's body, and they would realise how lucky they had been.

Death had passed among them, and they had been spared.

There was a sliding door into the garden. Hicks was waiting for him outside. He was wearing the same gear as Milton, but he was armed with a Beretta ARX 160, the modular assault rifle that the Italians preferred. He was standing by in the event that the drunken partygoers awoke. There had been no need to use it.

Milton exchanged a nod of affirmation with Hicks and descended the steps into the garden. The house was built in a style that would have been more at home in Malibu, minimalist in design, painted white and erected on stilts. They passed bamboo garden furniture and a hot tub installed on a veranda that overlooked the sea. Milton retraced their steps to the guardhouse and glanced in to see the bodies of the two guards that he had shot before they had even had the chance to take out their weapons. He kept on, passing the infinity pool and the body of the first guard; Milton had killed him with a silenced headshot from ten metres that had seen the man's lifeless body topple into the water.

The guards had been slow and lazy, as if the very thought of an attack on their patron was preposterous.

Milton led the way through the exit and onto the path that overlooked the ocean.

"All done?" Hicks asked in a tight, quiet voice as they calmly walked away.

"All done."

Milton looked down at the jetty at the foot of the cliff. The jet skis they had used to approach the property were tied up, bobbing up and down on the moonlight-flecked swells. He gazed out beyond them, into the infinite darkness of the sea and the sky, and wondered how many more Ali Tessemas there were, and how many of them had sent out overloaded boats on dangerous voyages that night.

"Let's go."

GET EXCLUSIVE
JOHN MILTON MATERIAL

Building a relationship with my readers is the very best thing about writing. I occasionally send newsletters with details on new releases, special offers and other bits of news relating to the John Milton, Beatrix and Isabella Rose and Soho Noir series.

And if you sign up to the mailing list I'll send you this free Milton content:

1. A free copy of the John Milton novella, Tarantula.

2. A copy of the highly classified background check on John Milton before he was admitted to Group 15. Exclusive to my mailing list – you can't get this anywhere else.

You can get the novella and the background check **for free**, by signing up at http://eepurl.com/b1T_NT

IF YOU ENJOYED THIS BOOK...

Reviews are the most powerful tools in my arsenal when it comes getting attention for my books. Much as I'd like to, I don't have the financial muscle of a New York publisher. I can't take out full page ads in the newspaper or put posters on the subway.

(Not yet, anyway).

But I do have something much more powerful and effective than that, and it's something that those publishers would kill to get their hands on.

A committed and loyal bunch of readers.

Honest reviews of my books help bring them to the attention of other readers.

If you've enjoyed this book I would be very grateful if you could spend just five minutes leaving a review (it can be as short as you like) on the book's page.

Thank you very much.

ACKNOWLEDGEMENTS

Thanks to the members of Team Milton for technical advice and support. Thanks to Pauline Nolet and Jennifer McIntyre for editorial assistance. And thanks to you for investing your time in reading this story. I hope you enjoyed it as much as I enjoyed writing it.

John Milton will be back.

ABOUT THE AUTHOR

Mark Dawson is the author of the breakout John Milton, Beatrix Rose and Soho Noir series. He makes his online home at www.markjdawson.com. You can connect with Mark on Twitter at @pbackwriter, on Facebook at www.facebook.com/markdawsonauthor and you should send him an email at mark@markjdawson.com if the mood strikes you.

ALSO BY MARK DAWSON

Have you read them all?

In the Soho Noir Series

Gaslight

When Harry and his brother Frank are blackmailed into paying off a local hood they decide to take care of the problem themselves. But when all of London's underworld is in thrall to the man's boss, was their plan audacious or the most foolish thing that they could possibly have done?

The Black Mile

London, 1940: the Luftwaffe blitzes London every night for fifty-seven nights. Houses, shops and entire streets are wiped from the map. The underworld is in flux: the Italian criminals who dominated the West End have been interned and now their rivals are fighting to replace them. Meanwhile, hidden in the shadows, the Black-Out Ripper sharpens his knife and sets to his grisly work.

The Imposter

War hero Edward Fabian finds himself drawn into a criminal family's web of vice and soon he is an accomplice to their scheming. But he's not the man they think he is - he's far more dangerous than they could possibly imagine.

In the John Milton Series

One Thousand Yards

In this dip into his case files, John Milton is sent into North Korea. With nothing but a sniper rifle, bad intentions and a very particular target, will Milton be able to take on the secret police of the most dangerous failed state on the planet?

Tarantula

In this further dip into his files, Milton is sent to Italy. A colleague who was investigating a particularly violent Mafiosi has disappeared. Will Milton be able to get to the bottom of the mystery, or will he be the next to fall victim to Tarantula?

The Cleaner

Sharon Warriner is a single mother in the East End of London, fearful that she's lost her young son to a life in the gangs. After John Milton saves her life, he promises to help. But the gang, and the charismatic rapper who leads it, is not about to cooperate with him.

Saint Death

John Milton has been off the grid for six months. He surfaces in Ciudad Juárez, Mexico, and immediately finds himself drawn into a vicious battle with the narco-gangs that control the borderlands.

The Driver

When a girl he drives to a party goes missing, John Milton is worried. Especially when two dead bodies are discovered and the police start treating him as their prime suspect.

Ghosts

John Milton is blackmailed into finding his predecessor as Number One. But she's a ghost, too, and just as dangerous as him. He finds himself in de ep trouble, playing the Russians against the British in a desperate attempt to save the life of his oldest friend.

The Sword of God

On the run from his own demons, John Milton treks through the Michigan wilderness into the town of Truth. He's not looking for trouble, but trouble's looking for him. He finds himself up against a small-town cop who has no idea with whom he is dealing, and no idea how dangerous he is.

Salvation Row

Milton finds himself in New Orleans, returning a favour that saved his life during Katrina. When a lethal adversary from his past takes an interest in his business, there's going to be hell to pay.

Headhunters

Milton barely escaped from Avi Bachman with his life. But when the Mossad's most dangerous renegade agent breaks out of a maximum security prison, their second fight will be to the finish.

The Ninth Step

Milton's attempted good deed becomes a quest to unveil corruption at the highest levels of government and murder at the dark heart of the criminal underworld. Milton is pulled back into the game, and that's going to have serious consequences for everyone who crosses his path.

In the Beatrix Rose Series

In Cold Blood

Beatrix Rose was the most dangerous assassin in an off-the-books government kill squad until her former boss betrayed her. A decade later, she emerges from the Hong Kong underworld with payback on her mind. They gunned down her husband and kidnapped her daughter, and now the debt needs to be repaid. It's a blood feud she didn't start but she is going to finish.

Blood Moon Rising

There were six names on Beatrix's Death List and now there are four. She's going to account for the others, one by one, even if it kills her. She has returned from Somalia with another target in her sights. Bryan Duffy is in Iraq, surrounded by mercenaries, with no easy way to get to him and no easy way to get out. And Beatrix has other issues that need to be addressed. Will Duffy prove to be one kill too far?

Blood and Roses

Beatrix Rose has worked her way through her Kill List. Four are dead, just two are left. But now her foes know she has them in her sights and the hunter has become the hunted.

Hong Kong Stories, Vol. 1

Beatrix Rose flees to Hong Kong after the murder of her husband and the kidnapping of her child. She needs money. The local triads have it. What could possibly go wrong?

In the Isabella Rose Series

The Angel

Isabella Rose is recruited by British intelligence after a terrorist attack on Westminster.

Standalone Novels

The Art of Falling Apart

A story of greed, duplicity and death in the flamboyant, super-ego world of rock and roll. Dystopia have rocketed up the charts in Europe, so now it's time to crack America. The opening concert in Las Vegas is a sell-out success, but secret envy and open animosity have begun to tear the group apart.

Subpoena Colada

Daniel Tate looks like he has it all. A lucrative job as a lawyer and a host of famous names who want him to work for them. But his girlfriend has deserted him for an American film star and his main client has just been implicated in a sensational murder. Can he hold it all together?